O9-AIG-660
LOST WORLDS

Also by Andrew Lane

Young Sherlock Holmes: Death Cloud
Young Sherlock Holmes: Red Leech
Young Sherlock Holmes: Black Ice
Young Sherlock Holmes: Fire Storm
Young Sherlock Holmes: Snake Bite

ANDREW LANE

MACMILLAN CHILDREN'S BOOKS

First published 2013 by Macmillan Children's Books
a division of Macmillan Publishers Limited
20 New Wharf Road, London N1 9RR
Basingstoke and Oxford
Associated companies throughout the world
www.panmacmillan.com

ISBN 978-1-4472-2799-1

1 3 5 7 9 8 6 4 2

A CIP catalogue record for this book is available from
the British Library.

Typeset by Nigel Hazle
Printed and bound by CPI Group (UK) Ltd, Croydon CR0 4YY

Dedicated to Helen Stirling-Lane, who has brought more light and happiness and contentment to my life than I thought possible. With all my love.

Dedicated also to my agent, Robert Kirby, who has been there for me virtually from the start and who came up with (assisted by his daughter, Maddie Dunne Kirby) many of the initial ideas, themes and characters in this book. Long may our association continue. Keep those champagne cocktails coming.

And with grateful thanks to Ralph Barraclough, Angela Burgess, Nigel McCrery, Polly Nolan, Sally Oliphant, James Pilborough and Joules Kilgallon, for keeping me sane through a very stressful period of my life. Thank you all.

CHAPTER one

Calum Challenger gazed in awe at the image on the computer screen. Well, to be fair, he gazed in awe at the image on the central one of the ten screens that hung, at different heights, suspended from articulated arms, in front of his work desk. The image was blurred and grainy, but that wasn't the screen's fault. His multi-screen, high-definition, hex-core computer system was the best that money could buy – and despite the fact that he was only sixteen he had access to a lot of money. An *awful* lot of money. No, the image was blurred and grainy because it had been blown up from a photograph taken with a mobile-phone camera at long range while the subject was moving. Even so, he could just about see what it was.

He leaned back in his chair. Five years he'd been waiting for an image like this to turn up. Five *years*. Now that it was here, captured in colour on his computer screen, he wasn't sure how he should react.

A cold breeze from the darkened expanse of the warehouse behind him caressed the hairs on the back of his neck. He didn't turn round. He knew that it was just a random gust of wind through a ventilation grille – the alarm systems would have gone off if anyone had actually broken into the warehouse. He was, as he almost always was these days, alone.

The screen showed a figure against a background of grass, bushes and rocks. Judging by the figure's shadow, the background was slanted – perhaps a hillside or a slope.

The interesting thing – the thing that had made Calum catch his breath in wonder – was that the figure didn't look human.

It was difficult to tell its size, with only the heights of the bushes with which to compare it, but Calum got the impression that it was about the size of a large man. It was stooped, with rounded shoulders and bowed arms that dangled in front of it. Its skin seemed to be covered with short red hair, with the exception of pale lines up its spine, down the inside of its forearms and beneath its jaw. He could have been looking at a big, hairy man with a stoop, except that the face was different. A thick ridge of brow pushed out over the eyes, like on a chimpanzee, and the teeth and jaw were pushed out slightly, but a distinct nose projected. Chimpanzees didn't have noses.

Calum drew a box round the figure's right hand with a couple of clicks of his trackball, and flicked the section of image inside the box to another of his screens. The result was pixelated almost to the point of incoherence, but he could just make out what looked like a thumb that was nearly as long as, but separate from, the rest of the fingers, and angled so that it could close against them. An opposable thumb – that was another thing that ruled out the possibility that it was a chimpanzee. Calum knew that their thumbs were much shorter than the rest of their fingers, making it easier for them to climb trees. Gorillas had opposable thumbs, but this wasn't anything like a gorilla. Some Old World monkeys, like mandrills, also had opposable thumbs, but they were all small – the size of a dog – and there was no way they could be mistaken for human. No, this thing was unique.

He ran his fingers through his long hair and interlaced them at the back of his neck. He supposed it could be a man in a mask and a hairy suit – like that 1967 footage taken in California, supposedly showing an ape-like creature locally known as Sasquatch, but which had turned out to be a hoax. That was the problem with these blurry photographs or jerky video clips – they could so easily be hoaxes. And yet . . . its forearms seemed longer in proportion to its upper arms, and to the rest of its body. Reduced to a silhouette, it just didn't *look* human. If the creature was a hoax, then it was a very well-constructed one.

The creature. He laughed suddenly, and the laughter echoed back to his ears from the cold brick walls of the warehouse. He was already thinking of it as *the creature*. Just a few moments ago it had been *the figure*. Somewhere in his mind, it seemed that he had already made a decision about the photograph's likely authenticity.

He could sense his heart beating faster than normal.

He felt slightly light-headed. Off in the distance the sound of London traffic drifted through the ventilation grilles, but Calum couldn't hear it. Mentally, he was listening again to his father's voice, deep and comforting, echoing over the gulf of time from five years before.

'You know, Calum, the original human species in northern Europe and central Asia was the Neanderthal. They were slow-moving creatures: large heads, bulbous foreheads and covered in hair. They were organized in clans, often living in caves, and had the intelligence to make fire and use tools. However, out of central Africa, at a time of particularly low sea levels, came Homo sapiens *– "thinking man" – our direct ancestors. They were descended from tree-dwelling apes and were smaller, more agile, intelligent and inventive. There was probably a time when the Neanderthals and* Homo sapiens *made room for each other, but, as the* sapiens *culture expanded, battles must have been fought for land and food and gradually the Neanderthals were driven to more mountainous and inhospitable regions and eventually, or so it's believed, made extinct. Remember the stories I told you about how American settlers treated Native American Indians? Or how Canadian settlers treated the Inuit, or Australians the Aborigines, or New Zealanders the Maori? The list goes on. It's a similar pattern. It's the spread of the dominant culture and the destruction of the weaker. But what interests me, Calum – and your mother, probably rightly, thinks I'm crazy – is the possibility that Neanderthal man may have continued to live and breed in small bands in extremely isolated locations surviving in some form even up to the present day. Wouldn't that be something? To find a*

Neanderthal and come face to face with a living descendant of the original inhabitants of Western Europe?'

That had been the last thing that his father had said to him. Apart from 'Goodbye'.

Breathing heavily, Gecko stood on top of the three-storey building and looked out across the rooftops of London.

The wind ruffled his hair. Down on the streets, where the ordinary people went about their business, it was warm and damp, but up here, where the wind scoured the city unobstructed, it was cool and fresh. And he could see the sky above and all around him.

His right foot throbbed where he had landed hard from his last jump, and he could feel a burn on his back where he had forward-rolled over a gravelled tarmac roof twenty minutes before, but they were minor distractions: badges of valour in the great game that was free-running.

He knew exactly where he was, but he still took a moment to orient himself. Making assumptions about what was on the roofs around him was a quick way to injury, or even death. He'd seen it happen before, to friends of his. Other free-runners. Things could suddenly appear – air-conditioning vents, pipes, piles of bricks stored somewhere out of the way, even pigeon coops, rabbit hutches or stretches of urban garden. If you jumped across a gap between two buildings expecting there to be a flat roof on which you could roll, only to find that someone had started building themselves an attic, you could find your day seriously ruined.

His sharp eyes scanned the gap in front of him. Everything looked the same as he remembered. The gap was about three metres across – an alley between this building and the next one. He had a feeling that the building on which he stood was an old fire station converted into an upmarket wine bar – the balustrade round the edge of the roof was ornate, sculpted from stone rather than moulded from concrete – but he didn't particularly care what was going on at street level. He just cared about the roofs, and the roof of the building on the other side of the gap was about a metre lower than this one. If he rolled left when he hit it, then he'd go through a skylight and plunge inside the building; if he rolled right, then he'd impale himself on a rusted pipe that had probably once been part of a ventilation system. In between the skylight and the pipe was a stretch of flat tarmac about a metre and a half wide and four metres long. He could hit the roof about fifteen centimetres in and roll, to absorb some of his momentum, then come out of the roll running, and vault across the low chimney that blocked his path. He knew that on the other side of the chimney there was a sloping section of tiles down which he could slide. At the bottom was a gutter. If he spun right and ran along the edge of the gutter, he would be in a perfect position to leap across the next gap and grab on to the fire escape of the five-storey building next door.

He paced five steps backwards, paused, took a deep breath and ran towards the edge of the roof.

As Calum remembered his father, pictured his face and heard his voice, he felt the old, familiar feeling of helpless grief well up within him. His chest tightened, and his breath caught in his throat. He could feel the tears behind his eyes, but he forced it all away, pushed it into the locked area at the back of his mind, which he kept for all the memories from that time.

To distract himself, he checked the source of the photograph again, just to be sure he knew where and when it had been taken. It was one of a bunch of images uploaded to a photo-sharing site by someone who claimed to be backpacking in the foothills of the Caucasus Mountains. Calum had found it by accident; or, rather, his automated internet search-bot applications had found it for him and flagged it up for his interest. *Look at this!* the caption said. *Never seen anything like it! One of the locals LOL?*

According to the date/time stamp, the image had been taken two days ago. With a couple of clicks of his trackball, Calum called up a particular and rather unusual piece of software that automatically checked the metadata of any photograph to see if there was a GPS tag attached. Many mobile phones had GPS chips that could locate the phone to within a couple of metres, and that data was often embedded in photographs. A window of the latitude and longitude digits appeared on the screen. He copied the figures and flicked them over to a third hanging screen – one with Google Maps running continuously. The rotating globe in the window suddenly expanded, as if Calum was plummeting from orbit towards the surface of the Earth. Within moments he was gazing at a picture of what looked like a dark green crinkled lettuce leaf sprinkled with mayonnaise, but which was probably ice-capped mountains seen from above. A label told him what he was looking at: *Caucasus Mountains, Georgia*.

Georgia – the former Russian republic, now a fully fledged country in its own right. Well, that matched the place where the backpackers claimed they were located. And, of course, if there were examples of the missing evolutionary link between apes and men still living somewhere in the world, a remote mountain range on the border between Europe and Asia was more likely than, say, a shopping centre in Essex – although, based on some of the TV programmes he'd watched recently, perhaps man-apes in Essex weren't as far-fetched as people might think.

On a whim, he copied the name of the girl who had posted the photograph online, and he flung it across to a fourth suspended screen. There it was immediately pasted into a specialized search program that he'd had written a few years before. The program took any name fed into it and cross-referenced that name with a whole range of databases – census information, school and university records, registers of births, deaths and marriages –

along with social-networking sites and then parsed the information to provide a description of that person's life in accessible form. Within thirty seconds, Calum was reading an essay about the girl who had taken the photograph, which contained information that even she had probably forgotten about.

Various pictures of the girl were scattered through the text, showing her at different ages. He skipped over them. What she looked like wasn't important: the fact that she was real *was*. All he wanted to know was that she had no hidden reasons for being in the Caucasus Mountains – like faking a sighting of a creature that looked like nothing known on Earth. He was gratified to find out that not only was she real, but she had been talking about her backpacking trip well in advance, and she had no interest in practical jokes, hoaxes or unknown creatures. She was taking a gap year before studying engineering at Warwick University. As far as he could tell, she was genuine.

His fingers hovered over the keyboard. Should he upload it to the website? It was speculative, certainly, but then what part of looking for evidence of previously undiscovered creatures still living in the world wasn't?

Before his brain had made a firm decision, his fingers hit the keyboard, starting up the app that would upload the photograph to his website. He quickly typed in a caption for the photograph: *Possible image of missing link in foothills of Caucasus Mountains. Is this the fabled Almast?* The app automatically linked the word *Almast* to the description already held on the website's database: the thousand words or so that he'd written two years ago about the Almast:

> The Almast is a supposedly man-like creature reputed to inhabit the mountainous regions of central Asia and southern Mongolia in small, hidden tribes. Although the Almast is not currently recognized or catalogued by science, there are numerous local stories and legends about it, dating back nearly seven hundred years. Almasti (the plural) are typically described as human-like and bipedal, about 150 cm tall and covered with reddish-brown hair. It is said that they have protruding brows, flat noses and weak chins. The descriptions are very similar to those of Neanderthal man. Is the Almast a lingering remnant of Neanderthal man, still alive in the modern day?

He gazed at the photograph again. Neanderthal? Or maybe one of the earlier forms of man, the ones that came before *Homo sapiens* – *Australopithecus afarensis*, *Australopithecus sediba* or *Homo erectus*?

He needed real evidence. He needed something he could hold in his hand.

A fifth screen – the one that he kept perpetually displaying his website, The Lost Worlds – flashed as the information on it updated. He swung his chair round so that he could see it. He kept an eye on it throughout the day in case someone uploaded a new photograph, or took part in one of the discussion forums that he moderated (or, to be honest, often left to moderate themselves). As he watched, the home page changed to display the new image – the one of the possible Almast. His caption ran beneath it.

Calum liked to think that, across the world, people were hunched in front of their computer screens staring in amazement at the image he had put in front of them. In his heart of hearts he knew that probably wasn't the case. Despite the fact that he had some ten thousand people who logged on to The Lost Worlds on a regular basis, he was enough of a realist to know that they didn't spend their lives hanging on his every word. Over the course of the next few days, most of the people who were interested in the same subject as he was would check the website out and see the new photograph. There would be some discussion, and perhaps, if he was lucky, someone else might have a snippet of information that they could add – another photograph, or a story they had heard from a friend.

If he was *really* lucky, then some university researcher would offer to organize an expedition to the Caucasus Mountains to look for the Almasti. The chances of that were slight, however. Cryptozoology – the study of creatures that either shouldn't exist at all or shouldn't *still* exist – was frowned on in academic institutions around the world. No researcher who valued their job or their reputation would ever get involved. Not obviously, anyway. He knew, from the ISP addresses of the computers that connected to his website, that about a third of his regulars were associated in some way with universities or colleges. Perhaps they were students looking for something unusual, something for a laugh, but he liked to think that there was a small core of zoology and palaeontology professors checking him out in their spare time.

And maybe, just maybe, one of them would take the plunge one day and get in touch with him.

Maybe this latest photograph would be the trigger.

'Now remember: be nice, smile if you can and try not to get too freaked at the way Calum moves around his apartment.'

Natalie Livingstone raised her eyebrows at her mother in what she hoped was appropriately withering teenage scorn. 'I'm always nice, I always smile and there's nothing in the world that can freak me out apart from mismatching shoes and handbag.' She paused, replaying in her head what her mother had said. 'Why – what's freaky about the way he moves around his apartment?'

Gillian Livingstone – *Professor* Gillian Livingstone, Natalie corrected herself in the same way that her mother corrected anyone who introduced her without the honorific – glanced at the rivet-studded metal door that separated the two of them from the apartment of this Calum Challenger boy. 'You know I've been taking an interest in Calum since his parents died, don't you? Between us, his great-aunt and I try to make sure that he can live the kind of life that he wants. They were my best friends, and I promised them that if anything happened I'd make sure Calum ate properly, got a good education, didn't spend all his inheritance on a Ferrari Testarossa and didn't mix in the wrong company.'

Natalie closed her eyes briefly. Parents were so stupid sometimes. She'd heard the story, like, *sooo* many times before. 'Yeah, I know. They died in a car crash three years ago. I remember when it happened.'

'Two.' A brief spasm of pain crossed her mother's face. 'Two years ago.'

'Right. Sorry.'

'What I didn't tell you is that Calum was in the car with them. He was fourteen – a year older than you were. He was . . . injured.'

Natalie had a sudden flash of horrible scarring, like from some gross horror film, and winced. She didn't like ugly things.

Her mother must have caught her expression. 'Oh, don't worry,' she said drily. 'He's not a monster who has to hide away from all human contact. Looking at him, you can't tell quite how serious the crash was. But when he moves . . .' She paused. 'Well, his spine was affected. There was nerve damage.'

'He has a broken back?'

'Not quite. It was never actually broken, but the damage to the nerves was so great that his legs are paralysed.'

Natalie thought for a moment. 'Oh, right. He's in a wheelchair. That's OK.'

Her mother shook her head. 'Actually, no. He's *got* a wheelchair – a very good, very expensive one, but he doesn't like to use it. He says it makes him feel like he's not on a level with anyone else.'

Natalie tried to imagine what Calum Challenger did without a wheelchair. The only thought that came to mind was just too stupid for words, but she said it anyway. 'So what does he do – *crawl* around the apartment or something?'

'Not quite. It's difficult to describe. Wait and see.' She reached out and pressed a series of keys on a security pad by the door. Somewhere behind it, Natalie heard a buzz.

While she waited for something to happen, Natalie looked around. Behind her was a large lift – one of those you see in American movies looking like they are only half made, out of wire mesh and metal struts, with those strange wooden doors that split horizontally in the middle and open up and down on some kind of pulley system, rather than side to side. The lift had brought them directly up from the door that led off the street – and 'street', Natalie thought, was a polite way of describing the narrow cobbled alley where they had parked. The lobby area where they were now waiting was lined in unpainted brick that was so old the corners were rounded and bits of them were flaking off. This place probably dated back centuries.

Her eye was caught by a movement above the lift. For a moment, she thought it might be a rat, and she was prepared to utter a dramatic '*Eugh!*' and demand that they left, like, *right away*, but she recognized it as a camera. A closed-circuit security camera. The movement had been the camera rotating so that it was pointed directly at her.

She turned her back on it, the way she turned her back on anything that didn't fit into her ideal world.

A few moments later the door opened.

The boy standing in the doorway was not what she had expected. He was tall – taller than her, and she was taller than average – and his nose and jaw were so perfectly formed that his face looked like something from a Greek statue. His hair was collar length and unkempt, but in a 'can't be bothered' way rather than a messy, 'can't look after myself' way. His eyes were a piercing blue, and he was standing strangely, slumped against the door frame with his left arm out of sight, but what she could see of his torso made her think of an inverted triangle – immensely wide shoulders and thick arms, a chest that narrowed down to a thin waist and legs that were much narrower than his arms.

'Professor Livingstone,' he said. 'I wasn't expecting you.'

Natalie's mother smiled. 'Nice to see you too, Calum. I was in London for a conference, and I had some spare time, so I thought I'd come over and see how you are.'

Calum was nodding politely, but his eyes were scanning Natalie's face. She could almost feel a spot of heat where his gaze touched, and she had to fight hard to maintain a steady, challenging stare back at him.'

'You brought your personal assistant?' Calum asked.

'No, I brought my *daughter*. Calum Challenger, meet Natalie Livingstone.'

'I suppose you'd better come in,' he said. He turned round clumsily, and Natalie saw that the arm that was out of sight behind the door frame was actually reaching up above Calum's head and holding on to a leather strap that had been screwed into the ceiling. As her eyes grew used to the dim light within the apartment, she saw that there were similar straps – like the ones she'd seen on buses, on the rare occasions she'd had to catch a bus – hanging in a regular pattern all the way across the room.

Just at the moment her mind worked out what they were for, and her lips formed an unplanned 'You have to be *kidding*!', Calum Challenger reached out with his right hand for another of the straps, and begin the process of swinging across the apartment, obviously expecting them to follow.

That, she thought as she watched him move away from them, would explain the arms and the shoulders. His upper-body strength must be amazing.

'Freaked?' her mother asked softly.

'Getting there,' she replied.

Exhausted, hot and sweating, Gecko swung in from the fire escape through the window into his flat.

It wasn't the main window, of course. He kept that closed for security reasons – burglary was a common problem in south London. He swung in through the smaller window on the top – the one he kept open for ventilation. It was barely large enough for a cat to get through, let alone a burglar, but he knew that if he came down the fire escape fast enough, grabbed the right metal strut in the right place, swung round and launched himself feet-first at the small opening then he could pass right through, flip in the air and land on his feet in the centre of the living room. There were maybe fifteen people in London who could do that – eight of them were squatting in the three-storey house where he lived, and none of the others were burglars. Trespassers, yes; risk-takers, certainly; but not burglars.

It all went perfectly up until the point at which his feet were supposed to hit the wooden floor of his living room. His speed down the fire escape was perfectly judged; his hands gripped the strut in the right place and didn't slip, and his body slid right through the open window like a letter through a letter box. His clothes didn't even touch the window frame.

The problem was that someone had put a chair in the centre of the room.

He hit it and his legs crumpled beneath him just as the chair toppled over, pushed by the force of his arrival. He hit the floor, tucking into an automatic roll, but feeling something in his shoulder tear. With luck it was just a few muscle fibres, rather than a tendon.

He came out of the roll in a crouch, hands on the wooden boards and feet braced, ready to push himself away and run. There was nowhere to run. A man stood directly in front of him, legs braced, hands on his hips. Another man was standing by the door to the hall. The closed door.

Both men had crew-cut hair and faces that looked like they had taken some beatings in their time. One of them was black, the other white. They both wore black jeans, T-shirts, leather jackets and sunglasses, even though they were indoors.

'Are you here to do the cable installation?' Gecko asked. He could hear the pain and the tiredness in his voice, but he couldn't help himself.'

The man in front of him smiled. 'Eduardo Ortiz,' he said. His voice had a foreign twang – Polish, perhaps. Maybe Russian.

'My name is Gecko. I have never heard of this "Ortiz".'

The smiling man in front of Gecko reached out his hand and took Gecko by the hair, pulling him upright. Gecko couldn't help noticing, in the few moments before the hand vanished from his sight and the pain began, that his knuckles were scarred and his little finger ended halfway.

'It wasn't a question. You are Eduardo Ortiz, also known as Gecko. A gecko is an annoying little reptile that can run up walls, yes? I looked it up in a dictionary.'

'No, really,' Gecko said through clenched teeth, 'I told you, I have never heard of him.'

The man twisted Gecko's head left and right. Gecko's scalp burned with the pain of the wrenched hair.

'Apart from us and you, there is nobody here. If this isn't your place, then what are you doing here?'

'Burglary?' Gecko ventured.

The man released Gecko's hair, pushing him backwards at the same time. Gecko stumbled, but caught himself before he could fall over.

'Funny you should mention burglary. We hear from friends of ours that you are very good at climbing walls and getting through small gaps.' He gestured to the tiny window. 'We would have asked for a demonstration, but we have seen the evidence ourselves. We want you to come and work for us. In a . . . private capacity.'

'Installing cable?'

The man shook his head. 'Not installing. Taking away. Money, jewellery, passports, iPods, mobile phones . . . anything you can carry.' He nodded towards the door. 'People out there take precautions if they think someone can get into their flats or houses. They lock their doors and windows, and they install alarm systems, but if they think it's impossible then they don't worry so much. But someone like you, who can get into impossible places . . . well, you would be quite an asset to us.'

'And who is this "us"?' Gecko asked.

The man shrugged. 'We are new to this country. From Eastern Europe, you understand. It is . . . a land of opportunity. We, for instance, have the opportunity to make a lot of money. You have the opportunity to not get your arms and legs broken. Everyone is happy, apart from the people who lose their money and jewellery and mobile phones, but even they can claim on their insurance, so they are happy as well in the end.'

'Can I . . . think about it?' Gecko asked.

'Do not think too hard. Thinking is a dangerous hobby. In Eastern Europe, we are fatalists. We believe that what happens is meant to happen. You are meant to work for us, committing burglaries. It is fate. Accept it.' He moved towards the door. His silent companion stepped to one side and opened it. 'We will return tomorrow for your answer, which will be "yes", but we would rather you came to that conclusion of your own free will than be forced into it here by us.' He stopped, and pointed a finger at Gecko's face. Either by accident or design, the way he held his hand made it look like he was miming a gun. 'Do not talk to the police. Do not talk to your friends. Do not talk to *anyone* about this. It is between ourselves, yes?'

'Yes,' Gecko said quietly, but he was talking to a closing door.

CHAPTER two

Tara Flynn's bedroom was like Tara Flynn herself – small, dark and chaotic. She sat on her bed, tablet computer propped up against a pillow on the duvet in front of her and a Bluetooth keyboard perched on her lap. Her long brown hair fell in front of her face like a curtain, shutting out the world.

A window popped up in the corner of the screen, accompanied by a soft chime. The words *How's it goin'?* were highlighted within it.

Tara clicked on the window, and typed a response: *No luck yet.* She pressed <return>, and an application on her tablet encrypted the message and sent it out over the ether.

She went back to what she was doing: attempting to find a way inside the security firewalls of a big and remarkably secretive company who called themselves Nemor Incorporated, but about which it was incredibly difficult to find out anything. She'd only discovered their internet presence by following a link from an email that had been revealed on WikiLeaks. Nemor Incorporated didn't seem to have an openly available, easily accessed website for those people that wanted information on what the company did, or wanted to apply for a job. It almost seemed like you needed to already know about the website in order to find it: you couldn't just look up the company name on Google or Bing and link to it. In fact, when Tara had tried to do just that she'd got no hits on the name, which almost made her think that Nemor Incorporated was actually paying the big search-engine providers to keep their name *out* of searches.

Another soft chime alerted her to a response – one that her app quickly decrypted before displaying it. Tara and her friends never communicated using unencrypted messages. Stuff that moved across the internet could be easily captured and read by anyone. That was how Tara and her friends got most of their information in the first place.

Nemor's some kind of big fish in commerce, that's for sure, the message read. *Their name crops up in emails from defence contractors, the US government, large tech companies – all kinds of places, some quite nasty. They're into something big. What are the chances you can get in?*

Tara snorted. *Chances are 100%, moron*, she typed, and sent the message.

While she waited for a response, she brought up the Nemor Incorporated website in her browser. There were some generic pictures of bright young people with neat smiles, neat haircuts and neat suits that looked like they'd been provided by an advertising company, and some close-ups of generic scientific stuff like silicon chips and chemistry-lab equipment that looked like they'd been ripped off from somewhere else on the internet – nothing which actually said what it was that the company *did*. There was a short paragraph that said absolutely nothing in 200 words, and a line of text that said: 'If you have a Nemor Inc. user ID and password, please log in now. If you wish to contact Nemor Inc., please use the contact email address below.' Two empty text boxes let people type in user IDs and passwords, if they had them. Below that was a hyperlinked email address.

Tara pinged the email address using one of her own apps, but the response came straight back: – *Error – this email address is invalid*.

Interesting. They didn't seem to want – or maybe expect – any incoming emails from members of the public. That kind of industrial secrecy made Tara and the other people in her group very suspicious.

She set another app working on the user ID and password boxes, cycling through millions of permutations of names and words picked randomly from the dictionary on the faint chance that some combination might accidentally be correct, but she wasn't holding out much hope. To get past this kind of authentication system you usually needed to know *something* about one of the employees – a name that you could use as a basis for generating a system username, and some personal information that would help identify a password, like their date of birth, or their partner's date of birth, or a favourite hobby or something. Here, she had nothing. Even the WikiLeaks references weren't specific enough.

Frustrated, she called up the HTML code underlying the website and glanced through it. The code was concise, neatly written and well documented. But there was something odd about it.

She looked closer. There was a hotspot on the site – a button that could be clicked, which led to a different site, but the button was the same colour as the background website colour, so it was effectively invisible. You had to know it was there if you wanted to click on it – just like you had to know that there was a company called Nemor Incorporated if you wanted to find their website in the first place.

Another soft chime, and a new message popped up in a window. *You want to hand it across to someone else to work on?*

No! she typed back. She knew that the loose affiliation of activists, anarchists and hackers that she hung out with – electronically, at least – had a whole load of computer experts who were more experienced than she was, but she felt like this was her baby. Investigating Nemor Incorporated had been entrusted to her, and she wanted to prove that she could do it, break their security. If they were part of the military/industrial/financial complex that effectively controlled the entire world through puppet governments and complicated financial transactions, then she wanted to do her bit to shut them down. If politics and democracy couldn't clean up the world, then it was time for the activists to have a go.

Now that she knew where on the website it was, she clicked on the hidden button. Her browser screen cleared, and the Nemor Incorporated front page wiped away to be replaced with a different screen. This one was much more impressive, and much more informative. Beneath a company logo that looked weirdly like a unicorn caught in the crosshairs of a telescopic rifle there were hyperlinks to other pages that appeared to be site maps, lists of company locations, lists of departments, subsidiary companies . . . all kinds of things. It was going to take her a while to filter the information.

Another chime, and a message window opened up. She glanced at it quickly, ready to put her friends off so she could work her way through the website she'd discovered.

Miss Tara Flynn, the message started, *you have found our hidden website. Congratulations. We need to talk to you.*

What the . . . ? She glanced around her bedroom automatically, suddenly suspicious that someone was watching her, but the door was closed and she was alone.

Who is this? she typed back after a few minutes of indecision.

The answer flashed back almost instantly. *This is Nemor Incorporated, Security Division.*

How did you track me? she typed, heart hammering in her chest. Nobody had *ever* managed to penetrate her own computer firewalls before. She'd thought she was impregnable.

Child's play, came the response. *Not even worth the time to explain. Let us get to the point – you are committing industrial espionage. You have two choices – face legal consequences, or agree to do something for us. We could use your particular skills.*

Tara took a deep breath. This was scary. If they knew *who* she was then they would know *where* she was, and that could lead to all kinds of unfortunate consequences.

She glanced again at her bedroom door. Somewhere out there, in the halls of residence, her college friends were drinking, dancing, talking and otherwise having fun. And in here she seemed to have awakened a serpent.

Still there? The text appeared suddenly. It almost seemed to be mocking her.

She reached out to the keyboard to type a response.

Like a stone gargoyle, Gecko crouched on the parapet that ran round the edge of a block of offices near the river. It was the highest roof he could get to by free-running. Free-runners were honour-bound to only use physical means of getting from place to place. Lifts and escalators were forbidden, and even stairs were frowned upon.

He supposed that he could actually climb up the *sides* of buildings, like a rock-climber, and get to higher roofs, but it would be risky – he might fall and kill himself. Yet it wasn't the risk that stopped him accessing the higher roofs; it was the fact that climbing slowly up the side of a building like a cockroach wasn't *beautiful*. Free-running was an art form. The running, the leaping, the rolling, the sliding and the controlled falling that ended in legs compressing like steel springs – they were like moves in a tennis match, or brush strokes in a painting. Each one had to be fluid and beautiful in its own right, simplicity hiding strength and complexity, but, also, they had to fit together into something greater than themselves. Climbing up a wall, fingers and toes scrabbling for cracks to hold on to, that had no beauty, no style.

His gaze scanned the distant horizon: a mishmash of buildings in different architectural styles, all of which went together to make up the London skyline. On his right there was a clutch of new tower blocks that had sprung up in the few years since he had moved to London: the Shard at London Bridge; the Strata apartment block at Elephant and Castle, with three wind turbines set into its roof; and the office block on the site of the old Baltic Exchange that was known as 'the Gherkin' because of its strangely bulbous shape. Gecko could think of other names for it.

He sighed. He knew that he was just trying to distract himself. He needed to make a decision: should he agree to work for the Eastern European criminals who wanted him to be their sneak-thief or should he just pack his few possessions and disappear, move to another flat in another area?

The problem was that if he just moved a little way away, they'd find him again, and next time they wouldn't be so polite. He supposed he could move out into the suburbs, or even to another part of England, but how would he be able to practise free-running then? He'd seen the outskirts of London – places like Pinner, or Nine Elms: rows and rows of two-storey houses like Lego blocks. Where was the challenge there? He supposed he could move to a different city, like Liverpool or Manchester – they had a whole set of different-sized buildings with their own different challenges – but they also had their own criminal gangs, and pretty soon there would be someone else looking down at him, making gun-shapes with their fingers. He could find somewhere smaller – a town or a village – but he'd probably be able to get from one side to the other via the rooftops in ten minutes. Where was the challenge? Where was the *art*?

He shook his head. Good sense told him that if he wanted to keep on free-running then he had to stay in Central London, and that meant he had no choice but to become a thief.

Could he? Was he really capable of sneaking around in people's bedrooms, riffling through their private possessions for something his Eastern European masters could sell for a quick profit? What would happen if he got caught? He'd be locked up in a cell two metres square. No chance of free-running there. He'd go insane.

Two options, neither of which ended well for him. One impossible choice.

Abruptly, he stood up. He needed to run. He needed to feel the wind whistling past his ears and see the ground flashing past far below his feet.

He raced left, towards the edge of the roof. There was a route in that direction he'd rehearsed before, one that was challenging enough to take his mind off his problems for a while.

Reaching the edge of the building he jumped on to the parapet and used his momentum to carry him out into empty space.

He fell: feet first and arms extended, wind pulling his hair back into a comet's tail behind his head. His target was a small patch of tiled roof two metres away vertically and four metres away horizontally. He hit it, the impact taking his breath away and sending shockwaves up through his chest. He let his legs take the strain of landing. His forward motion continued, and he rolled head over heels, scraping his spine on the hard tiles but coming out of the roll in a pumping run. The next building abutted this one, separated by a metal railing. He vaulted the railing. The metal was cold beneath his fingers. He kept running, diverting round a central vent without breaking stride, taking huge gulps of air to keep his blood oxygenated.

A three-metre gap separated this building from the next one. It was just too far to jump – maybe if it had been lower he'd have managed it, but it was on the same level as the roof he was pounding across. Workmen had put a girder across the gap at some stage in the past. Cables hung beneath it, secured by plastic ties. Gecko leaped on to the girder and ran across the gap like a man on a tightrope.

This roof was a crazy paving of flat sections, sloping sections, sunken skylights and sudden vertiginous drops that formed ventilation shafts. Gecko jumped and dodged his way across the various obstacles, on the verge of over-balancing several times, and darted round a central pyramidal section of glass that topped a lobby far below. The next building was higher than this one – no chance of landing on the roof this time. Instead he let his eyes scan the face of the building as he raced towards the edge. A nanosecond before the last safe moment to stop he saw that the window straight ahead and one storey down was empty of glass. It had been like that for as long as Gecko could remember.

He leaped into empty space.

His trajectory carried him in a perfect parabolic curve. He brought his legs up to his chest and curled his arms round his knees as the wall of the building opposite zoomed towards him. Brick . . . more brick . . . and then the open window! His curled-up body fitted perfectly through the space. As the frame passed his face he explosively uncurled. His feet hit the windowsill so hard that spikes of pain jolted up to his hips. His thigh-muscles absorbed the impact and rebounded like springs, projecting him in a flat dive along the central corridor of the deserted building. He extended his hands in front of him. His palms hit the wooden floor, and he let momentum carry him in a series of flips past empty doorways and graffiti-covered walls. Maybe a shocked face – red-rimmed eyes and a straggly beard – gazed at him from one of the empty doorways, perhaps not. He was past too quickly to say for sure. He came out of the flips in a run, grabbed a banister at the end of the corridor and yanked himself sideways into a stairwell, nearly dislocating his shoulder in the process.

The sound of his feet pounding the stairs echoed like thunder through the building and through his skull. He descended two levels, then emerged on to a lower floor and raced back down the corridor, heading towards the building he'd just come from, but diverting halfway along into a room with a door hanging drunkenly from its hinges. A stained, torn mattress shoved into a corner and a burnt area of floorboards, as if someone had been cooking in the centre of the room, were the only two things he noticed as his feet carried him racing across the space towards the lone window. Like the one two floors up, it was bereft of glass. He jumped through the space like a hurdler, knowing (because he'd done that run so many times before, each time getting slightly further than the last) that the building got narrower as it went up and that the ceiling of the floor below formed a balcony-like roof outside the window through which he'd just jumped. He raced to the edge of the roof and jumped again, this time over the gap between the derelict building and a warehouse next door.

The warehouse roof was tiled, and it sloped from one side to the other. This was the furthest he'd got by free-running before, and he stopped to catch his breath and to work out what his next move would be – either this time or next time he did the run.

The tiled roof was punctuated by a series of rectangular skylights made of frosted glass. The glass was patterned with a grid of wires, presumably to make it stronger. Each skylight had a metal pipe projecting up from beside it, and each pipe was capped with something that looked like an upside-down flower pot. Something to do with ventilation, Gecko assumed.

He leaned on one of the pipes while he took a series of deep breaths. He could feel the burn of the lactic acid build-up in his muscles.

The trouble was it didn't matter how far he ran – his dilemma had no problem keeping up with him. The same question still loomed large in his mind – what should he do about the Eastern European gangsters who wanted him to become their pet burglar?

No. Push that to one side. Worry about that later. Now was for free-running.

Gecko was just in the process of straightening up and looking around to see what was accessible from where he was standing when an electronic voice spoke right next to his ear. 'Warning! Warning! Intruder detected!'

The shock made him step back inadvertently. His heel caught against the lip of the nearest skylight. He fell backwards, hands desperately clawing at the air, and crashed through the skylight, the slivers of flying glass rising above him like a swarm of glittering insects.

Calum had said goodbye to Professor Livingstone and her daughter, Natalie. Now he sat in the darkened living area of his warehouse apartment, holding a bottle of Coca-

Cola in his hand and sipping occasionally. It came from a bottling plant in Mexico, and he had it shipped across the Atlantic especially for him. The Mexican production process used cane-sugar sweetener, rather than the lower cost high-fructose corn syrup that was used to sweeten Coke everywhere else in the world. He found the taste cleaner and sweeter. It was something that made his life more bearable, which he could afford, so he bought it. And it was healthier. Either Professor Livingstone didn't know about his little extravagance or she was letting him get away with it. At least it wasn't a Ferrari Testarossa.

His arms ached. He wasn't used to moving around the apartment as much as he had for the past hour or so, while Professor Livingstone and her daughter had been present. He'd also been conscious of swinging around like a monkey in front of a girl who was about his own age and stunningly beautiful, if overly made-up and dressed like a Barbie doll. He'd tried to make the swinging look effortless and controlled, and had ended up pulling a muscle or something. He definitely had a pain running down his ribs that hadn't been there before.

He swilled the Coke in the bottle and took another sip. Professor Livingstone's visit had disturbed him. He didn't see his guardian that often; when she did visit it was usually on the back of a conference or seminar that she was attending in London. She would pop in, check that he looked healthy and that the place was tidy, ask what he'd been up to and then leave. He knew she had the power to check his use of the bank accounts that had been set up for him and to veto any unusual payments, but he was careful not to abuse the financial freedom he'd been given. The two of them had a reasonably good relationship – not like mother and son, but more like aunt and nephew. He only vaguely remembered her from before the accident, but he knew that she had been a good friend of his mother and father, and he knew that she felt as if she was paying tribute to their memory by looking after him – she and his great-aunt between them. He just wished she wouldn't. He was perfectly capable of looking after himself.

And why had she brought her daughter with her? Calum had never met Natalie before, and wasn't sure that he ever wanted to again. She was obviously more used to a sunny Californian shopping-mall environment than a rainy London street and a warehouse that dated back several hundred years and which still smelt of rum and tobacco and the other things that had been shipped out along the Thames from its loading docks. He'd spotted her looking around with barely disguised distaste; glancing at the bare brick walls and the wooden floorboards that had absorbed all kinds of spills from various cargoes in the past.

It was probably a good thing that she hadn't gone down to the ground floor, where Calum stored a lot of the stuff that had been passed through generations of the Challenger family to Calum's great-grandfather, Professor George Challenger.

Now there was a man who wasn't frightened of arranging speculative scientific expeditions to exotic foreign countries in search of specimens of things that nobody else believed still existed. Calum had heard stories from his father that George Challenger had, back in the 1880s, mounted an expedition to South America which had uncovered evidence that some prehistoric reptiles still existed, in numbers large enough to sustain a stable population. The stories told of Professor Challenger bringing back a live pterodactyl and displaying it in London, to the disbelief of the scientific and journalistic establishments. Calum had trawled through as many old newspapers from the time as he could locate, however, and had not found any reference to Professor Challenger or live pterodactyls. You would have thought that live pterodactyls would have rated at least *some* mention.

It was because of Professor George Challenger, and the stories that his father had told him, that Calum was obsessed with the possibility of extinct animals still alive in the world. Not just prehistoric reptiles, but mammals, insects, fish . . . anything. That's why his website was called *The Lost Worlds* – paying homage to the book *The Lost World* that the writer Arthur Conan Doyle had written about his great-grandfather's South American expedition – although most people took it to be a work of fiction rather than what it was: a near-journalistic piece of non-fiction.

His fingers clenched on the bottle as his memory

flashed up a picture of the cover of the book *The Lost World* by Michael Crichton – a more recent piece of fiction, sequel to Crichton's previous novel *Jurassic Park*. Both had been made into films, which meant, as far as Calum was concerned, that his great-grandfather's memory was being eroded away, bit by precious bit.

Which brought Calum back to the ground-floor storage area in the warehouse, where his great-grandfather's boxes were stored. Hundreds of crates, left over from the various adventures that Professor George Challenger had undertaken. Who knew what was down there? Dinosaur skulls? Giant eggs? Calum dreamed of going down there one day with a crowbar and opening up as many crates as he could, just to see what was inside, but the ground floor wasn't set up for his particular means of moving around, and he refused to get into a wheelchair to do it. That would be like giving up.

He took another sip of his Coke, frowning when he realized that he'd finished the bottle. He put it down with a sigh and levered himself off the sofa with his arms, reaching up to the nearest leather strap and swinging across to the kitchen area to get another one.

An artificial voice suddenly blared out through the apartment, jolting him. He nearly missed the next strap, which would have sent him sprawling to the floor.

'Warning! Warning! Intruder detected!'

Something crashed through the skylight overhead.

Calum twisted round, staring in shock as a body

plunged downward and hit the sofa where he'd been sitting, sending a cloud of dust mushrooming through the apartment. Fragments of glass followed it, raining down like a meteor storm.

CHAPTER three

Calum quickly cancelled the alarm and swung across to look at the person who had fallen through the skylight. He was worried that they would be dead from the impact, or the shock, but the boy on the sofa was still breathing. He looked about the same age as Calum. A burglar, obviously, but one taking a cleverer route than most of the other people who tried to break into the warehouse.

Calum fished his mobile phone out of his jeans. He had the local police station on speed dial.

He stared down at the boy on the sofa. Maybe he ought to call for an ambulance. Uncharacteristically, Calum wasn't sure what to do.

'*Meu cabeca dói!*' the boy slurred. He was smaller than Calum, with coffee-coloured skin and black hair. He was slight, but Calum could see the muscle development in his arms and legs.

'You were breaking into my apartment,' Calum said, wondering if the boy could understand English.

'I was not breaking in.'

'You were on the roof.'

'Roofs are common property. They are like pavements.' The boy's voice was getting stronger, and he was staring around the apartment.

'No.' Calum was firm on this point. 'Roofs are private property, and if you climb on them then you're trespassing,'

The boy frowned. 'I was just passing across. Using your place as a staging post, you know. Then your alarm went off and I fell through the skylight. I ought to sue you!'

Calum looked him up and down. The muscular development, the tight clothes that wouldn't restrict movement, the expensive high-end trainers . . . He thought he knew what this boy was doing.

'*Parkour*?' he asked. He'd heard of the discipline before.

The boy looked up at him with a frown. 'Hey, *parkour* is serious, hardcore stuff,' he said. 'I am a free-runner.'

'What's the difference?'

'*Parkour* is all about efficiency. It is about finding the lowest-energy route around obstacles. Free-running is about the art, and about self-development. If it is not beautiful, it's not free-running.' The boy raised an eyebrow. 'You obviously know a bit about this stuff.'

Calum shrugged. 'I've seen it in films, and played computer games with it in.' He cocked his head to one side, gazing at the boy, evaluating him. His face was open and honest, although it was currently screwed up into a pained scowl, and he was making no moves to conceal his identity, escape or threaten him. Calum didn't think he was a thief.

'What's your name?' Calum asked.

The boy struggled to a sitting position. 'You can call me Gecko.'

'Have you got a *real* name?'

'What – so you can report me to the police?'

Calum just remained silent, and waited.

'What the hell – enough people around here know me, know what I do and know where I live. They even did a feature on me in the *Big Issue*.' He shrugged, and winced as a spasm of pain shot through his shoulders. 'My *real* name is Eduardo Ortiz.'

'Brazilian?' Calum guessed.

Gecko nodded. 'Came over to England ten years ago with my mother. She is a cleaner. Works on the stock exchange, believe it or not.' He shook his head. 'She is always looking down at floors, carpets and skirting boards. Never looks up at the sky. I keep telling her there is a whole new world up there, but she doesn't even know what I'm talking about.'

'I'm Calum. Calum Challenger.'

Gecko gazed around the apartment. 'You live here by yourself?'

'Yeah.'

When Calum didn't elaborate, Gecko went on. 'What is it with all the straps hanging from the ceiling, then? Are you in training for something?' He looked over at Calum, and seemed to suddenly spot the way that Calum was standing awkwardly, with one hand braced on the back of a chair and the other casually entwined in one of the straps. His gaze travelled up and down Calum's body, taking in the overdeveloped arms and shoulders and the comparatively underdeveloped muscles of the legs. 'You have a problem?'

Now it was Calum's turn to shrug, and the pain was inside rather than outside. 'Car crash, a couple of years back. I was paralysed. My parents were killed. I spent a long time wishing I'd been killed along with them.'

'Never wish for death,' Gecko said, shaking his head firmly. 'It spends all its time slinking around, watching us from the shadows. Never invite it into the light.'

'It's OK. I got over it.'

'So I see.' Gecko ran his hands along his arms, down his chest and stomach, and then along his legs. 'Not much damage done, I think.'

'You were lucky,' Calum pointed out.

'I twisted when I fell, to minimize injury, and I kept my muscles relaxed.' He smiled slightly. 'Of course, none of that would have done me any good if I had landed on concrete. I was lucky you put your sofa there.'

'Actually,' Calum admitted, 'I put it there because the skylight was there. More light to read by.'

Gecko's attention was caught by the ten-screen computer display in Calum's workspace area. 'Sweet system,' he said with awe in his voice as he crossed over to take a closer look. 'That is a high-end gaming set-up. I have seen stuff like this before – only with fewer screens.'

'I don't use it for gaming,' Calum replied. 'Not often, anyway. Some of the stuff I do needs really good graphics and processing power.'

'Video editing?' Gecko guessed. 'Or are you hosting a web service?'

'A little bit of both.' Calum shifted position, aware of the muscle he had pulled when Professor Livingstone and her daughter were there. 'You want something to drink?'

'Do you have Coke?'

Calum smiled, despite himself. 'Have *I* got Coke? Prepare for a surprise, Gecko.'

As usual, Tara Flynn was hunched over her tablet. This time, however, she wasn't in her college room. She was in the campus library.

She wasn't there for information or for the peace and quiet. She was there because her own room had been invaded. And she hated it.

She'd been at college for almost a year now, studying a combined degree in History of Art and Graphic Design. She was only fourteen, but the college had taken her in early, partly because of her impressive exam results and partly because she had hacked their admissions database and changed her age. It wasn't that she felt any great calling towards making art; more that she wanted to be a computer-games designer – preferably working full time on some massive multi-player online role-playing game – and she knew she already had all the computing skills necessary for the job. What she lacked was the ability to quickly create a character graphic, or build a world that actually looked realistic, down to the waving of the grass. The course kept her interest, and it was fun, but she didn't seem to be engaging with the other students. They avoided her, for some reason, and she couldn't find a way to break into their little cliques. Her room was where she retreated to, a sanctuary. And now someone had got inside – virtually, not in reality, but it still felt like an invasion.

She had to decide what to do. She'd started out trying to destabilize those big financial and defence companies who seemed not to care that their activities were grinding entire countries into poverty, but now it seemed as if she was going to end up working for one of them. That, or face jail. She didn't know enough about the legalities of her situation, but what she did know was that these big companies had a lot more money behind them than her family did, and they could hire a lot more lawyers with a lot more experience and a lot fewer moral qualms. They could crush her, if they wanted. The only reason she'd got away with her hacking activities for so long was because she was beneath their notice, like a mosquito quietly sucking blood from an exposed leg. But she'd bitten too deep, and now they had her in their sights.

She felt desperate. She felt as if she didn't have anywhere to turn, anyone to talk to. She supposed she could get in contact with her hacker friends, but they were just presences on the other end of an electromagnetic wave. They might be in the next room to her in the halls of residence or they might be on the other side of the world. She would probably never know.

Her tablet was on the table in front of her. It suddenly flashed into life as another message came through.

Books are so very old fashioned, don't you think? How did people ever manage to find what they were looking for without the use of a decent search engine?

A pause, and then:

Have you come to a decision yet? Time is ticking away, and we have solicitors to instruct.

She typed in a response: *You're blackmailing me!*

The reply came so quickly that her hand was still lifting away from the tablet's touch-sensitive screen. *Of course we are. You seem surprised.*

Tara took a deep breath. *What is it you want me to do?* she typed.

The answer took a few seconds this time. *There is a website at www.thelostworlds.com. We want you to investigate it for us. We want you to find out everything you can about it. We want to know who set it up, who administers it, who updates it and who is viewing it on a regular basis. We also want a copy of all the images and text on the site.*

Tara frowned. That sounded suspiciously easy. *Can't you do that yourselves?* she typed.

Of course we can, but it might be traced back to us. Far better if we use a dupe who has no connection to us.

She had to admit it made sense. *And when I get that*

information for you, I'm clear? You won't ask me for anything else?

The letters that arrived on the screen were just pixels, assembled into patterns. They had no emotional context, no overtones, but somehow she knew that they were lies. *Of course not*, they said. *After this, if you leave us alone, then we will leave you alone.*

Tara sat there for another twenty minutes, waiting to see if the disembodied communicator was going to send her anything else, but there was nothing. Eventually she tapped her finger on the website address that she had been sent: www.thelostworlds.com.

The site seemed on the surface to be someone's attempt to pull together lots of information about creatures that might exist out in the world somewhere but were either thought to be extinct or had never been identified by scientists. There were links on the home page to information on things she'd heard of, like the Loch Ness Monster (which might be some kind of aquatic dinosaur – a *plesiosaur*, apparently), and the Sasquatch (which she knew was a big hairy ape-like creature in the forests of America, but which was more likely to be a hoax, she found). But there were also links to things she'd never heard of – everything from bacteria in frozen underground lakes that had been sealed away from the rest of the world for hundreds of thousands of years to something called the *chupacabra*, or 'goat sucker', which was supposed to be (according to eyewitness reports from Mexico and Puerto Rico, at least) some kind of hairless dog or large rat that sucked blood from livestock. The overall term for these things, Tara discovered, was *cryptids*, and whoever was behind this website was fascinated by them. Not just that though – he (and she was positive that it was a man) was very even-handed. If there was evidence about the cryptids, then he would report it fairly. The various photographs and mangled corpses that turned up as *chupacabras*, for instance, were almost always eventually identified as coyotes with severe mange.

It all looked innocent. It looked like the hobby of someone with an obsession and a lot of time on their hands. But if Nemor Incorporated thought there was something odd about it then she had to investigate.

After all, she thought bitterly, she worked for *them* now.

'Well, what's so fascinating about these . . .' Gecko hesitated for a moment, trying to find the right words. 'These *espécies ameacadas de extincao*?'

The kid with the paralysed legs – Calum Challenger – had been telling him about his hobby – finding creatures that were supposed to have been extinct for thousands of years or which had never been known about in the first place. Well, 'hobby' probably wasn't the right word. 'Obsession' was closer to the mark. Gecko knew the signs of obsession. He'd run across rooftops until his lungs burned, jumped across gaps that he shouldn't have been able to cross and generally pushed things too far, all in the cause of his own obsession – free-running. But that was about beauty and freedom of movement. Trying to find dead stuff – that was just lame.

Calum shrugged. He was sitting on the sofa, now that it had been cleared of glass, and both he and Gecko had drinks. 'I guess it has to do with my parents,' he said softly. 'My father was a palaeontologist.'

'A what?'

'He studied fossils. His particular field was the early evolution of the human race.' Calum smiled. 'He used to talk to me for hours about what he was doing, and what he hoped to prove. At the beginning I only understood a fraction of what he was saying, but as time went on I picked up more and more. It was his life – his passion.'

'What about your mother?' Gecko asked.

'She was a geneticist. She was trying to find ways of curing disease by modifying the human genome.'

'I'd say you were lucky they ever met,' Gecko pointed out. 'It is like he is at one end of the football field and she is at the other. My father was a janitor and my mother is a cleaner. Same world.'

'You would think,' Calum replied. 'But they met at a scientific conference. My mother had got interested in whether our remote ancestors had genes which might have protected them from diseases like cancer. She asked my father about the chances of finding DNA samples from some of the predecessors of *Homo sapiens*, like *Australopithecus afarensis*, *Australopithecus sediba* or *Homo erectus*. She even wondered whether *Homo neanderthalis* might have some genetic material that could prove useful.' He smiled, obviously remembering some story his parents had told him. 'They talked all night. By morning they'd realized two things – they could work together on this project, and they were in love.'

Gecko shook his head. He was getting lost. 'This genetic thing,' he said. 'I do not understand it.'

'It's pretty simple,' Calum said. 'Genes are the plans for what we are – what *any* living thing is, right? They're like little sections of blueprint that tell chemicals and cells how to work together to make something – like an eye, or a hand, or a tentacle. The great thing about genes is that they pretty much don't care if you mix and match them.'

'What do you mean?'

'Let me give you an example. A few years back scientists managed to move certain genes in a fly's DNA around so that instead of growing antennae, it grew an extra set of legs out of its head. They just replaced the "antenna-making" gene with a duplicate copy of the "leg-making" gene.'

'Yes, I think I saw that film,' Gecko said drily. 'It didn't end well for mankind.'

Calum shrugged. 'That was just an example, to prove that genes could be moved around. There's no actual *need* for a fly with legs growing out of its head.'

A thought struck Gecko. 'Does that make it a spider instead?' he asked.

'What do you mean?'

'Well, I remember at school, we were told that the difference between insects and spiders was that insects had six legs and spiders had eight legs. But if this modified fly had eight legs – six of them where they should be and the seventh and eighth ones sticking out of its head, doesn't that make it a spider instead?'

'No,' Calum said firmly. 'It doesn't work like that.'

'Why not?'

Calum's mouth was setting into a shape that Gecko was beginning to recognize as indicating he was annoyed. 'Just accept it. It was still a fly.' He took a deep breath. 'Other scientists moved genes from one animal to another. They took a gene from a jellyfish that caused it to glow, and inserted it into a mouse. The result was a glowing mouse.'

'Easier to catch,' Gecko pointed out. 'They can't hide in dark corners.

Calum's mouth twisted into that shape again. 'That wasn't exactly the point.'

Gecko raised his hands in surrender. 'OK. I understand. Scientists can move these genes around, within the same animal or between animals. So what?'

'So, what if we could find a gene that protects its owner from some terrible disease and incorporate it into human DNA?' Calum asked, leaning forward.

'Would we still be human?'

Calum flicked his head, as if to brush the question away. 'Of course we would. We'd be human, but better.'

'*Tá bom*,' Gecko conceded, although the thought of

fiddling around with the blueprint of the human body made him uneasy. 'But how does this connect up with your search for these animals?'

Calum nodded. 'Take the horseshoe crab. It's one of the oldest creatures known. By "oldest" I mean that it's been around in the same form, without noticeably evolving, for millions of years. Unlike any other creature, its blood is blue, not red, because it's based on copper-containing haemocyanin rather than iron-based haemoglobin.' He paused, and took a breath. He was staring ahead now, not looking at Gecko. 'The horseshoe crab's equivalent of the white blood cells found in human blood are incredibly efficient at neutralizing bacteria. They have to be, because the seas where the horseshoe crab lives are like bacterial soup. Humanity is facing a crisis in controlling bacteria – most of our antibiotics are losing efficiency as the bacteria get used to them. If we can find a way of synthesizing this factor from horseshoe-crab blood – if we could even splice it into our own DNA, or splice it into a cow's DNA so the antibiotic is expressed in the cow's milk – we might never get ill or die from an infection again.'

Gecko nodded slowly. 'My brother died from an infection,' he said slowly. The memories were still raw. 'He scratched his leg on a rusty nail when he was climbing over a fence. He developed tetanus. It –' he caught his breath, feeling his throat constrict in unexpected grief – 'it was not a good way to die.'

'There are a lot of bad ways to die,' Calum pointed out.

'If we can reduce them . . . find ways to avoid them . . . then that's got to be a good thing.'

'And you reckon some of these undiscovered animals might have genes that could help save people's lives?' Gecko nodded. 'That is a noble way to spend your life.'

Calum looked away. 'Maybe not completely noble,' he said softly.

'What do you mean?' Gecko noticed the way Calum's hand clamped on his leg, and suddenly understood. 'It's the nerves, isn't it? You think there might be a gene out there, in some undiscovered creature, that could help regenerate your nerves.'

Calum shrugged awkwardly. 'Your namesake, the yellow-headed gecko, can grow a new tail if the old one gets bitten off. Salamanders can regenerate entire legs if they lose them. Maybe, somewhere out there, is a way for me to . . . to walk again.'

There was silence for a few moments, both boys preoccupied with their own thoughts.

'You need any help?' Gecko asked eventually. 'For the sake of my brother, I want to do something.'

'Can you organize an expedition to the Caucasus Mountains to look for a possible missing link between apes and humans?' Calum asked.

'No,' Gecko said. 'I think I can quite honestly say that I cannot do that.' A thought struck him. 'Hey, do we have any of these supposedly undiscovered animals in Brazil? I never heard of any.'

Calum thought for a moment. 'There's something called the *mapinguary*,' he said. 'People say it's a giant sloth-like creature that has a really strong unpleasant smell. And there's the *minhocão*, which is supposed to be a giant black worm, some twenty-five metres long, with scaly skin and two tentacles coming out of its head.'

'That's just a story for children!' Gecko protested. 'The *minhocão* is supposed to be able to uproot trees and destroy houses, but nobody has ever seen one!'

'The last eyewitness reports are about a hundred and thirty years old,' Calum conceded, 'but they were taken seriously at the time. The trouble is that there are no photographs and no sketches, and it's difficult to see how an animal that large could survive in numbers big enough to keep a population going without anybody noticing.' He paused, and shrugged. 'Still, there's always hope.'

Gecko was about to ask Calum how he managed to fund all this work when a soft alarm started pinging over at Calum's computer station.

'What's that?' Gecko asked. 'Someone else on the roof?'

Calum shook his head. 'Not that kind of alarm. Someone's trying to hack into my website.'

'You have a website?' Gecko asked. 'What kind of website?'

'A website all about the undiscovered creatures we talked about.' Calum pulled himself off the sofa and started to swing across to the computer desk and the multiple screens.

'Why would someone want to hack into a site about animals that don't even exist?' Gecko asked, standing up and following Calum. 'Banks, I can understand. Nobody likes banks. Defence companies, yeah. But extinct animals? *Isto é loucura!*'

'Good question.' Calum slipped into the seat in front of the keyboard.

'I have another good question.'

'Yeah?' Calum grunted distractedly.

'Why do you have an *alarm* that tells you when someone's trying to hack into a website that nobody in their right minds would want to hack into? What exactly are you trying to protect?'

Calum turned in his seat and locked gazes with Gecko. 'Maybe there's other stuff on that website,' he said. 'Hidden stuff that I keep there.'

Gecko shrugged. 'You should use a safe deposit box, like normal people.'

Calum turned back to his screens and keyboard. His fingers flew across the keys. Gecko watched, entranced, as the various screens in front of them all started displaying different things: maps of the world with lines crossing back and forth, scrolling computer code, black and white images from security cameras, all kinds of things.

'So who is it?' he asked eventually. 'The CIA? MI5? The

Royal Society for the Prevention of Cruelty to Horseshoe Crabs?'

Calum was frowning. 'The IP address keeps bouncing around,' he said. 'It's difficult to track, but it seems to be coming from a wireless device just across the river.' He pressed a few more keys. 'St Catherine's College of Art, library building,' he said. 'Fourth floor.' His balled fist crashed down on his leg. 'Damn it – if I report it to the police they'll treat it as some kind of joke, but there's no way I can get out there and check for myself!'

'I could go,' Gecko said, surprising himself.

Calum turned round to stare at him. 'You'd do that? Why?'

Gecko shrugged. 'Like you said: fourth floor. I know that building. Once I get across the river, there is a route that will take me all the way. I can look in through the windows without anyone noticing me.'

'You're not answering the question. You just told me *how*. What I want to know is: *why*?'

Gecko smiled. 'Because it will be fun.'

Tara had downloaded all the web pages – text, pictures and hyperlinks – to her flash drive for later analysis, and for sending on to her unknown handler at Nemor Incorporated. Sitting in the library, alone in the study booths that lined one wall, she still had no idea *why* she was doing it, though. There was nothing at all unusual about the website. It showed a certain amount of obsessive-compulsive behaviour, as well as a good sense of design, but it was innocuous. Harmless.

Was it some kind of test, designed to see whether she would follow orders? Or was there something more to it, some hidden secret that she just hadn't stumbled across yet?

On a whim, she checked the size of the directory on the flash drive where she had saved the files – and drew her breath in. The directory was *much* larger than it should have been, given the number of pictures that she'd downloaded. The pictures would have taken up most of the space – text took hardly any space at all – but based on the resolution of the images, the whole thing should have been only a couple of gigabytes. Not the *eleven* gigabytes eating up her flash drive.

There was something else there. Something hidden.

She was about to trawl through the various sub-directories one by one, looking for any file names that seemed out of place, when she realized she was being watched.

It was a tickle on the back of her neck, like a psychic breath of air on her skin. She didn't know *how* she knew, but it was a certainty.

Without moving her head, she let her gaze roam around the deserted library area. Someone could have been hiding between the shelves of books, but that wasn't the direction that the feeling was coming from. It was more towards the far side of the room – where the windows were. There wasn't anywhere to hide there – it was an open area. That meant the watcher was somehow *outside* the window – like maybe a small remote-controlled drone or something!

Someone from Nemor Incorporated? It had to be. They were watching her, checking up on her for whatever purpose they had in mind!

A sudden flash of anger burst through her like a shock wave. What the hell did they think they were doing? She was a *student* for heaven's sake! She had *rights*!

Part of her wanted to cross straight to the windows, fling them open and have a shouting match with whoever was out there, but another part of her – the more sensible part – had a better idea. She stretched her arms above her head theatrically, and checked her watch in a way that would be obvious from the other side of the room. She wanted to make it look as if she was taking a break. Leaving her tablet on the work surface in the study booth, having activated an app that would sound an alarm if anyone disturbed it, she got up and walked off towards where the vending machines were located.

From the vending machine in the lobby she bought a packet of crisps and a can of drink. Holding them, she walked back into the library, but instead of heading for her booth she moved rapidly down one of the aisles between the bookshelves, anger driving her to run as fast as she could. At the end she turned right and moved quickly along the ends of the shelves.

When she got to the last bookshelf, she was by the

windows. Without hesitating – without even thinking – she climbed up on the windowsill. Slinging open the window, she stuck her head out and glanced sideways, along the line of windows.

She was right. Someone was crouched on the sill outside the fourth window along – just where he could observe the seat in which Tara had been sitting. His hands were clamped on the stonework of the building, stabilizing him. His clothes and hair were dark. He was just a silhouette against the sky.

'Not content with spying on me electronically, you have to do it in person?' she called. 'You want to tell me just what you think you're doing? What harm have I ever done you?'

The figure turned to look at her. It was just a kid: barely older than she was! His hair was long and shiny, and his eyes were the darkest, most soulful eyes she had ever seen.

'I think you have got things the wrong way round,' he said. His voice held a slight accent. 'You have been spying on someone else.'

'I have *not*,' she said, but a sudden flash of guilt washed some of the anger away. What if this boy didn't have anything to do with Nemor Incorporated? What if he was something to do with www.thelostworlds.com instead? But how could that be true? How could someone have traced her hacking and got here so fast? And why was he outside the window?

The boy looked at her hands. She realized that she was still holding the drink and the crisps.

'Do you mind if I come in?' he asked. 'I could do with a bite to eat. All this running and climbing really builds up an appetite, you know?'

'And what then? You arrest me for hacking? You report me to the college authorities?'

He shrugged: a smooth motion of his shoulders. 'Not exactly. I think there is someone you need to meet.'

'A friend of yours?' she asked sarcastically.

The boy seemed to treat her question more seriously than it deserved.

'Well,' the boy said, 'I think he is. I think he is going to be a friend to both of us.'

CHAPTER

four

The two of them stood side by side in the rackety lift that linked the ground floor of the warehouse to Calum's apartment. Gecko could feel anger radiating from the girl standing beside him. He could have fried onions with the force of her emotion. She was furious – but there was something else, some other feeling hidden beneath the anger. Fear?

Just looking at this girl – Tara Flynn, she had said her name was – he could tell that she wasn't built for free-running. Her muscle development was all wrong, and she slumped rather than stood upright. With posture like that he guessed she didn't get much exercise. Her skin was pale as well, indicating that she didn't get out in the sunlight very often. And she wore glasses, which would have thrown her depth perception off completely in the unlikely event that she'd try to jump from one rooftop to another. No, judging by the skill with which she'd been hitting her keyboard, he guessed she was one of those techno-zombies – *internautas*, as they were called in Brazil – that he kept seeing through windows of flats or office blocks at night – faces illuminated by the ghostly glow of LCD screens. If he'd tried to lead her across the rooftops, it would have ended with her splatting into the pavement at some speed.

The lift juddered to a halt and Gecko pulled the doors open. The two of them stepped out into a small hallway. There was a metal door ahead of them, set into brick, with a security-code pad beside it. Gecko typed in the code that Calum had given him earlier, and the door clicked open.

Tara glanced at Gecko. There was a scowl on her face. 'This had better be worth it,' she muttered.

'Hey,' he pointed out, 'this wasn't my idea. You're the one who tried to break into the website.'

'Websites are visible to anyone on the internet,' she said defensively. 'They're effectively public property. I wasn't doing anything wrong.'

'Actually,' Calum's voice called from inside the apartment, 'that's like saying that because the outside walls of a building face on to the public streets then the entire building is public property. The logic doesn't stand up to more than a few seconds' scrutiny. It's a fallacious argument.'

Tara's scowl intensified. Grinning, Gecko led the way inside.

Calum was in his computer chair, facing the door. The ten screens behind him silhouetted him dramatically. Presumably that was intentional. Gecko thought it made him look like a villain in a James Bond movie.

'It's like Gecko here thinking that because my roof is accessible by jumping from a nearby building, that makes it all right to run across it,' he went on. Gecko felt the grin slide off his face. 'The technical term in that case is actually "trespassing".' He stared at Tara. 'I'm not sure that "breaking and entering" covers what you did, but "electronic theft" probably does.'

'I didn't steal anything,' Tara said defiantly.

'You downloaded the entire contents of my website on to a USB drive.' Calum's voice didn't have any obvious emotion in it, but Gecko could tell that behind the words there was some anger, but a lot of curiosity as well.

'That wasn't stealing – it was copying,' Tara said defensively.

'What made you do that? Were you doing it for money, or just for kicks?'

'It wasn't a *what*,' Tara said. 'It was a *who*.'

There was silence in the large room for a few moments while Calum seemed to consider her words. Abruptly he said: 'Would you like a drink? There's Coke in the fridge over in the kitchen area.'

'It's good stuff,' Gecko confirmed.

'Gecko, could you grab three bottles for us?'

Gecko was about to protest that he wasn't a slave, but then he remembered the trouble Calum had getting around the room. The kid wasn't going to be able to carry three bottles back from the kitchen area himself, not while hanging on to the ceiling straps.

As Gecko headed over towards the huge double-doored fridge that dominated the kitchen he heard Calum say, 'Please – take a seat. You're making the place look untidy. The sofa is comfortable. Just be careful of the broken glass.'

He heard Tara moving towards the sofa. She obviously glanced upward, because she said, 'What happened to your skylight?'

'Someone dropped in.' Gecko turned his head to see that Calum was nodding in his direction.

Tara sat on the sofa – primly, on the edge – and Calum twisted his chair and pushed against the computer table with his right hand. The chair scooted across the wooden floor, ending up just across from the sofa. He twisted his body again so that he was facing the girl. It was obvious to Gecko that Tara had realized there was something wrong with Calum, but she didn't say anything. Her gaze flicked to the straps that hung from the ceiling, then to Calum's muscular development. She was quick on the uptake – Gecko would give her that.

He walked across to join the two of them. He passed out two of the bottles, then slumped in the opposite corner of the sofa to Tara.

'Got a thing against doors, I take it?' she asked him.

He shrugged. 'Getting into and out of rooms is a problem,' he said. 'Doors are a solution to that problem. They're not the *only* solution though, despite the fact that ninety-nine people out of a hundred think they are. And in most cases they aren't the most interesting or the most graceful solution.'

'Yes, talking about graceful but unorthodox methods of entry,' Calum said, 'let's get back to the website, and your rather skilful attempts to crack it.'

'It wasn't an *attempt*,' Tara protested. 'I succeeded!'

'Debatable.' Calum shrugged. 'But the important question is *why*. You indicated just now that you were doing it on behalf of someone else. Who are you working for?'

'I'm not *working* for anyone,' Tara protested. She was quiet for a few moments. Gecko could see from her expression that there was some kind of battle going on inside her mind. 'What I mean is I wasn't being paid,' she finally admitted. 'I was blackmailed into it.'

'Blackmailed by who?' Gecko asked, intrigued.

'*Whom*,' Calum corrected.

'Sorry?'

'It's "blackmailed by *whom*". Not "*who*".'

'Oh.' Gecko shrugged. 'Sorry. English is only my fifth language.'

Tara hadn't registered the byplay between Calum and Gecko. She was huddled on the sofa, staring at the floor. Gecko and Calum waited for a few moments. Eventually she said: 'Look, it was some dodgy corporation called "Nemor Incorporated", OK?'

'Never heard of them,' Gecko said.

'They keep themselves out of the news and off the internet, apart from some corporate rubbish that doesn't tell you anything interesting.' Her shoulders straightened with pride. 'There's a group of us who are trying to get inside their corporate firewall and find out if they're doing anything wrong so we can expose them to the world's media.'

'Computer hackers?' Gecko asked, nodding. 'Like those LulzSec people you hear about. Or WikiLeaks.'

She sniffed. 'WikiLeaks just publish stuff they're sent by insiders, and LulzSec just try to crash other people's systems for giggles. We're more serious than LulzSec and more activist than WikiLeaks. We try to break through the firewalls and scoop up whatever we can find that might be embarrassing or against the law, and then release it to the public.'

'Illegally,' Gecko pointed out.

'We answer to a higher morality,' she said, as if reciting the words from a script. 'If companies breaking the law use the law as a shield, then the law needs to be circumvented in order to catch them.'

'What do you call yourselves?' Calum asked.

She shook her head disdainfully. 'Why is it that the first thing people want to know is what we call ourselves? We don't have a name. We don't *need* a name. We're just . . . us.'

He nodded. 'OK, I can appreciate your motives. I can even approve of them . . .'

'Oh, gee, thanks for the endorsement,' she said with fake wide-eyed enthusiasm.

'. . . But it doesn't explain how you came to be here.'

She wriggled uncomfortably. 'This company, Nemor

Incorporated, realized that I was hacking them. And really quickly too. Instantly. They must have some real computer expertise at their end. They emailed me and offered me a deal – I was supposed to hack your website or they would report me to the police and have me arrested. They said they chose me because I had no connection to them, and nothing I did could be traced back to them.' She paused, and smiled slightly. 'I'm also better than anyone they have on their books, but they didn't admit that.'

Silence, for a few moments.

'What have you done,' Gecko asked Calum, 'to attract the attention of some big multinational company?'

Calum's face reflected a mixture of concentration and confusion. 'I don't know,' he admitted. 'I've never heard of Nemor Incorporated. I know that my guardian – Professor Livingstone – does consultancy work for some defence contractors, but I've never heard her mention them. I don't know why I would have turned up on their radar screens. It's not like I do anything that overlaps with defence or military interests. I'm just interested in creatures that are either thought to be extinct or not yet registered by biologists.'

'They were particularly concerned,' Tara added, 'with anything that might be hidden within your website. And there *is* something hidden there, isn't there?'

Calum glanced sharply at her. 'You spotted that?'

'It wasn't hard to spot.'

'You need to show me how to cover my tracks.'

'First,' she said, 'you have to break my connection to Nemor.'

Again, silence for a few moments while Calum and Gecko considered what she had said.

'You sure you want to cast your lot in with us?' Calum asked.

'I don't work for corporations,' she replied firmly. 'Not through choice.'

'So what makes you think I can help you break free from this unfortunate arrangement you've got yourself into?'

Tara glanced at Gecko. 'He told me you were smart.'

Calum smiled. Gecko hadn't seen him smile before, and he liked it. The smile made Calum's serious face light up into something boyish. 'I am,' he said. 'I'm actually *very* smart.'

'And very modest about it as well,' Gecko murmured.

'Much as I would like to take credit for what's about to happen,' Calum said, 'honesty compels me to admit that it's nothing to do with me. Well, not directly, anyway.'

Tara frowned. 'What do you mean?'

'I mean that Nemor Incorporated realized instantly that you were hacking their mainframe, yes?'

'Yes . . .'

'So they're keeping an eye on you.'

'OK . . .'

'Which means that they know you are here, right now.'

This time, the silence was so heavy that it could have drowned out the sound of church bells.

The sun weighed down on 'Rhino' Gillis like a dull weight, and the air was heavy and humid. Breathing was like trying to suck air through a towel that had been soaked in hot water and then clamped over his face.

He stood at the bottom of King Street and gazed around casually, feeling the sweat prickling down his back. He made it look as if he was glancing at the shops and the street signs, trying to work out which photographs he wanted to take with the camera slung round his neck, but his surroundings weren't really what he was interested in. He was actually considering the people around him, working out which of them wanted to kill him.

King Street was the spine running up the centre of the historic district of Alexandria, a part of Washington DC – the capital city of America, and therefore by definition the most powerful city in the world. The Alexandria district had been one of the first areas settled by travellers, several hundreds of years ago, and many of the buildings were obviously old and in need of restoration. The street ran from the marshy banks of the Potomac River – which cut Washington DC in half – and up a shallow hill all the way to the King Street metro station at the top. It was lined with hotels, restaurants and the kind of tourist shops that sold expensive scented candles, or hats that would be worn for a couple of days on holiday and then lost or forgotten about.

Rhino could never understand why, out of all the places that settlers could have stopped and set up a capital city in a newly explored country, they had chosen an unhealthy, mosquito-infested swamp that was far too hot in summer and far too cold in winter for humans to endure with any degree of comfort. Why not keep travelling for a while and find a better place? Wouldn't that have made more sense?

People puzzled him. They always had. People made strange decisions that couldn't be explained by logic. That was why he preferred guns, and engines, and things that either worked the way you expected them to or broke down in predictable ways and could be repaired. That was what he was good at. That, and rescuing hostages from captivity.

Rhino realized that he was standing outside a restaurant. The sign above the door read *The Fish Market*. He remembered eating there before, several years ago. It had been a celebration dinner after he and some colleagues had completed a tough mission rescuing a bunch of backpackers and aid workers from a criminal group in one of those African countries that seemed to measure its history not in years but in the number of times its government got overthrown and replaced. His colleagues had been retired American Special Forces personnel, which was why Washington had been chosen as the best location for the mission to start and finish. They mostly lived inside the ring road called the Beltway that encircled the city, hoping that the Secret Service, or the FBI, or the CIA would call on them for some Top Secret and highly deniable mission in the Middle East or North Korea, and filling in the time with paid hostage-rescue jobs.

'Why do they call you Rhino?' one of the men asked him.

'I used to play a lot of rugby when I was younger,' he answered. At the blank looks, he added: 'Rugby – it's like your American football, except without the padding and the constant stopping. Anyway, the team I played on used to joke that I had no real talent for the game – my one skill was to run fast with my head down and barge my way past the opposing players. They said I reminded them of a rhino charging. The name stuck.'

'So what's your real first name?' the man pressed.

'You know,' Rhino replied, 'it's been so long since I've used it that I just don't remember.'

That wasn't true – his name was on his passport, of course – but he preferred 'Rhino'. It suited him.

Now, a few years later but back in the same location, he caught sight of his reflection in a shop window as he scanned the passing crowd for signs of pursuit or danger. He was still under thirty, muscular and without an inch of fat on him. The chinos and the polo shirt he was wearing were suitably anonymous. His sunglasses hid his eyes effectively, and the baseball cap he wore cast a shadow on his face. His lightweight cotton jacket was loose enough to allow him to conceal a weapon either in a shoulder holster or tucked into the back of his chinos, but today he was unarmed. Today was not meant to be a day for problems.

He didn't know the people tailing him. He had noticed them out of the corner of his eye when he had left a restaurant called the Charterhouse. He had been eating alone, passing the time before a meeting with a potential client later that afternoon. Emerging from the restaurant, he had seen two people glance at him at the same time then look away. It was a subtle sign, but Rhino had been trained to pick up on subtle signs. He had started to walk away, not obviously looking at the two people but using reflections in car windscreens and shopfronts to keep an eye on them. They had both set out after him within a few moments of him hitting the pavement. Interestingly, they hadn't looked at each other. That meant they had a certain level of training, enough that they could avoid checking with each other all the time, but not enough to stifle that initial impulse to look at their quarry as soon as he emerged from his hiding place. Professional, but not expert.

Of course they might have been completely independent of each other, but the chances were slim. It made more sense to assume that he was being targeted by a team.

But who *were* they? Rhino quickly ran through the options. He doubted that they were official – he hadn't broken any American laws that he knew about, and he tried as much as possible to stay off official radar screens. Local criminals, maybe, looking to mug an unwary tourist for his camera? Probably not – they had ignored the various better-dressed people who had left the restaurant before

Rhino, but they had registered him and started moving as soon as he came through the doors. They had been waiting specifically for him. No, as uncomfortable as the thought was, Rhino was pretty sure that his followers had something to do with the unofficial hostage-rescue business in which he worked. The kidnap gangs in Africa often had links to gangs in America – finance flowed one way, drugs the other. If he had to guess, then he would say that one of the gangs from which he'd rescued hostages had put out a call to have him found and killed. Him and, he supposed, the other members of his team.

He started moving up King Street, towards the distant metro station. His 'friends' followed. One of them was directly behind him, about ten metres back, while the other was paralleling Rhino's course on the other side of the road.

He had to assume they were out to kill him. The hostages that he and his colleagues rescued in Africa and elsewhere were usually being ransomed by their captors. Some governments would quietly pay millions of dollars to get their citizens back alive, and if the governments wouldn't pay then families or employers would often raise the cash. Hostage-taking was fast becoming the major source of income in some Third World countries. And what Rhino and his colleagues did was stop that payment from reaching the gangs.

Passing the Marriott hotel on his left, Rhino thought momentarily about dodging inside, dashing across the lobby and losing himself in one of the many branching corridors that would lead into the bowels of the building. There were bound to be back exits and ways down to the underground car park, or he could break into an empty storeroom and wait there until everyone chasing him had given up and gone home. He dismissed the idea straight away. He didn't know how many people were following him. It might just have been the two that he had seen, or it might have been more. If *he* had been in charge of a pursuit, he would have already scouted the ground out and worked out all the places where the quarry could make a sudden dash for freedom. Hotel lobbies were an obvious option, and he would have stationed operatives with mobile phones or personal radios in each lobby, just in case.

That was the problem with pursuit operations – they were very labour-intensive, if done properly. To follow one man effectively took a team of about fifteen people, minimum.

He kept moving, hoping that somewhere up ahead he could find an opportunity to break and run.

The darkened glass frontage of the hotel gave him a perfect opportunity to glance sideways and get a better view of the pair following him. They were both male, and both dressed anonymously: T-shirts with sports-team logos, lightweight waterproof anoraks that could hide a variety of weapons, jeans, trainers. Definitely not FBI, CIA or Secret Service then: they wore suits to everything. One of his pursuers wore a blue baseball cap, while the other had a pair of bright orange trainers that looked so new and so inappropriate that he must have bought them himself, recently, and loved them so much he had to wear them everywhere. Rhino labelled the two of them as Blue and Orange. It helped him keep track of them in his mind.

Orange was about twenty metres behind Rhino. He was talking, muttering a rapid stream of words. There wasn't anyone nearby, so he was either chatting to himself or speaking into a hidden microphone. When he raised a hand and pressed something more firmly into his ear, Rhino knew that he was communicating with his controllers – or with Blue – using some kind of miniature microphone and earpiece system.

Rhino's gaze flickered around, trying to spot Blue. The man had vanished while Rhino was cataloguing what Orange was doing.

When something sharp scratched his stomach, Rhino suddenly knew where Blue was.

'Keep walking,' a voice said in his ear: harsh and low. 'Otherwise I'll slice you from navel to ribcage and let you bleed out on the street.'

'How?' Tara asked. 'How do they know I'm here?' Her tone was level, but Gecko could hear the stress in it.

'Oh, various ways,' Calum replied blithely. 'The most obvious is your mobile phone. I'm guessing it's on right now, which means it's broadcasting your location to the world.'

'Not mine,' she said. 'I'm a hacker, remember? I know

how to use and abuse anything with a silicon chip in it, and I know how to protect myself. The first thing I did when I got this phone was to deactivate any apps that sent my location, or any other information about me, to anyone else.'

'But your mobile-phone company can still track which cell you're in, and an expert can use other techniques to tell roughly where you are in that cell – like, which cell you were in before. If you move from cell A to cell B, then they know you're on the A side of cell B.' Calum thought for a moment. 'What about Wi-Fi? Does your phone automatically try to link into any Wi-Fi network it can find?'

Tara nodded. 'I tend to do a lot of work in coffee shops and the like. Saves 3G roaming charges if I can piggyback on any local networks. I'm a poor student – I need to save all the money I can.'

Calum nodded decisively. 'Then anything you email will show up as being sent from my IP address. Just send them a message saying that you've downloaded the Lost Worlds website, and asking them what they want you to do with the data.' Tara looked at him for a long moment, then at Gecko. Her expression didn't change, but she seemed to soften suddenly. 'I guess . . .' she said. She reached inside her jacket and took out her mobile phone. Her fingers danced across the keypad. 'OK, it's done. I hope you know what you're doing.'

Calum pushed himself back across the room towards his impressive computer desk. As his fingers tapped the keyboard of his multi-screen array, Tara asked Gecko: 'What's he up to?'

'Search me,' Gecko said.

'Right,' Calum said, pushing himself back across the room. This time he was holding a wireless keyboard. 'Now we wait.'

'For how long?' Tara asked.

'Probably a matter of seconds.'

He was right. Tara's phone pinged to alert her to the arrival of a new email. She quickly opened it up.

The ten screens over Calum's computer desk all suddenly moved on their spidery support arms. They twisted and joined up, edge to edge, to form a supersized rectangular array that was flat-on to the three of them across the room. The screens flickered, and an email browser program appeared, with the newly arrived message displayed clearly so they could read it.

Your instructions were clear, the message said. *You were supposed to hack the website, not infiltrate the building. We have other, more skilled, operatives for that kind of operation.*

Tara glanced at Calum. 'Clever trick,' she said. 'You realize that's a private message?'

'Oh, please,' he murmured. 'By all means let's have a conversation about privacy and security – but not right now, OK?' His fingers typed something into the keyboard without looking at it. 'Ask them how they want the files you stole delivered.'

She typed the message into her phone.

Moments later: *The problem is that we can't trust anything you send us now. You appear to have defected to the enemy camp. Our arrangement is null and void.*

Tara's face fell. 'What have you done? They're going to report me to the police!'

'I doubt it,' Calum replied calmly. 'They pressurized you into committing a criminal act. They can't shop you to the police for hacking *their* website without you telling everyone that they wanted you to hack *my* website. Both sides now have something to hold over the other.'

'I should have worked that out myself,' Tara chided.

The screens flashed, and a new message appeared. *Your new friend will have explained by now that we cannot hurt you without you causing us some minor and temporary embarrassment. Pursuing you is not worth the trouble – not yet. We will, however, meet again, and when that happens we will determine an appropriate form of punishment for your betrayal. We have long memories.*

The words seemed to echo in the silence of the room like a struck bell. Tara glanced from Calum to Gecko and back. 'That's a bad thing, right?' she said in a small voice.

CHAPTER

five

As the knife blade scratched his skin, Rhino Gillis cursed silently and clenched his fists. He had been looking so hard at Orange that Blue had managed to catch up without Rhino seeing him. He wouldn't normally fall for something like that. Was he getting old and out of practice, or was he just jet-lagged?

He glanced down at his stomach. A hand was pressing a small, wickedly curved knife against him. It had already sliced through his shirt, and he could feel a trickle of warm blood from where the blade touched his skin.

'Where are we going?' he asked. He tried turning his head to look at the man with the knife, but the man pressed the knife harder into his stomach and muttered, 'Don't try to look at me. Just keep moving forward. There's a van at the next intersection: we're all going to get inside it nice and simply.'

'Then what?'

'Then,' Blue said, with an amused tone in his voice, 'there're some people that want to have a talk with you.'

'What about?'

'Don't know and don't care.'

'A movement in the corner of his eye jerked Rhino's attention to the left. Orange had just come alongside the two of them.

'Nice trainers,' Rhino said.

Orange scowled at him. 'What do you mean by that?'

'I'm just saying.'

'No talking,' Blue snapped.

'But he's makin' smart-mouthed comments 'bout mah trainers!'

Blue growled deep under his breath. 'Don't matter what he says about those stupid trainers of yours. He ain't gonna be in a position to mouth off about anything soon.'

'Look, is this about that parking ticket I got last week?' Rhino asked mildly, trying to keep the conversation going while he thought of ways to escape.

'Do we look like traffic wardens?' Orange asked.

'Well, you're certainly not the fashion police,' Rhino responded drily. 'Not with trainers that colour.'

He could feel Orange bristling with righteous indignation. He was right – the man was defensive about his new acquisition. Other people were probably making jokes – people in his gang. That gave Rhino a slight edge – and he had to be very precise and quick about exploiting it, otherwise he would end up in the van. And once he was in the van his chances of escape would be considerably smaller than they were now.

'You got some kind of death wish?' Orange snarled.

Rhino could see that he was staring directly ahead and scowling. He wasn't thinking about Rhino, or his mission. He was obsessively brooding over the insult to his fashion sense.

Rhino noticed two women up ahead, talking. They were wearing expensive clothes and sunglasses, and they were both holding tiny poodles in their arms.

Rhino stopped walking abruptly. The knife pulled away from his stomach as Blue moved forward. Blue caught himself quickly, realized what was happening and turned towards Rhino. His knife hand automatically reached out, trying to re-establish contact with Rhino's skin.

Rhino grabbed Blue's wrist and jerked it sideways, towards Orange.

The knife was already moving in that direction, thanks to Blue's automatic response to Rhino's dead stop. All Rhino had to do was help the knife on, and aim it.

At Orange's right arm.

Orange suddenly found his colleague's knife embedded in his forearm. He stared at it in disbelief. Blood bloomed on the sleeve of his green anorak. 'What the . . . ?'

While Orange and Blue were distracted, Rhino stepped towards the two chatting women and grabbed the poodle from the arms of the nearest one.

'Excuse me,' he said. 'Sudden emergency.'

The poodle squirmed in his hands, snarling. Both women turned to stare at him, their mouths twin 'O's of surprise.

Blue realized what Rhino was doing and reached for him with a claw-like hand. So Rhino threw the poodle into the man's face.

The dog twisted in mid-air. Blue brought his arms up automatically to intercept it, and it sank its teeth into his hand. He cried out and tried to push the animal away, but it was locked on to his palm and wouldn't let go. Rhino could hear it growling, deep in its throat.

'Sorry,' he said to the second woman as he snatched her dog. 'I really do need a matched pair.'

This one he just pushed at Orange as the man gaped in amazement at what was going on.

Panicking, the dog fastened its teeth on Orange's nose.

Orange screamed: a high-pitched whistle of pure shock.

Rhino reached out and pushed Blue and Orange in opposite directions. The men stumbled and fell, each one still with a dog latched on to some vital part of his anatomy. Smiling at the two shocked dog owners, who were staring in disbelief at what was going on, Rhino sprinted away.

Behind him he could hear snarling, shouting and, if he wasn't mistaken, the sound of the two women hitting Blue and Orange with their handbags. He didn't look back. He kept running, then dodged down a side street.

He diverted down an alleyway that separated two warehouse-like buildings. There were some plastic bins a few metres down, and he ducked between them. He could feel his breath rasping in his chest, and his pulse hammering in the arteries of his neck and in his temples. Despite all his training, despite all the exercise he did on a regular basis, sudden exertions like this would always drain his energy.

He listened above the sound of his own ragged breathing for the noise of footsteps running after him. There was nothing. Somewhere in the distance he thought he could hear voices raised in anger, but nobody appeared to be chasing him. Hopefully the two dog-owning women were so busy with Blue and Orange that the two thugs hadn't had an opportunity to get away. They wouldn't dare use weapons. Not on members of the public. That would immediately involve the police.

He cursed under his breath. His cover was comprehensively blown. He needed to get out of Washington in a hurry.

The best thing he could do was go somewhere remote – back in England, if he could get to the airport and on to a flight without getting intercepted – and go to ground for a while. Get out of circulation until the fuss had died down. The way criminal gangs worked, something else would come along to distract their attention. Pretty soon he would be yesterday's news, and nobody would waste time or money looking for him.

Time or money. That was the problem. Rhino had time, but he didn't have money. Financing these kidnap-rescue operations took a lot of cash, and the profit margin wasn't that big. If he wanted to keep going, then he had to take any job that came his way. He couldn't afford to take a break for too long. And, of course, there were other ex-Special Forces soldiers wandering around trying to get into the same business. Work came through personal recommendations, and it was time-sensitive. If he was out of the game for a few months, lying low to avoid getting tracked and caught, then someone else would come along and take the jobs that would have been his. And then, when he got back into the game, it wasn't just the criminals who would have forgotten about him. His prospective customers would have done so as well.

The bottom line was he needed a job that would take him out of circulation for a while, and he needed it fast. But where was that job going to come from?

'Don't worry,' Calum said to Tara. 'They're playing games with your mind.' Gecko watched as he typed furiously into his wireless keyboard, then let out a frustrated breath. 'Blast it, they're using an anonymizer. Obvious, I suppose, but I can't trace the email back to a location.'

'First thing I thought of.' Tara shrugged. She was trying to look casual, but her face was shadowed with worry. 'They're not technological muppets – that much is certain.' She glanced from Calum to Gecko and back again. 'So what exactly is it that I've got myself into here? What is it you do that's attracted the interest of these Nemor people?'

Calum opened his mouth to explain, but Gecko stopped him with an upheld hand. 'Hey, can I do this one? Just to see if I understand it properly?'

Calum shrugged. 'Knock yourself out.'

'Right.' Gecko turned back to Tara. 'Your man here is a one-person ecology project, but he is not interested in cuddly pandas or the like. He is trying to locate and protect species that either science doesn't know about, or that science thinks are already extinct.'

'That much I got from a quick scan of his website.' Tara raised an eyebrow. 'I guess the question is: *why?*'

Gecko glanced at Calum, who nodded. 'Because there might be stuff in their DNA that could cure diseases, or help us in other ways.'

'And,' Calum added, 'because it would be a tragedy if a species died out due to global warming or endemic pollution without us even knowing that it was there.'

'Even though it might be a really small beetle, or some kind of ugly, spiky fish or something,' Gecko continued. At Calum's frown he went on: 'Hey, be honest – not all creatures are as cute as pandas.'

'And that's half the problem.' Calum shrugged. 'There's definitely a pecking order in cryptids.'

'Cryptids?' Tara asked.

'Animals that are just rumours, or just legends. Everyone wants there to be a plesiosaur in Loch Ness, or pumas living wild in Hampshire, but it's the unknown stick insect in Bolivia that's more likely to have genetic material that can be used for the benefit of mankind.'

'That's exploitation,' Tara said firmly. She seemed to sit straighter on the sofa, and her face took on an aggrieved expression. 'Nobody owns the DNA of another creature. We all own the rights to our own genetic material.'

'Even ugly, spiky fish?' Gecko asked.

'*Especially* ugly, spiky fish,' she responded angrily.

Whoops, Gecko thought, that obviously hit a nerve. Maybe she thinks of herself as a spiky fish. Best leave that analogy well alone in future.

Calum held up a hand. 'Look, nobody in this room wants to exploit these creatures. I know what you mean – there are some companies out there who, if they can genetically sequence a newly discovered creature, will try to copyright all the data and then use it to create new drugs and new medical treatments so they can make a profit. And they'll stop anybody else from benefiting. That's just wrong.' He shook his head. 'No, if a new creature is discovered, then its DNA should be sequenced and released as widely as possible so that everyone can benefit from it. And the population of creatures has to be protected from deliberate theft and from environmental pressures. All of that is fundamental.'

'So who gets to do that genetic sequencing?' Tara asked. 'It's not like you can buy the kit down at Maplin. Big biotech companies already have the equipment, ready and waiting, but they aren't well known for their acts of charity.'

Calum shrugged. 'Universities are the best option, especially if they're incentivized with a grant from an outside body.' He raised his hands to forestall Tara's immediate objection. 'A no-strings-attached grant, of course.'

'Do you think,' Gecko asked, 'that this Nemor Incorporated might be one of those companies? Do you think they might be wanting to copyright and own some of that DNA that is wandering around out there waiting to be discovered, and they do not appreciate your desire to make the information freely available to everyone?'

That thought effectively killed the conversation for a few moments.

'That hadn't occurred to me,' Calum said slowly. 'You think that Nemor might want to get a head start on finding, capturing and exploiting any cryptids that get discovered?'

'It is a thought.'

'Quite a disturbing one.' Calum shook his head. 'I wish I hadn't put the Almast photograph up on the website now.'

'Almast?' Gecko and Tara asked at the same time.

He waved his hand in an apparent attempt to indicate that the information wasn't important. 'It's the name given by the people in Georgia to a local legendary creature that looks like a cross between an ape and a human.'

'"Georgia" as in the southern state of the USA?' Tara asked.

Calum shook his head. '"Georgia" as in the former Soviet republic, bordered by Russia, Turkey, Armenia and Azerbaijan. The Almasti are supposed to live in the South Caucasus Mountains,' Calum went on, 'which are generally taken to be the division between Europe and Asia. Some people have thought for a while now that the Almasti legends might be a kind of local memory of a tribe of some kind of primitive prehumans still living in isolation – Neanderthals, or something similar. I'd never taken the stories seriously until someone uploaded a photograph to a file-sharing site.'

He tapped on the wireless keyboard, and a blurry photograph appeared on the multiple-screen array. Gecko stared at it, fascinated. Just like Calum had said, it seemed to show a creature that was somewhere between chimpanzee and human, caught in an unguarded moment as it was walking between two boulders on a sloping patch of ground.

'Incredible,' he breathed.

'You've checked for artefacts?' Tara asked.

'Artefacts?' Gecko asked.

'Traces in the data showing that it's been manipulated,' she answered. 'Hard edges, pixelation, mismatching contrast and saturation levels, that kind of thing.'

'I checked,' Calum said. 'The image is completely undoctored, as far as I can tell. That figure you can see in the photograph was actually there, on that hillside.'

Tara gazed critically at the screens. 'Could have been a man in a suit.'

'Unlikely,' Gecko found himself saying. 'Look at the way the weight is thrown back. Look at the relative length of the forearms compared to the upper arms. If that's a man, then it's a man with severe muscular and skeletal issues.'

'And you're an expert on the way people stand?' Tara asked scornfully.

'Yes,' he said simply. 'I'm a free-runner. I know more about human anatomy and the way it works than most medical students. I have to. For me it's a matter of survival.'

'So, we're agreed that it's a real image,' Calum said. 'The question is: what do we do about it? If you'd asked me an hour ago, I would have said that I'll try to raise interest and funding through my website for an expedition to Georgia to look for the Almasti, but that could take years to arrange. If Nemor Incorporated *is* sniffing around, then they could get people out there within a few weeks. And if they find the Almasti, then the consequences could be catastrophic.'

'They'll stop any information reaching the public,' Tara said bleakly. 'They'll probably take as many of the Almasti as they can and lock them up in cages in a laboratory. They'll treat them like animals while they take samples of blood, spinal fluid and bone marrow for testing. If the Almasti do exist, then they should be celebrated, not incarcerated.'

'They should be allowed to live free,' Gecko said quietly. 'Out in the open. Not in cages.'

Tara's expression was fierce. 'We need to do something.' She stared challengingly at Calum. 'You swear that you don't want to harm the Almasti?'

He nodded soberly. 'If they exist . . . *if* they exist . . . then all I want to do is to get some photographs, take some cell samples and make sure that they're not in the way of any forest clearance or dam-building programmes.'

'And you're not going to turn them into a tourist attraction?' Gecko asked.

'Quite the reverse – I want to protect them from any interference from the outside world, no matter how well-intentioned.'

'And these cell samples.' Tara was still staring at Calum. 'How invasive would they be?'

'Just a simple swab of the inside of the mouth. No discomfort, and just a few seconds to do.'

'And you would ask their permission?'

He frowned, as if the question hadn't occurred to him before. 'I suppose,' he said cautiously. 'If I could communicate my intentions to them. I must admit, until now I'd been thinking about new species of beetle or fish, not something that might have an opinion on what I was doing. But yes – if the Almasti exist, then they must have some degree of intelligence, and that means they have the right to make their own choices.'

Gecko felt a kind of pressure in his chest. He could suddenly see a way out of his predicament. The feeling was a bit like the mixture of fear and anticipation that he got just before he performed a jump that he'd never done before. But the leap he was about to take was a psychological one, not a physical one. Although the consequences if he got it wrong might be just as dangerous.

'Look,' he said slowly, 'I have got an idea. Call me stupid if you want, but I think I could go to Georgia and take a look around for you. See if I can find this

Almast.' He swapped to Brazilian Portuguese to make sure that he was expressing himself in the right way. '*Eu gostaria de voluntaria com minha especializacao*,' he said, and then carefully translated the words for Calum: 'I would like to volunteer my services.' He bowed slightly, formally.

Tara gazed at him as if he was mad. Calum, on the other hand, looked at him the way a scientist might stare at a bacterial culture in a Petri dish that had just done something unexpected.

'Why would you do that?' he asked eventually.

Gecko shrugged. 'It sounds like it might be an interesting challenge.'

'No, you're going to have to do better than that if you want me to commit funding to this hare-brained scheme.'

Gecko sighed. 'Look, I am in a little bit of trouble, here in London. I mentioned I am a free-runner, yeah? Well, there is some Eastern European criminal gang that want me to steal stuff for them.' He sniffed. 'Cannot say I am that much in favour of the idea. Even ignoring the fact that it is against the law, I would be taking all the risks while they take all the profits. It is a mug's game, but they have made it clear that I am not really in a position to say no. There is a certain amount of pressure being applied – the kind of pressure that can result in broken arms and legs. And if my arms and legs are broken then where does that leave me? Free-running is my life. It is who I *am*.'

He realized that his voice was getting louder, and that he was staring intently at a spot on the wooden floorboards as he spoke. He hadn't realized how much worry he'd been bottling up until he'd uncorked it and allowed it all to come spilling out.

'So I think that the best thing I can do is clear out for a while. Wait until they have found some other sucker to work for them. The question is: where?' He gestured up at the broken skylight. 'When I was up there, I was sorting through my options. I did not think I had any. Now you have caught my interest. If you can spring the cash for a plane ticket, I can head out into the wilds of Georgia and scout the place out for you. Take some photographs, talk to people, see what they say.' He raised his gaze and glanced at Calum. 'Look, I will come back and report. Honest.'

'I don't doubt that.' Calum raised an eyebrow. 'I was just wondering why exactly you're so confident that you can make it by yourself in a foreign country.'

Gecko shrugged. 'I have done it before. I used to live in France. Before that I was in Brazil. My father is dead, and my mother is working most hours in the day. I am used to being by myself in a foreign country, and surviving.' He frowned as a thought struck him. 'Hey, what language do they speak in Georgia?'

'Seventy per cent of the population speak Georgian as their first language,' Calum replied. 'It's the country's own indigenous tongue, which the Russians never managed to eradicate when they were in control. Ten per cent speak Russian, while the remaining twenty per cent speak a variety of languages like Armenian and Azeri. English is quite widely taught in the schools.'

'Well, if I cannot get by in English, then I can make myself understood in Russian,' Gecko said with some relief. 'I learned it a while ago. I guess most of the population, especially the older ones, will speak Russian.'

'Make sure you speak it with an accent,' Calum cautioned. 'I don't think the ethnic Georgians have much love for the Russian people.'

'I want to go too,' Tara said quietly.

Gecko and Calum turned to stare at her. '*What?*' they asked together.

'I said I want to go too.' She was looking down at the sofa, but she raised her gaze towards Gecko defiantly. 'What – you think you're the only one with a good reason for getting out of the country for a while? This Nemor Incorporated have got me in their sights. They won't forget what I did – or rather, what I didn't do – for them.' She glanced over at Calum. 'I hear what you say about them having more important things to do with their time, but I don't believe it. In my experience, big powerful corporations get that way by always looking after the details. I'm a detail, and I don't want to be. So I think I need to get out of the country for a while. Vanish from the grid.'

Calum looked genuinely amazed, and Gecko felt his own jaw drop open in surprise. He wasn't sure how he felt about having a companion on his travels. On the one hand it would slow him down, but on the other hand it would be nice to have someone to talk to.

Calum was shaking his head, although it seemed to Gecko that there was some reluctance in the movement. 'No, this is stupid. You're both teenagers. I can't ask you to go and do this for me.'

'You're not asking us,' Tara pointed out. 'And besides, *you're* a teenager, and if you *could* go then you would, wouldn't you?'

Calum didn't say anything or move his head, but the expression on his face told Gecko that Tara was right.

'You'd need some kind of guide,' Calum said slowly. 'Someone who knows the area.'

'We can find someone local,' Gecko said, but Calum shook his head.

'There's no way to know whether we could trust a local guide. It would have to be someone English, someone who comes with a recommendation, who happens to know the area. Not easy to find.'

'But you've got an idea, haven't you?' Tara asked shrewdly.

'I have,' Calum agreed, 'but I need to make a phone call . . .'

Natalie Livingstone was lying face down on one of the two single beds in the hotel room when her mother's iPhone rang.

'Mom!' she called out, her voice muffled by the duvet. 'It's your phone!'

'Can you answer it?' a voice called back from the bathroom.

Natalie sighed. She reached out from her position and felt about blindly until her fingers curled round it just as it rang again, sending vibrations through her hand.

'Yeah?' she said into it.

'Professor Livingstone?' The voice was familiar: male, young, tentative.

'No, sorry, she can't come to the phone right now.' She put on an exaggerated Personal Assistant voice. 'Can I take a message?'

'Er, yeah. It's Calum. Calum Challenger.'

She suddenly connected the voice with the boy she'd met earlier: the one with the absurdly broad shoulders and the stupidly floppy hair, the boy who was obviously crippled but didn't want to use a wheelchair – which she could totally sympathize with.

She turned over so that her voice wasn't muffled by her face-down position. 'Oh, hi – it's Natalie.'

'Hi, Natalic. How arc you?'

She looked around. The hotel room was four-star, of course, but it was a hotel room, just like any other. Only the view through the window changed. From here she could, if she bothered going across to the window, see down on to Regent's Park. Apparently there was a zoo in Regent's Park – at least that's what her mom had said. Natalie had replied that if she wanted to go to a zoo then she'd magically turn herself back into a six-year-old. Her mom had snapped back that Natalie often acted like a six-year-old, and they had argued until her mom had thrown her hands up in the air and said, 'I haven't got time for this. I'm going to have a bath. Don't leave the room.'

'Oh, I'm just peachy,' she said.

'Professor Livingstone cramping your style?' he asked.

'Like you wouldn't believe. You don't know how lucky you are.' She realized what she was saying just as the words were coming out of her mouth, and if she could have swallowed them back up she would have done. 'Jeez, sorry. I didn't mean . . .'

'It's OK,' he said. 'I've got used to people saying things without thinking. In a way, that's probably better than them trying to avoid the subject altogether.'

'Who is it?' Natalie's mom called from the bathroom.

'It's Calum!' Natalie shouted back.

'Calum *Challenger*?'

'Yeah.'

'Ask him what he wants. Is everything OK?'

'She's asking what you want,' Natalie said into the phone. She ran a hand through her hair.

'That's a tricky one. Is there any chance she can ring me back?'

'I doubt it. She's likely to stay in there until her skin gets all wrinkly, then she's going to spend half an hour and use an entire tub of moisturizer to make it all unwrinkly again. And then she's going out to dinner with a bunch of men in suits with dandruff on their shoulders while I get to spend the evening alone apart from room service and whatever movies the hotel's entertainment system will allow me to watch.' For a crazy moment she thought about inviting Calum over to hang out for a while, but just for a moment. She already knew how much effort it took for him to move around his own apartment. God knew how he would be able to get across London to the hotel.

'Sounds like fun.' A pause while he obviously considered his options. 'OK, can you ask her two questions?'

'Sure.'

'First question – if I give her a sample of DNA, would she be able to get its entire genome sequenced and analysed for me?'

That was not the kind of question Natalie had been expecting. 'Uh, right. let me ask.' She moved the phone away from her mouth and yelled, 'Mom, Calum wants to know if you can sequence a genome for him.'

A long silence, then: 'Why?' her mom called back.

'Just "because", I guess.' She brought the phone back to her face. 'Did you hear that?'

'I did. Good answer.'

'Thanks.'

'Tell her that I might be able to get my hands on a DNA sequence from a previously unknown animal, and I want to evaluate it for genes that might be useful, but I don't want some big corporation to do it. I want a university to have a crack, so that the results are available to everyone.'

'Oh. OK.' She moved the phone away again and called out: 'I was right – he says "just because".'

'I very much doubt that's actually what he said,' her mom's voice called back, 'but yes, in *principle*, I can get it done.'

'She says yes,' Natalie relayed back. 'What's the second question?'

'Can she recommend someone who can act as a guide in the south-eastern area of Europe, specifically Georgia?'

Taking a deep breath, Natalie relayed the question.

'Intriguing question. Tell Calum that there's a man I've used before as an expedition guide to remote areas of the world. He's ex-Special Forces. I know he's visited that area of Europe. I can get him to give Calum a call, if that would be OK – as long as Calum promises to tell me what exactly he's up to.'

'That's brilliant,' Calum said as Natalie put the phone back to her ear. He'd obviously picked up the answer. 'What's his name?'

'What's his name?' Natalie called out.

'Gillis,' her mom shouted. 'I don't know his first name, but everyone calls him "Rhino".'

'Sounds like a fun kinda guy,' Natalie responded, although she wasn't sure whether she was talking to her mom or to Calum.

'You know, your mother is pretty amazing,' Calum said on the phone.

'I guess. Was there anything else you wanted?'

'No. Oh, wait – yes, there is.' Calum paused for a moment. Natalie got the impression that he was trying to phrase a question in the right way. 'Can you ask her if she knows about a company called Nemor Incorporated?'

'Mom – Calum wants to know if you've heard of a company called Nemor Incorporated.'

Natalie suddenly heard a lot of splashing from the bathroom. A few seconds later her mother appeared, wrapping herself in a towel. The expression on her face was . . . concerned? Angry? Maybe a combination of both.

Gillian Livingstone snatched the phone from her daughter's hand.

'Calum – this is Gillian. We need to talk. I've got a dinner tonight that I can't miss, so we'll be over at nine o'clock tomorrow morning.'

A pause while Calum obviously said something.

'Very well, after lunch then. Give your great-aunt my regards. And, Calum – don't do *anything* between now and then.'

She ended the call and stared out of the window.

'What *has* he got himself into this time?' she muttered, as if Natalie wasn't there.

CHAPTER

six

Sunrise was shining horizontally across the city when Calum woke up. It cast the canyons between the buildings into deep shadow but caught the tops of those same buildings with rosy highlights.

Calum didn't need an alarm. Whatever time he told himself to wake up just before settling down to sleep, that's the time his eyes opened.

For a few minutes he lay in bed, letting the vague ghosts of his dreams fade away. He felt vaguely sad. He had dreamed about running again. He could still remember the sensation of rushing through a field of wheat, letting the tall stems thrash against his body and the wind push his hair back from his forehead. He could still feel the impact of his feet against the soft soil.

Those were feelings that he might never experience again, unless he could somehow cure the paralysis that had affected his legs since the car crash. He knew the odds of the Almasti's genetic structure containing the answer were slim, but it was a start. If not the Almasti, then some other unknown inhabitant of planet Earth's more remote regions would hold the answer. He was sure of it.

And that meant there was something he had to do.

He pulled himself to a sitting position and reached for his mobile phone. He pressed the number 1 and held it down until the phone dredged a telephone number from its memory.

'Yes?' a deep voice said.

'Mr Macfarlane – it's Calum Challenger. Sorry to trouble you. Could I have the car round as soon as possible?'

'Of course, sir,' Macfarlane's voice said. He didn't even sound surprised, even though Calum hadn't spoken to him for months. 'It's no trouble at all. I take it you will be visiting your great-aunt?'

'That's correct.'

'Will you be needing the—'

'Yes,' Calum interrupted. He didn't like hearing the word. 'Bring it. You know the code to get in.'

'I do, sir. I'll be there in forty-five minutes.' A dialling tone replaced his voice.

Calum put the mobile back on his bedside cabinet. He pulled himself out of bed and swung across the apartment to the bathroom. Thirty minutes later he was showered and dressed, and preparing breakfast.

Forty-four minutes and fifty seconds after he had put the phone down he heard the bell of his front door chime. 'Come in!' he yelled. Whoever was outside typed a set of numbers into the security system, and the door opened.

'Good morning, sir,' said the man standing in the doorway. 'It's good to see you again.' He was short – very short – and bald, and he wore a three-piece suit that had obviously either been made to measure for him or had originally been intended for a chunky twelve-year-old attending a bar mitzvah or acting as a pageboy at his sister's wedding. His deep voice was completely at odds with his size.

And he was pushing a wheelchair in front of him.

'Good morning, Mr Macfarlane,' Calum responded. The sight of the wheelchair provoked a sinking feeling in his stomach. He hated it. He hated everything that it represented. The trouble was that the world outside the walls of his apartment was not designed for him. There were no straps hanging from ceilings, and no convenient places to lean, or to sit. That's why he didn't leave his apartment if he could possibly help it.

The trouble was that Merrily Challenger – his father's aunt – didn't like Skype, or any form of conversation that didn't take place with two people in a room together. Preferably with a pot of tea and a plate of cakes.

'Are you ready, sir?' Macfarlane enquired.

'I suppose,' he grunted.

He pulled himself to his feet and swung across to the door. Reluctantly he lowered himself into the wheelchair. 'Let's go,' he sighed.

As the door closed behind them, and as Macfarlane pressed the button to call the lift, Calum listened out for the *clunk* as the security system locked the door behind them, and the *beep* as the alarm activated. That should keep everything safe until Gecko returned to repair the skylight.

As the two of them descended in the lift, Calum found himself wondering why it was that he had taken to Gecko so quickly. Gecko and Tara. The three of them seemed to fit together in some fundamentally simple way, as if they were parts of some greater whole and had been seeking each other out without realizing it. He felt comfortable with them. Relaxed. And that wasn't a feeling he normally got around other people. Neither of them appeared to pity him because of his paralysis. In fact, they both seemed to hardly notice it, which was the way he liked it.

Other people had tried to make friends with him since the accident – befriending him on Facebook, or 'accidentally' bumping into him on those rare occasions when he went out, but he knew what they really wanted. It was obvious. His parents had left him a considerable fortune in their will – money that Great-Aunt Merrily was looking after for him. One day soon he would inherit that money, and he would suddenly appear on various lists of the richest people in the country. Money attracted friends like sugar attracted wasps. He could see through them, and he avoided them. He would prefer to be without friends than to have friends who were keeping one eye on the calendar, waiting for him to inherit. But Gecko had fallen into his life – literally – in a way that was so dangerous, so liable to have caused a serious injury, that it had to be accidental. And Tara had arrived almost by accident as well – nobody could have anticipated that Calum would have sent someone looking for her when she attempted to hack his website, and nobody could have anticipated that Gecko would bring her back to Calum's apartment rather than watch her to find out what she was trying to do. No, it would take a conspiracy of massive and convoluted proportions to arrange for the two of them to arrive in his life at the same time. It had to have been coincidence, which is why he had trusted them so quickly.

The two of them had left shortly after he had spoken to Professor Livingstone, the night before. They had both been reluctant to leave. Gecko said that he was going to sleep at a friend's place, and Tara had said that she was going to take the almost unheard-of step of switching her computer off. The second from last thing that Calum had said to them was: *Be back here at lunchtime tomorrow*. The last thing that he had said to them was: *Bring your passports.*

The doors of the lift opened and Macfarlane pushed Calum out of the building.

His great-aunt's car was parked just outside the warehouse. It was a Bentley SUV – one of a few demonstration models that the company had built with a view to moving into a new area of luxury car design. It also had a hybrid petrol/electrical engine – Calum's great-aunt had wanted one of the test models with the standard V12 engine, but Calum had persuaded her that a hybrid engine was better for the planet.

Macfarlane moved the wheelchair beside the Bentley

and opened the rear door. He moved away and fussed with the boot while Calum laboriously levered himself out of the wheelchair and into the car. His great-aunt's chauffeur knew, from long experience, that Calum did not like to be helped, or even watched.

When Calum was seated in the back of the Bentley, Macfarlane folded up the wheelchair and stowed it in the boot. He climbed into the driver's seat and started the engine.

'Would you like some music, sir, or would you prefer silence?'

'Music,' Calum responded curtly.

'Anything in particular, sir? I have been transferring quite a number of albums on to my MP3 player.'

He thought back to Tara, the night before. 'I don't suppose you have anything emo, darkwave or post-rock?'

Macfarlane considered for a moment. 'I have King Black Acid, Dead Can Dance and Mogwai. Which would you prefer?'

'Surprise me.'

The car started, purring away from the kerb, and music began playing: an instrumental wash of guitars, drums and vocals that somehow made it sound as if the music was being played underwater. Macfarlane took them down several streets that seemed too narrow for the SUV and then pulled out on to a wider road that led out of London. Calum leaned back into the luxury of the leather seats and relaxed.

Great-Aunt Merrily's house was an imposing building on the edge of Richmond Park. It was built of a reddish stone. The view from the front door was one of carefully manicured lawns and ordered trees. Once upon a time those lawns would have been the house's own grounds, but now it was a public park. Great-Aunt Merrily still had some influence, however, and there was a boundary fence around the house to stop people just wandering in on the assumption that it was a tea room or a gift shop.

Macfarlane slowed to a halt on the gravel drive outside the house. He retrieved the wheelchair from the boot, then opened the rear door to the SUV and waited, looking off into the distance, while Calum manoeuvred himself into it. The chauffeur then struggled to push the wheelchair across the gravel, causing a sound like a torrent of rain hitting the surface of a river, and leaving two deep V-shaped tracks leading from the car to the front door.

A wooden ramp had been built from the drive to the front porch, taking up a quarter of the stone stairs that had been there for several hundred years. Macfarlane manfully pushed Calum up to the top, then through the doorway into the relative coolness of the house.

'I'll leave you in the sitting room, sir. Your great-aunt will be down in a moment.'

'I presume you told her that I was coming?'

'As soon as I received your phone call, sir. I wouldn't have wanted to surprise her. I know how much she looks forward to your visits.'

True to his word, Macfarlane wheeled Calum into a room that was crammed with old furniture and older paintings, then quietly withdrew. Calum levered himself out of the wheelchair and on to one of the sofas. He considered trying to fold the wheelchair up and hide it behind the sofa, but he decided that an action like that would be trying to take a point too far.

After five minutes or so his Great-Aunt Merrily entered the room.

As usual, she was in a rush. She always seemed to be moving from one place to another at speed. Calum wasn't sure that he had ever seen her settle down or relax. She was a small, delicate woman, and today she wore a startlingly modern blue silk blouse and a green skirt. She reminded him of a hummingbird – seemingly in motion even when she was standing still.

'Calum!' she exclaimed. 'How delightful. You should have given me some warning – I would have prepared a meal. Or maybe baked a cake. Are you staying?'

'I'm afraid not,' he said.

'Let me look at you.'

He threw his arms wide. 'Here I am.'

'You've lost weight. Are you eating properly?'

He recalled the pizzas he'd ordered the night before for himself, Tara and Gecko. 'Yes, I am,' he said.

'Good. It's so easy to slip into eating junk food these days.'

'Although having your own cook is a good way to avoid

the temptation,' he pointed out. As his great-aunt frowned, he added, 'I saw Gillian Livingstone yesterday.'

'Oh, did you?' His great-aunt sniffed audibly. 'And how was she?'

'Still working as hard as ever. She's coming over this afternoon as well – that's why I have to get back.'

'If she had a man in her life, she wouldn't need to work so hard. And what about that daughter of hers?'

'Natalie?' Calum felt himself blushing. He couldn't help it. 'Yes,' he said casually, 'she was there too.'

'That girl has too much money and too few inhibitions. I would have brought her up very differently.'

'Yes, I'm sure you would.' Calum shivered for a moment, imagining the resulting fireworks if Natalie had been brought up by his great-aunt. 'Perhaps it's best for both of you that it never happened that way.'

Before his great-aunt could respond, the door opened and a maid entered carrying a tray bearing a pot of tea, two cups, a jug of milk and a plate of cakes.

'You're staying for tea and a bite to eat, of course?' Merrily Challenger said as the maid put the tray on a side table and withdrew. She smiled fondly at him. 'So tell me what's been going on in your life. How's that website of yours?'

'The Lost Worlds?' Calum asked, cringing inside. He wished he'd never told his great-aunt about the website. He'd mentioned it a year or so ago, just to make polite conversation during a lunch where she had insisted on telling him all about the accomplishments of remote relatives he was never likely, and never wanted, to meet. He'd realized while he was speaking that she didn't really understand what he was talking about, but every time he'd seen her since she had asked him about it, in the same way she might ask about some passing hobby like learning the guitar or collecting stamps, or whether he'd got a girlfriend yet. 'Yeah, it's . . . going well.'

'Good,' she said briskly. 'Have you managed to find any of those poor lost animals yet?'

He winced. He was pretty sure she'd got the wrong idea about the website. He had tried to explain as best he could that he was helping coordinate a search for missing species, but somehow during the conversation his aunt had translated 'missing' into 'lost', and he was pretty sure she now thought he was engaged in looking for cats, dogs or parrots that had wandered off from the family home.

'Actually . . .' he said delicately, 'that's not quite the kind of thing I'm doing. It's more like . . . a conservation project. You know – trying to look for creatures that are on the verge of extinction, and helping save them.'

'Oh, how lovely,' she said. 'You know, I've always had a soft spot for giant pandas. Ever since I was a girl I wondered how evolution could come up with a colour scheme for their fur where the only place they could possibly hide was on a zebra crossing. There can't be many of those in their natural habitat.'

Calum raised his eyebrows in surprise. That was a

surprisingly sharp comment. Maybe she *had* understood what he'd been saying after all.

'Actually,' he replied, 'I'm more interested in creatures that haven't yet been discovered, or that are supposed to already be extinct but which still survive in little colonies somewhere remote.'

She smiled at him. 'Bless you, Calum, I think you think your great-aunt is rather simple in the head. I do know what it is that you're doing. I've even logged into your website once or twice and taken a look. It's very impressive, you know. You are doing exactly the kind of thing that your dear mother and father would have wanted you to do. They would have been proud.'

Calum felt a lump form in his throat. He hadn't expected the conversation to turn so personal so soon.

'Well,' he said, blinking a few times so that his eyes would dry out, 'that kind of leads me on to something that I wanted to ask you.'

'Ah, this wasn't a social call then?' she said gently. He could sense the sadness behind the words.

He smiled reassuringly. 'It wasn't *just* a social call. I do enjoy your company, you know. It's just . . . it's not easy getting here. Not with . . .' He let the sentence trail off, but patted his right leg.

'I know. I understand. You don't like admitting to any weakness. Your dear father was just the same. He was asthmatic, you know, but he never let that hold him back. And I'm glad that you do make the time to come. Now, what is it that you need? I presume it's money? It usually is.'

'It's money,' he confirmed.

'I do hope it's not for a Ferrari.'

He sighed. How many times? 'No, it's not for a Ferrari. I want to send some . . . friends of mine abroad.'

'A holiday! How lovely! And how considerate of you!'

'Not exactly a holiday. They're going to go and check out a rumour that a particularly rare . . . animal . . . has been seen in Georgia.'

She clapped her hands together in delight. 'Wisteria and mint juleps and men with white hats and white suits!'

'No, not the American state of Georgia,' he corrected. 'The former Soviet republic of Georgia. It's near Turkey.'

'Oh.' She sounded crestfallen. 'That doesn't sound like much fun.'

'It's not meant to be fun – it's meant to be a serious scientific expedition.'

'But . . . a former Soviet republic? Isn't that dangerous?'

He shook his head. 'Georgia's very stable, apparently. Unless you go to the borders you can be pretty sure nothing bad is going to happen. And besides, my friends are going to be accompanied by an experienced guide. They'll be perfectly safe.'

Calum had crossed his fingers, and moved his hand down behind his leg, where his great-aunt couldn't see it.

Great-Aunt Merrily gazed at him, frowning. 'You

aren't planning to go yourself, are you? I really couldn't approve of that.'

'No,' he sighed. 'No, I won't be going.'

She tipped her head to one side and stared at him. 'This is important to you?'

'Yes.' He took a deep breath. 'Yes, it's important.'

'And how much do you think you will need?'

He had totted the figures up in his head the night before, while he was trying to get to sleep. 'With flights, and hotels, and equipment, plus the payment for the guide, as well as insurance and inoculations . . . I think –' he swallowed – 'fifty thousand pounds ought to do it.'

'That seems an awful lot,' she said quietly. 'I'm sure the hotels in Georgia can't be that expensive.'

'There is some special equipment that I need to get hold of – research equipment. And there's going to be a guide as well – I can't let them go by themselves. So, all in all, it isn't cheap.'

She nodded. 'Very well then. I can see that you have your heart set on this. I will transfer the money to your account later on, while Mr Macfarlane is driving you home.'

He let out a breath that he hadn't known he was holding. 'Thank you.'

'And now help yourself to another cup of tea and a cake, while I tell you what your cousin twice removed has been up to . . .'

Calum managed to stay awake for the next couple of hours while his great-aunt gave him an exhaustive rundown of the events that had befallen various members of the Challenger family. She made sure that he was eating properly, that he was getting regular check-ups at hospital and that he was going to the dentist at least once every six months – everything that great-aunts were expected to do. In the absence of parents, of course.

All the time she was nattering on, he was thinking about the practicalities of getting Gecko and Tara to Georgia. Which airlines flew there? What were the hotels like? Would they need visas? Was it going to be safe for them? So many questions.

Eventually he said goodbye to his great-aunt. She hugged him tight, bending down to get to him in the wheelchair. 'Take care, Calum. I do worry about you.'

'I know,' he said. He patted her shoulder. 'I'm fine. Really I am.'

She gazed at him for a moment. 'Why do I have a feeling that there's something more going on here than you are telling me?'

'That's paranoia,' he pointed out.

'Your father used to say, Calum, that just because you're being paranoid it doesn't mean that someone *isn't* out to get you.'

The door to Calum Challenger's apartment was open a crack when Tara arrived.

She had slept uneasily in her college room, thinking about what had happened the day before. Had she really agreed to travel to a former Soviet republic with a boy she'd only just met and a guide whose name was the only thing she knew about him? It had seemed to make more sense when it had been agreed. Now it seemed crazy.

Eventually she had realized that the only way to see whether it was all true, and not just a hallucination, was to head back to Calum's apartment. So she did.

She pushed the door open and stepped inside.

Calum was sitting in front of his computer screens. In front of him stood a woman. She was, Tara estimated, middle-aged, slim and attractive, and she was dressed with understated expense – silk blouse, tailored jacket and tight chino trousers. Her hands were on her hips and she was obviously in the middle of a very polite rant.

Tara suddenly spotted another person in the large apartment. Over in the kitchen area a girl of about her own age was pouring herself a glass of water. She was thin – almost painfully so – and her smooth brown tan was obviously the genuine article, rather than something that came out of a bottle or a tanning salon. She had long blonde hair that curled just as it hit her shoulders. She seemed to sense Tara watching her, looked up and nodded slightly in acknowledgement.

A rise in the volume of the discussion between Calum and the woman caught Tara's attention. She raised her eyebrows at the girl in the kitchen and moved her attention back to the discussion. Or argument, as it was turning out.

'. . . can't possibly intend sending two teenagers that

you've only just met to a country whose primary language neither of them speaks and whose northern border is still the subject of a violent dispute!'

'For a start, I'm not "sending" them,' Calum said calmly. 'They don't work for me. I'm not paying them. All that happened was that I explained about the Lost Worlds website, and this possible sighting of a Neanderthal-like creature in the foothills of the Caucasus Mountains, and they volunteered to go and take a look.'

That wasn't *quite* the way Tara remembered it, but she decided not to say anything. That was a conversation they could have later. Especially the part about not being paid.

'What's the legality of this?' the woman challenged. 'Surely they count as unaccompanied minors? The airlines will refuse to fly them!'

'They'll be accompanied by this Special Forces guy you've recommended – Rhino Gillis,' Calum pointed out. 'And they'll have letters signed by their parents or guardians allowing them to travel in his company. Gecko has already talked to his mother, and she's apparently happy to let him travel wherever he wants. Her only stipulation is that she meets Rhino Gillis first.'

Gecko must have already arrived, then. Tara looked around, but couldn't see him. A noise from above made er look up at the ceiling, and the skylight. Gecko was up there, fitting a new pane of glass to replace the one through which he'd crashed. He caught sight of her, and smiled.

'"Gecko"?' the woman said scornfully. 'What kind of name is that?'

Calum was a model of patience. 'His real name is Eduardo Ortiz, and he's used to travelling alone. He's done it before. He's gone back and forth between here and Brazil a couple of times.'

'And this girl? What do her parents say?'

Tara stepped forward. '*This girl*'s parents don't say anything,' she interrupted bluntly. 'My dad's in prison and my mum's in and out of rehab so often that they reserve a room for her.'

The woman had the grace to look embarrassed. 'Sorry – I didn't realize you were there.'

'Obviously not.'

'You are . . . ?'

'Tara. Tara Flynn.' She raised an eyebrow questioningly. 'And *you* are?'

'Gillian Livingstone. I'm—'

'Professor Livingstone is my guardian,' Calum interrupted. 'She looks after me. She and my great-aunt, anyway. They work in parallel to keep me on the straight and narrow.' He waved at Tara. 'Hi – thanks for coming back. I was getting worried.'

'So if your mother and father are . . . not available,' Professor Livingstone said, 'who exactly is *responsible* for you?'

'I'm responsible for myself. I look after myself.'

Gillian Livingstone was persistent. 'But in the absence

of your parents you must have some legal guardian, surely?'

'There's a social worker.' She shrugged. 'Actually, there have been a whole string of social workers. There's a high turnover, apparently.'

'Then surely we should be talking to them?'

Calum raised an eyebrow at the use of the word 'we', but obviously decided not to interrupt.

'After several occasions when I ran away, including one when I got as far as Bahrain,' Tara said calmly, 'along with a couple of overly dramatic episodes of self-harm, my social worker and I came to an arrangement. If I went to college, got good reports from my tutors, didn't do anything obviously illegal and phoned them every three days without fail, they would pretty much leave me alone to live my life the way I want. I'm sure they'll write a letter of authorization for me to go abroad if I ask nicely, and if they know I'm going with someone responsible. Oh, and I've got a passport.' She smiled. 'I had to, in order to get to Bahrain.'

Professor Livingstone stared at Tara for a long moment. Tara stared back, not confrontationally, or even defensively, but without blinking or looking away. Eventually the professor nodded slightly, and turned back to Calum.

'Well, you seem to have got this all sewn up. Merrily has already told me that she's given you a line of credit. I suppose I'll have to go along with it – reluctantly.'

'Thank you.' Calum smiled, and Tara was struck by

how much better he looked. With the borderline-sullen expression taken off his face, his eyes seemed to sparkle.

'Has Rhino made contact yet? I phoned him yesterday, just after we spoke.'

Calum nodded. 'Yes – he emailed me last night.' He frowned. 'I've got to say he sounded quite tense.'

'I gather he's had a spot of trouble in the USA. I think he is glad of the opportunity to leave.'

'When does he fly in?'

'Ah. That's something I wanted to speak to you about – assuming I couldn't persuade you to change your mind, that is.'

'Since when have you ever been able to change my mind once it's been made up?'

The professor's mouth twitched in what might have been a smile had she not quickly suppressed it. 'In that respect, as in so many others, you take after your father. Anyway – once I described the mission, the location and –' she glanced at Tara and then upward at Gecko – 'the rather unusual composition of the party, he suggested that there was a new piece of equipment that the US army are working on that might come in useful. I pulled some strings, and they're willing to lend one of them to you, as long as they can analyse the readings from it when it comes back. They're keen to give it some real-world experience.'

'Sounds interesting, if a little puzzling. Are they going to send it over, or is Rhino going to collect it?'

'Slightly more complicated than that – there's a full day's training course involved. Rhino suggested that you go over and join him on the course, but I pointed out that it would be impractical.'

'This equipment – is it technical?'

Gillian Livingstone nodded. 'Very. I've got a couple of documents in my bag that will tell you all about it – give me a minute and I'll let you read them.'

'Then Tara ought to go out and meet Rhino,' Calum said firmly. 'They can do the course together.'

Tara blinked a couple of times as her brain slowly processed the information. 'You want me to go to *America*?' she exclaimed.

Professor Livingstone looked at her watch. 'Too late today,' she said. 'We'll aim for tomorrow. The flight will leave at lunchtime. You won't need a visa. Rhino will meet you at Dulles Airport, and drive you to where the course will be taking place. It's called the Aberdeen Proving Ground – it's just up from Baltimore. Driving distance. Part of the US Army Research Laboratories.' She glanced at Calum, whose mouth was hanging open slightly. 'Buck up, Calum. If you want to arrange an expedition, there's a lot to do, and a lot to think about.'

Calum glanced at Tara. 'Are you OK with this?'

She considered for a moment. Getting the chance to play with high-tech US military equipment for free? Maybe take some photos?

Ah, yes. That might be a problem. Her . . . reputation.

'Sounds great,' she said. 'But . . . don't I need some kind of . . . security clearance?'

Professor Livingstone shook her head. 'The equipment has been developed by a major international company for whom I do some consultancy work. *New Scientist* have covered it. *National Geographic* printed photos. I think there's even a Discovery Channel documentary that mentions it. I'll sort out your entry visas and I've already vouched for you and Rhino, so getting to play with it won't be a problem. Besides, you're trustworthy, aren't you?'

'Totally,' said Tara, crossing her fingers behind her back.

Calum frowned. 'Actually,' he said, 'talk of a major international company reminds me – you never answered my question about Nemor Incorporated. *Have* you ever heard of them?'

A shiver ran up Tara's spine at the mention of the company. She glanced over at Professor Livingstone, whose face was smooth and expressionless.

'No,' she said calmly. 'The name's a mystery to me.'

She was holding her right hand casually behind her back, and Tara had the sudden and disquieting thought that maybe *her* fingers were crossed.

CHAPTER

seven

The arrivals and departures hall at Dulles International Airport, some thirty miles out of Washington DC, was a cavernous area with a curved concrete roof. It felt airy and oppressive at the same time, which, Rhino Gillis thought, was quite a feat of engineering. Fortunately it was air-conditioned, which was a relief considering the marshy heat outside.

A row of check-in areas dominated the centre of the building, covering almost every airline that Rhino could think of and quite a few that he couldn't. Wherever he looked there were armed police officers wandering around, conspicuous in their dark blue uniforms and caps. Slightly less obvious were the undercover air marshals in their blazers and slacks. They might just have been businessmen or politicians on their way home, if it weren't for the slight bulge of a holster beneath the jacket of each one, and the uniformity of their hairstyles. Given the continuing likelihood of terrorist attacks directed against American aircraft, Rhino wasn't surprised to see them, but he did think they could do more to blend in.

Rhino was blending in. He was wearing his usual faded chinos and polo shirt, with a lightweight canvas jacket over the top. He stood at the top of the escalators that led up from the luggage-reclaim area with a sign on a pole. The sign read *Mr Desponda* in large letters, and *Trent Office Machinery* in smaller letters underneath. There was no Mr Desponda, as far as Rhino knew, and probably no Trent Office Machinery either, but the sign gave him a level of anonymity. There must have been thirty other people – taxi drivers and chauffeurs – standing around with signs. He was just one of the crowd.

He glanced around, making it look as if he was just checking for the fictitious Mr Trent. In fact, he was keeping an eye out for Blue and Orange, or their friends. He was pretty sure that he'd shaken off any attempt to follow him, and he had spent the previous night in an anonymous roadside motel under an assumed name rather than go back to the rather more upmarket room he'd been staying in previously, but there was always the off-chance that the gang who were looking for him – whoever they were – had thought to stake out the airport. There might be gang members stalking through the crowd now with his photograph in their hands and a silenced gun or a knife beneath their jackets.

Rhino had thought about disguising himself, but in his experience false beards, wigs and moustaches were more likely to attract attention than to deflect it. The only disguise that Rhino was wearing was a pair of plain glasses and a baseball cap. He was relying on the fact that every second man in the crowd was in the same get-up. It was the standard American blue-collar look.

The flight from London had arrived about twenty minutes ago. If this Tara Flynn was quick retrieving her baggage, then she should be appearing at any moment.

Professor Livingstone had emailed a photograph of the girl to his smartphone. It had obviously been taken with a camera phone when she hadn't been expecting it: she was looking away and she had her mouth open, as if she was just about to say something. She shouldn't be hard to recognize, he mused. Not with hair dyed that violent shade of black, the ear piercings, the heavy eyeshadow and the suggestion of a lip stud. She looked to him like a typical goth – self-absorbed and ready to blame the rest of the world for anything she didn't like. She was nothing like the kinds of people that he usually accompanied on missions and expeditions. The next few days were going to be . . . well, interesting to say the least.

He still didn't quite know what Professor Livingstone had got him into. If he hadn't needed money and the chance to get out of the country quickly, then he wouldn't have accepted the job. Nursemaiding a couple of kids on a trip to a former Soviet republic didn't sound like his kind of thing.

The only consolation was that it was paying well. The kid who was apparently funding the expedition to Georgia had agreed to his price without trying to negotiate Rhino down. Rhino respected that – he prided himself on pricing a job realistically, but with enough of a profit margin to make it worth his while and to cover any unexpected eventualities. When potential clients tried to get him to reduce his prices, he tended to lose respect for them very fast. Particularly in the hostage-rescue game, where arguments over money often made him wonder if the families or the companies who hired him actually wanted their relatives or their employees back again.

A girl was rising up on the escalator from the luggage-reclaim area beneath the arrivals and departures hall. Her hair was coal-black apart from a purple streak above one eye, and she wore a leather jacket over a purple T-shirt with some band logo on it, and black jeans. He guessed she was pretty, but she seemed to be doing quite a bit to disguise it. She had a rucksack slung over one shoulder, and she was looking around as if expecting to meet someone.

Rhino subtly angled his 'Mr Desponda' sign towards her. She saw it, caught his eye and nodded. Obviously Gillian Livingstone had given her the information about what to look for. Rhino nodded back discreetly. He was going to have to be careful. She didn't have his training, and she didn't know that he was effectively on the run, but he got the impression from the way she looked and the way she dressed that she kept her emotions well under control. When she got to the top of the escalator she turned towards him.

'Hi,' she said. 'I'm Tara.' She looked at the sign, and smiled slightly. 'Or rather, I'm Mr Desponda.'

'Hi. I'm Rhino.' He extended a hand and she shook it with a firm grip. 'Good flight?'

'I guess. Calum booked me a Business Class ticket. I was surrounded by businessmen in suits and ties. They spent the whole flight putting together presentations and spreadsheets on their laptops, while I just played games and read books. Of course, they got a free glass of champagne, while I had to make do with an orange juice. I suppose the food was OK, if you like things that don't taste of anything.'

'It's the lower pressure. It does something to the taste buds. Nothing tastes of anything on an aircraft. No problems with the flight attendants, considering you were travelling on your own?'

'They didn't seem to mind. One of them asked me if I was being met in Washington. I told her "Yes", and she left me alone after that.'

'Good stuff.' Rhino paused, and glanced around again. It was an automatic reaction. Nobody appeared to be paying them any undue attention. 'I've got a hire car outside. Are you OK if we head straight for the Aberdeen Proving Ground? I've booked us into a hotel for the night, and then tomorrow it's an eight o'clock start.'

Tara grimaced. 'Early. Ouch.'

'Don't worry – you can sleep in the car. Jet lag heading in this direction isn't too bad. It's heading east that it gets you.' He reached out a hand. 'Let me take that bag for you.'

She pulled away. 'Thanks, but I've got my tablet in here. I never let anyone touch it, if I can help it.'

Rhino nodded. He didn't like letting anyone take his kit either. 'Fair enough. You OK to walk for five minutes?'

'Sure.'

The parking area was down a pedestrian exit ramp and across a road used mainly by buses and taxis dropping people off or picking them up. The heat and the humidity hit them both like a wet rag in the face as they walked out into the open.

'Wow!' Tara exclaimed. 'Is it always this brutal?'

'Half the year it's too hot with one hundred per cent humidity and the other half it's too cold with snow drifts a half a metre deep. There are two nice days a year – one when the weather is moving from hot to cold and the other, six months later, when the weather is moving back from cold to hot.'

Rhino had hired a Pontiac Trans Am in an anonymous white. 'Nice,' was Tara's only comment as she climbed into the passenger seat.

As they pulled away from the parking space, Rhino kept his eyes peeled for any cars that set off just after they did. A red Cadillac and a grey BMW followed him out of the car parking area, but he could see that one of them held a Hispanic family and the other was being driven by an elderly lady. Tentatively he ruled both out as potentially hostile. By the time he had navigated through the maze of roads that surrounded the airport and got on to the Dulles Expressway, he was as sure as he could be that they were safe.

'How much do you know about this thing we're going to see?' he asked Tara.

'I just know that it's a piece of high-tech kit that will help us on the expedition,' she replied. 'How much do you know about the expedition?'

He laughed. 'Just that it could use this bit of high-tech kit.'

'OK, how long's the drive to the Aberdeen Proving Ground?'

'Four hours.'

'Great – we both have a lot to talk about, then.'

Tara wriggled in the leather seat of the car, unable to believe just how comfortable it felt.

The car was heading down a wide . . . well, motorway was what she would have called it in the UK. What was it over here? An interstate? An expressway? It was four lanes across, and all the cars on it looked bigger and sleeker and more colourful than she was used to at home. Every car seemed to be a Chevrolet, a Cadillac, a Dodge or a Pontiac. These were just names she had only ever read about before in books or magazines, but now she was surrounded by them.

The buildings lining the . . . expressway? . . . were equally unusual. They all appeared to be designed to be unique, rather than back home where so many buildings looked the same. It was wild and crazy. It was America.

She had to keep telling herself that she was in America, otherwise she would have decided that she was dreaming.

Two days ago she had nothing to look forward to but college work, and maybe going out to see a band or something. But now, here she was in a big, fast car heading towards a high-tech demonstration where she was expected to be some kind of expert. It was mad!

'Are you OK?' Rhino asked.

'Yeah. Just got carried away with the craziness of the moment.'

He laughed. 'Yes, I get that sometimes. Every now and then I have to look around, take a deep breath and remind myself which country I'm in and what exactly it is that I'm supposed to be doing. So – apart from the craziness, how *are* you feeling? Any jet lag?'

She frowned, trying to analyse her feelings. 'I think my body is still working on UK time. It feels later than it is. I keep wondering when dinner will be, but I guess it's only mid-afternoon here.'

'We'll stop for a bite to eat in a while. The sunshine will help you adjust to the new time zone.'

'But apart from that I feel OK. Not tired or anything.'

'Good.' He paused for a second as he changed lanes. 'So – who's going to go first?'

'Go first?'

'Explaining to each other what we're doing here.'

'Oh, right. I guess I could go first. How much do you know?'

'Only what Gillian Livingstone told me,' Rhino said. 'You've met her, right?'

'Yes. Kind of.'

He smiled. 'What does that mean?'

'I mean we've not really had a chance to talk.' Apart from her wanting to know who was 'responsible' for me, Tara added in her own mind. 'She seems quite . . . impressive. What's the story with her?'

'She's a technology consultant,' Rhino explained. 'She runs her own firm. Big international companies and consortia come to her for advice about what they should invest in, and what they ought to be researching. "Horizon-scanning and future-proofing", she calls it – looking out for what's going to be important in five, or ten, or twenty years and making sure that the people she advises are ready for it.' He laughed. 'Hang on, I thought *you* were supposed to be doing the talking!'

'Sorry.' She glanced sideways at him, and was struck by how young he looked. Based on what Gillian Livingstone had said, back at Calum's apartment, Tara had been expecting some grey-haired, heavily tanned army veteran, but if she'd seen Rhino at her college she could have mistaken him for one of the students. His hair was dark and close-cropped, and his eyes were a piercing shade of blue, but it was his smile that struck her. He seemed to be continually and genuinely amused by what was going on around him.

Only his hands gave him away, she thought. They were solid and calloused, and covered with small white scars. They looked like the hands of a man who had climbed rock faces and dug tunnels and got into fights.

Rhino glanced sideways and met her gaze, and she blushed.

'Yeah, this expedition,' she said quickly, 'it's all the idea of this guy called Calum. Calum Challenger.'

'He's the disabled kid who Gillian is supposed to be mentoring, isn't he?'

'Yes, but he doesn't seem to need, or want, much mentoring. He's got very clear ideas about what he wants to do, and I don't think he lets much get in the way. He's got this thing about creatures that science doesn't know about – either because they were supposed to have died out, like, thousands of years ago, or because they live somewhere so remote that they've never been discovered and catalogued. It's a family thing, apparently. His great-grandfather was a famous explorer, and his parents did the same kind of stuff.'

'Nice to have a family business,' Rhino observed.

'Calum has evidence that there's something living in the foothills of the Caucasus Mountains. It's a photograph of some kind of man-ape. He says it might be a Neanderthal, or a missing link between apes and humans.'

'A fake?' Rhino asked. 'Or maybe a misidentification of something like a thin, starving bear?'

She shook her head. 'I've seen it, and I'm pretty sure it's not a fake. The proportions are wrong for it to be a man in a hairy suit. I've run some tests on it, and the image hasn't been doctored in any way. And it doesn't look anything like a bear, or a timber wolf, or anything whatever. No, I'm pretty sure that it's real.'

'And what does he want to do with this thing, if we find it? Does he expect us to bring one back?'

'Nothing like that. Ideally he wants a sample of genetic material so that he can get it analysed in a laboratory. He thinks that the DNA of this creature might contain some kind of resistance to diseases and infections, or maybe it can fight off cancer. He thinks that if he can get these bits of DNA isolated then he can start to develop treatments that will help people. Apart from that, I think he just wants to make sure that these things are protected, that they're not exploited by anyone.'

She paused, an image of Calum Challenger floating in her mind.

'Actually, what he really wants,' she continued, more quietly, 'is something that can regenerate nerves. He was disabled in the car accident that killed his parents.'

'Yeah, I remember Gillian telling me about that. So why not just tell a university, or a TV channel, and let them fund an expedition?'

'Because it would take too long, and the chances are that nobody would believe him anyway – not based on one photograph and some local legends.'

'Fair point, I guess. So he's funding all this himself?'

'He inherited a lot of money from his parents when they died. I think it's all tied up in a trust fund or something, but he can access it if his great-aunt agrees. He must be a hell of a smooth talker, because he convinced her to release the money for the expedition.'

'He's not planning on coming himself, is he? I really don't think the foothills of the Caucasus Mountains is the best place for someone in a wheelchair, and with the best will in the world I'm not carrying him all the way.'

Tara shook her head. 'No, he's resigned to not being there. Although he did get excited by this technology that we're going to see. He thinks it'll help him see what we're seeing.'

'It might just do that,' Rhino said non-committally.

'So what is it? Some kind of high-definition camera system?'

Rhino just smiled. 'You're cold.'

'A remotely piloted drone that he can steer, so that it follows us around?'

Now he laughed. 'Warmer, but not close.'

'Well, what is it, then? I'm going to see it tomorrow anyway.'

Instead of answering the question, Rhino said, 'So Calum's not coming. Who is? You?'

'Me, and Gecko.'

'Gecko?'

'His real name is Eduardo Ortiz. He's a free-runner,' she said proudly.

Rhino's eyebrows rose in surprise. 'He must be fit then. Free-running needs a lot of muscular strength and stamina, as well as a good cardiovascular system. He might just come in useful.'

'Unlike me,' Tara said quietly, turning her head to stare out of the window.

'Sorry?'

'Look, I'm under no illusions. I'm not in what you'd call good physical condition. You're probably thinking that I'll hold you back.'

Rhino glanced sideways at her. 'Don't do yourself down,' he said gently. 'From what I can see, you're only carrying a couple of pounds excess weight, and you managed the walk to the car in heat that you're not used to without getting out of breath. When we get back to the UK, I'll take you and this Gecko kid through some training sessions, but I don't foresee any problems. You won't hold us back.'

'Thanks,' she whispered.

'No problem.' Silence for a few minutes, then: 'Do you really want me to spoil the surprise and tell you what we're seeing tomorrow?'

'Yes, please,' Tara said primly.

'OK, it's an experimental automated robotic system being tested for US soldiers in Afghanistan and elsewhere. The idea is that it carries all the kit and clobber that the soldiers normally have to carry, allowing them to concentrate on their mission and not get tired.'

'Like a mechanical donkey,' Tara said.

Rhino snorted. 'I wouldn't let the company who've built it hear you put it quite that way if I were you. But essentially, yes – it's like a mechanical donkey, only it's faster, it never gets tired and it never refuses to go another step unless it has a carrot. The problem it's been built to solve is that soldiers in armies today are carrying more kit than ever before, and in hot weather and direct sunshine that can seriously compromise their ability to do their jobs. Today's marines, for instance, are carrying more weight than a medieval soldier in full armour.'

'And this thing is what – remote-controlled?'

He shook his head. 'That's the clever part. It's fully robotic. If you tell it to follow you, it'll follow you. If you tell it to go to a certain map reference, it'll set off on its own. It's fully independent. If it discovers that a route is blocked, then it will try to find another way around. If it comes under attack, it'll retreat until it is safe. It's a really clever piece of kit.'

'Battery life must be a problem,' Tara mused. 'I bet it can't go for more than a couple of hours without a recharge.'

'That's where you're wrong,' Rhino said. 'The company is claiming that they have some kind of super-efficient solar cells that can keep it going.'

'Now that,' said Tara, 'I really have to see.'

It was dark in the apartment. Outside the windows, the sky was black and dusted with a scattering of stars. The sun had set some hours ago, and the apartment had gradually drifted through deepening shades of red and purple to the point where the only light was that cast by the multiple computer screens.

Calum stretched his arms out and rocked his head from

side to side. He'd been working at the computer for several hours straight, and his muscles were protesting that they hadn't been used for a while. Not only that, but his eyes felt grainy and hot from focusing for so long on something just a few centimetres away. He turned his chair to the side and let his gaze refocus across the room.

To where Gecko was barely visible, sitting on the sofa. In the cold blue glow of the screens he looked like a ghost. Calum nearly leaped out of his skin.

'How long have you been there?

'About an hour,' Gecko responded. 'You know, you get very caught up when you are concentrating on something. I could probably have come in here with a full marching band and you would not have noticed.'

Calum shrugged, trying to calm his suddenly panicked heartbeat. 'I can get a bit obsessive about things, I guess. Lose track of time.'

'What were you doing?'

'I was checking out flight details and hotels for your trip to Georgia. The best option seems to be to fly from Heathrow to Frankfurt, and then get another plane from Frankfurt to Tbilisi.'

'Why Tbilisi?' Gecko asked. 'I thought we were going to Georgia?'

'Tbilisi is the capital of Georgia, just like London is the capital of England.'

'Ah. OK.'

'I've found a hotel for you and Tara. It's got a restaurant, so you won't have to go out for breakfast, lunch or dinner if you don't want to.'

'I like trying new foods,' Gecko said. 'Although I am not sure if Tara feels the same. She strikes me as a veggieburger and fries kind of girl.'

Calum laughed and went on: 'After I sorted out the flights and the hotel, I spent a while checking to see if anyone else had reported seeing this man-ape creature in the Caucasus foothills.'

'And have they?'

'Not so far.' Calum shrugged. 'I'm not sure whether to be pleased or sorry. It would be nice to have some kind of independent confirmation that there's something unusual out there, but then again, I don't want anyone else getting in before we do.' He frowned, and stared at the dark shape that was Gecko. 'But you're trying to distract my attention. The big question is: even without the marching band, how exactly *did* you get in.' He turned his head to check the apartment door. It was shut and locked. 'You couldn't have hacked the code for the security system. That's Tara's field of expertise.'

Gecko smiled and glanced upward. 'I came in through the skylight.'

'What, *again*? I didn't hear the sound of breaking glass.'

'Don't worry – I have not done any more damage. No, when I replaced the skylight yesterday I did the sensible thing and made sure it had a lock on it. And then I did the other sensible thing, and made sure I had a copy of the key.'

He paused. His expression was invisible in the shadows, but it sounded to Calum as if he was suddenly unsure of himself. 'Look, it seemed like a good idea at the time, but maybe I went too far. I will give you the key back. I understand that you might want to control who comes and goes around here. It is just that . . . with the free-running, I kind of forget that people get touchy about their personal space. When I am running across the roofs, I think of it all as being public property.'

'Yes, just like Tara and the internet,' Calum said darkly. He was silent for a moment, considering what his feelings were exactly, and he was surprised to find that he didn't mind Gecko dropping in unexpectedly. Considering how much he valued his privacy, and considering how little time he'd known Gecko, he was actually pleased that the boy was there. He'd forgotten what it was like to have friends, and it was a feeling, he realized, that could become addictive. 'Don't worry about it. I'll just have to make sure I lock the bathroom door when I'm inside. The problem with living alone is that you get into bad habits, and leave doors wide open when maybe you shouldn't.'

'More information than I really needed.' Gecko laughed. 'Any news from Tara yet?'

Calum shook his head. 'Her flight should have landed a little while ago. Professor Livingstone's pet travel guide should have let her know if there was a problem and Tara didn't turn up, but I'm not expecting anything to go wrong.'

'You trust her to be OK out there?'

'Yes, I do. Which is strange, considering how little I know either of you, but I'm pretty sure that both of you can survive by yourselves wherever you go. You're both loners, and you're both very competent in different ways. She'll be fine.' He paused. 'It's this Rhino Gillis who worries me.'

'Why?'

'Because I don't know him. I've never met him. I have no sense of whether or not I can trust him.'

'Professor Livingstone seemed quite impressed by him. She recommended him, didn't she? She has used him before?'

Calum nodded. 'She's done quite a lot of work in what used to be the Soviet Union – not just Russia, but Kazakhstan, Uzbekistan and the rest, and she's used him as a bodyguard. There are lots of scientists and researchers left over from Soviet days out there who want to start up their own companies, and there are lots of bright young kids who can write good computer code and want to work on computer security. She thinks that in a few years' time the economic balance of power will shift back from China and end up somewhere in Eastern Europe.'

'I'm surprised she hasn't tried to use that fact to get on board your expedition,' Gecko said. 'You know, make sure that Tara and I don't get into any trouble while managing to fit in some business meetings at the same time.'

'Ah. Funny you should mention that.' Calum abruptly turned and picked up a remote control from the desk in front of him. He waved it towards the ceiling and pressed a button, and the lights in the apartment bloomed into life. Gecko blinked in the sudden glare. 'Actually, I got an email from Professor Livingstone earlier. She said she'd been thinking about it, and she's realized that she can arrange some business meetings in Tbilisi to coincide with your trip.' Seeing Gecko's face, Calum hurriedly added, 'She's not going to go along with you, or even travel with you, but she'll be in the area at the same time in case you get into trouble. She has resources that might be helpful.'

'Well, that's OK,' Gecko said cautiously. 'She obviously feels protective of you and she wants this expedition to succeed. I can relate to that.'

Calum tried to keep his face from showing any emotion, but he must have failed because Gecko picked up on something.

'What is the professor doing with her daughter?' he asked. 'Natalie – that was her name, wasn't it? She was quite a looker. I presume she is leaving Natalie somewhere with friends?'

Calum didn't say anything.

'Or sending her back to whatever boarding school she is at?'

Still nothing.

'Or maybe she's taking Natalie with her and letting her stay in the hotel while she goes off to her meetings?'

Calum couldn't stop himself from reacting any longer.

He closed his eyes for a long moment, and shook his head. 'No, Professor Livingstone said that she doesn't trust Natalie if she's left to herself. She's a bit of a party animal, apparently. Natalie held a party a year ago, in an apartment in Washington DC, and some gatecrashers arrived and trashed the place. Lots of expensive artwork ruined, and the carpets were so stained by drinks that they had to be ripped out and replaced. Professor Livingstone says she's not going through that again. And she doesn't want Natalie to be alone in a hotel for hours on end, because she might go out shopping and max out her credit card on shoes she'll never wear.'

'I have such a bad feeling about this,' Gecko moaned.

'Professor Livingstone said the only way she'd agree to this expedition going ahead was if Natalie went along with you.' Calum shrugged. 'It's non-negotiable. The professor wants Natalie with her in Georgia, which means that Rhino Gillis has to look after her. That means she has to go with you.'

Gecko just stared at Calum. 'When were you going to tell us?' he asked eventually in a far-too-calm voice.

'Probably when you were sitting on the aircraft and it was too late to back out,' Calum admitted.

'Has she ever been on an expedition like this before?'

'Have you?'

Gecko shrugged. 'I have spent nights alone in the rainforest in Brazil. I can look after myself. Natalie looks like she will not go anywhere that has not got air conditioning and a juice bar. Does she know that you cannot wear high heels when you are hill-walking?'

'Look, I doubt she's any happier about it than you are. Sadly, it's something we're going to have to live with. The professor said she'd get in touch with my great-aunt and have the plug pulled on the finance if I argued.' Calum paused, trying to tell from Gecko's expression whether this was going to torpedo the entire expedition. He hoped not: this was the closest he'd ever got to finding one of the cryptids he'd been hunting for so long. 'Are you OK with this?'

Gecko stared at him in silence for a while. 'I suppose I have to be,' he said. 'But I don't like things being kept from me. I like to make informed decisions.'

'Understood,' Calum said, relieved. Desperate to change the subject, and get over the sudden heavy awkwardness in the apartment, he said: 'I spent some time researching Nemor Incorporated while I was on the net. I've found quite a few references to them in other people's blogs and tweets, but very little *from* them. They like to keep a very low profile. Companies are supposed to make public things like who's on their board of directors, and who their major shareholders are, but I can't seem to get that information for Nemor. I wonder what exactly they have to hide.'

'They're probably running some kind of huge offshore tax-avoidance scheme,' Gecko said. 'Isn't that what all big companies try to do – avoid paying as much tax as possible?'

'You're beginning to sound like Tara,' Calum complained.

'Hey, just because she is a little nerdy does not mean she does not know what she is talking about.'

CHAPTER eight

The sky was blue, the sun was bright and the leaves on the trees lining the road were every possible shade of red, orange and yellow. Tara was entranced as Rhino drove the hire car towards Aberdeen. America was proving to be wonderful, and she was enjoying being with Rhino, and that was odd. Generally she despised armies as old-fashioned remnants of an imperialist political mindset, and she was contemptuous of the kind of people who joined up just to follow orders or who thought that spending billions of pounds on vastly complicated military systems that might never be used was a good idea. She hadn't been looking forward to this visit, despite the opportunity to play around with some high-tech kit. She had only agreed to do it because Calum had asked her to, and she felt like she owed him something. But Rhino had overcome her misgivings with his easy smile and his quietly competent manner. He didn't act the way that she'd imagined soldiers acted.

They'd got to the small motel late the night before. It looked strangely familiar to Tara, and it took her a few moments to realize that she'd seen places like it in every horror film that she'd watched over the years. People in those films tended to book in for the night and vanish before morning, falling prey to zombies or vampires or demons. But Tara had been so exhausted that she hadn't cared about the supernatural risks. She and Rhino ate a quick meal in an all-night diner across the road, and headed for their separate rooms.

She noticed now, as they drove, that his gaze kept flicking to the rear-view mirror, even though there were no other cars on the road that early.

'Looking for pursuers?' she joked.

'Hey,' he said, 'you never know. It's the unexpected things that get you.'

Like zombies and vampires and demons, she thought, but she kept quiet.

Rhino shrugged. 'It's like one-way streets. I always look both ways when I cross one. I'm pretty sure that if I ever get run over it'll be because a car came at me from a direction I wasn't expecting, not one that I *was* expecting.'

'Do you always think that way?'

'I always look for the threats, I anticipate what might go wrong before it does, and I don't take anything for granted. It's what keeps me alive.'

'So,' Tara teased, 'you'd be ready if I suddenly lunged at you with a penknife?'

'You're right-handed,' he said calmly, 'and you're sitting on my right. That means you would have to reach across yourself to stab me, which would be clumsy and slow. Besides: your jeans and T-shirt are so tight that there's no chance of you hiding a knife in them, which means that the only place you *could* hide a knife is in the outside pockets of your leather jacket, and that's on the back seat. Given all of the above, I feel safe. *Relatively* safe, anyway. Everything is relative.'

'Oh,' she said, deflated. 'You know, you take the fun out of everything.'

'I don't like surprises,' he said. Tara saw his eyebrows lift as a thought occurred to him. 'Then again, I'm sitting in a car with a fifteen-year-old goth, preparing for a trip to a former Soviet republic in search of a mythical missing link between apes and humans. I wasn't expecting *that*.'

'Yeah, but do you *like* it?'

He laughed. 'I'm getting used to it.'

They passed a sign saying *Army Research Laboratory – Aberdeen Proving Ground: next left*. A few seconds later, Rhino steered the car across the road and into a side road that almost immediately terminated at a security barrier and a security hut. Soldiers in grey combat fatigues converged on the car. They all had semi-automatic rifles. Tara suddenly felt very small and very scared.

'Don't worry,' Rhino said reassuringly. 'This is my area of expertise.'

He rolled his window down and smiled up at the soldier who loomed over him, gun held half ready at his side. 'Morning!'

'Sir, please turn off your ignition,' the soldier rattled out. As Rhino complied, he went on: 'ID, please, sir.'

Rhino reached down to the storage unit between the front seats and pulled out two passports – his and Tara's. He handed them across. 'We're here for the demonstration.'

'Wait here, sir.' The soldier quickly checked the passport photographs against their faces, then crossed to the security hut. He handed the passports to a colleague, who cross-checked the names against a printed list on the table in front of him. He nodded. The first soldier returned to the car and handed the passports over.

'Thank you, sir. Please follow the signs to Parking Area Green. Have a nice day.'

'Thanks.'

Rhino started the car and drove towards the barrier. It lifted into the air just before the bonnet touched it, and Rhino drove into the base.

'Well, that was simple,' Tara said. 'I was expecting a full body search!'

'Five Ps,' Rhino said.

'Sorry?'

'Standard military strategy. *P*rior *p*reparation *p*revents *p*oor *p*erformance. What it means is, make sure you've arranged everything early. In this case, Professor Livingstone emailed our names and passport numbers to the organizers of the demonstration, and they put us on the security list. As long as we have our passports with us, we're OK.'

They drove around a wide curve, and then down a

tree-lined avenue that was lined with armoured vehicles. There must have been a couple of hundred of them, in two long rows. Most of them were tanks, or things that looked like tanks, but there were others that Tara couldn't even identify. Some had no turrets, some had several turrets, and at least one had a gun that looked wide enough to fire beer barrels from one side of London to the other.

'It's called the Mile of Tanks,' Rhino said. 'I thought you'd be impressed. These are all experimental vehicles. Only one of each of them was ever built. You like it?'

'No,' Tara said quietly. 'Part of me feels a bit scared by the amount of military firepower that's on display, and part of me is angry at the amount of money it costs to build a single complete and functional armoured vehicle just as part of an experiment.'

'Oh.' Rhino grimaced. 'Sorry. I keep forgetting that you're not a military brat.'

'I'm not *what*?'

'A military brat. Nothing personal – it just means those kids who grew up around the military. Me, I love this stuff.'

There was silence in the car for a few minutes as Rhino drove through a landscape of close-cut lawns and white-painted two-storey buildings, following the signs for Parking Area Green. There were, Tara noticed, also Parking Areas Blue, Red, Black and Purple. She guessed that there were a lot of cars on the base, which indicated a lot of people.

Parking Area Green turned out to be at the end of a

road that seemed to be leading towards the edge of the base. They stopped in the shadow of trees, next to a collection of ten or so cars. Small signs had been hammered into the earth, pointing towards a path that led into the forest. They read: *ARLENE Demonstration*.

'ARLENE?' Tara asked as Rhino locked the car.

'*A*utomated *R*obotic *L*oad-carrying *En*vironmental *E*quipment,' Rhino replied. 'That's the thing we've come to see. This is the USA – they love acronyms.'

He led the way along the path through the forest. It ended in a clearing. A prefabricated hut had been built near the trees. A dark opening in the front of the hut looked big enough to drive a car through. From somewhere behind the hut, Tara could hear the *chug chug chug* of a portable generator.

A group of men was standing next to the hut. Some of them were wearing suits, and some were wearing uniforms, but they all had close-cut hair. A few of them turned as Rhino and Tara appeared. They glanced at Rhino, then at Tara, then looked away. And then they looked back at Tara again, and frowned. She guessed that the goth look was not the usual style of dress at these demonstrations.

'Here,' Rhino said. He handed her a pair of sunglasses. 'Wear these.'

'Protection from bright lights?' she ventured.

'No,' he said. 'Because it looks cool.'

He slipped on a similar pair of sunglasses as they approached the group of observers.

A grey-haired man broke away from the group and moved towards them. 'My name is Chesterson – Brad Chesterson. I'm the technical director of the company that makes ARLENE. You must be the two visitors that Professor Livingstone requested be given access.' His eyes were a faded blue, Tara noticed, and his skin looked as if it was permanently tanned. 'We had to pull a few strings to get you accredited this late in the day.'

'And we're very grateful,' Rhino replied smoothly.

'Who exactly are you representing, if I may ask?'

Rhino made a movement of his head that wasn't quite a shake, and wasn't quite a shrug. 'A potential user,' he said quietly. 'One who wants to remain . . . discreet.'

'Ah, I understand,' the man said. Clearly he didn't, or he had made an assumption of his own based on what Rhino had said. Either way, he seemed satisfied. He turned to the rest of the group and announced: 'Gentlemen . . .' He turned back to look at Tara. 'And ladies . . . it's time to start. I won't beat about the bush. I don't have to tell you how much equipment our soldiers are carrying right now, in Afghanistan and in other theatres of war. What with weapons, armour, rations, radios, binoculars, video cameras, personal sensor systems, battery packs, ration packs, medical packs, water bottles and entrenching tools, it's as if each man is carrying another man on his back. This situation has crept up on us bit by bit. Each new piece of equipment that we give to our soldiers is heavier than the piece it replaced. Every new piece of electronic equipment uses a different battery. Things have got to the stage where we are losing more soldiers through heat exhaustion, muscle strain and fatigue than to improvised explosive devices and small-arms fire. This situation cannot go on.' He paused for effect. 'That is why we have, on behalf of the US Army Research Labs, developed ARLENE. Now, I could spend the next ten minutes describing ARLENE to you, but I think it would be much better if I just let you see it.' He turned his head towards the prefab hut that the group was standing in front of. 'Corporal Higgs – if you please!'

A soldier emerged from the hut. He was wearing the kind of sand-coloured camouflage uniform and helmet that Tara was used to seeing on news reports, but he didn't have the big backpack that she remembered from the broadcasts. He just carried a semi-automatic rifle. He ignored the group of watchers, and turned back to the hut.

'ARLENE – follow!' he called.

And something walked out of the hut after him.

It looked to Tara like someone had built the skeleton of a prehistoric animal out of stainless-steel rods, pistons, cables and lengths of black elastic. It stood shoulder-high to the soldier, and it was about the width and the length of a single bed. It had six legs, but these legs were articulated with hip joints and knee joints and ankles. Where a living creature would have a head, this thing, this device, had a thin neck that was topped with a selection of sensors – video cameras, infrared cameras, microphones and radio aerials. Where a living creature would have a tail, this thing had a radio antenna. Solar cells glittered across its surface, forming a kind of intermittent skin. Packs had been strapped to its sides, attached to convenient hooks and anchor points, partially covering some of the solar cells. They had been arranged so that the weight balanced out, left and right.

'OK,' Tara said. 'Kinda impressed now.'

'ARLENE,' the corporal said, 'mission mode: reconnaissance. Follow me at a ten-yard distance.'

He set off at a fast walk across the clearing towards the far trees. ARLENE obediently waited until he was ten yards away, and then ambled after him, matching his speed exactly. Tara had expected it to sound heavy and clanky, but apart from a slight hiss as the pistons expanded and contracted there was almost no noise. In fact, she thought that the soldier was making more noise than the robot.

The corporal reached the trees and vanished into the shadows. ARLENE stopped for a moment. Its sensor 'head' scanned back and forth for a few seconds, weighing up alternative paths, and then it followed him.

'Mom, are you *serious*?'

Natalie Livingstone knew that she had that whiny tone in her voice again, the one that drove her mother mad, but she didn't care. In fact, she was glad. If there was one time that she wanted to put a dent into her mother's invisible protective shield, it was now.

'Yes, Natalie, I am completely serious. I am always

completely serious. I don't have time to be trivial or humorous. You should know that by now.'

They were in a black London taxi, heading back to Calum Challenger's apartment. It was morning, and everywhere Natalie looked she saw men in suits and ties walking along the sidewalk. No, not the sidewalk – the *pavement*. Stupid word. A sidewalk allowed you to walk along the side of the road. What the hell did a *pavement* let you do?

'But, Mom, you promised that as soon as you'd given your speech at this conference thing we'd head back home. To Los Angeles.'

'That was the plan.' Gillian Livingstone gazed out of the taxi window at the passing crowds as if on the lookout for business opportunities. 'Plans change. Get used to it.'

'But Savannah is having an epic pool party on Friday. *Everyone* is going to be there. Everyone who matters. And if I'm not there people will think *I* don't matter any more.'

Natalie's mother shook her head, still not looking at her daughter. 'That's just stupid. Nobody will think any less of you because you aren't at this party. And, besides, people have parties all the time, especially in LA. There'll be another one along before you know it.'

'When we were at home, you said that you had to be at this conference in England. When I asked you why, you said that it was an important conference, and that lots of important people were going to be there, and you said that if *you* weren't there then people would wonder if you were still important. And I said that there'll be other conferences, and you said that there wouldn't be any conferences as important as this for a while.' Natalie took a breath. 'Well, that's what Savannah's party is going to be like. It's really, *really* important.' She paused, trying to force her eyes to well up with tears and hoping that her mother might turn her head for long enough to notice. 'You don't want my social development to be affected, do you?'

That hit a nerve. Natalie knew that her mother was paranoid about her having a wide circle of friends and lots to do. Natalie suspected that her mother had grown up without many friends, probably due to the fact that she was so intelligent and so career-oriented, and she didn't want Natalie to turn out the same.

'I'm sorry,' Gillian said quietly, and this time she did turn away from the taxi window and – hurrah! – she *did* notice the tears in Natalie's eyes. 'I understand that this seems like the end of the world to you, but it's not. It's really not.'

'What if I flew back to LA by myself?' Natalie asked. She'd found that if she presented her mother with a reasonable alternative then she usually caved.

Not this time. 'I'm not having you back in Los Angeles without a chaperone. I can't trust you.'

'What about Dad? I could stay with him. *He* could look after me. I haven't spent much time with him recently.'

Gillian looked away, out of the window again. Natalie could see from her reflection that her mother was angry; her lips had thinned, and she was frowning. 'Your father needs more looking after than you do. I wouldn't trust him with a kitten, let alone a teenage girl.'

Natalie knew from her mother's tone of voice that there was no point in pursuing that line of argument. Whatever feelings had existed between her mother and her father had burned out a long time ago. He ran a moderately successful landscape-gardening business in LA, and seemed happy to just drift along in the sunshine, enjoying himself and not thinking about the future. Gillian Livingstone, on the other hand, lived in the future. She rarely thought about anything else.

There was silence in the taxi for a few minutes. Looking out of the window, Natalie recognized Trafalgar Square. They turned right down a wide, long avenue that was lined with old-fashioned buildings.

'I don't suppose you'd let me stay here in London?' she asked quietly. 'I could hang out with Calum Challenger while you're doing your stuff in Georgia.'

'Not going to happen. I like Calum, and I trust him, but he's a teenager and so are you. I'm not leaving the two of you alone together.'

Natalie wrinkled her nose. 'Mom, *please*! I've only just met him. And, besides, he's . . .'

'What?'

'Well, you know.'

She could tell from her mother's reflection that Gillian knew *exactly* what her daughter was getting at, but she was going to make Natalie say it. 'He's *crippled*! He can't move his legs!'

'And that matters *why*? Professor Stephen Hawking is completely immobile, but he still managed to leave his wife and move in with his nurse.'

'Who?'

Her mother sighed softly. 'Every now and then I can hear your father's genes in your voice,' she said. 'This is one of those times.'

'I'm not interested in Calum. Not like that.'

'He's handsome. And you can't help but admire his upper-body muscular development. And he's frighteningly intelligent.'

As if that mattered. 'Mom, let's drop the subject, all right?' She shrugged theatrically. 'If you really think it's safer for me to be on some stupid ecological field trip with a couple of teenagers I've hardly met in the wilderness of a foreign country where I don't even speak the language than going to a party with my friends in my own home in my home country, then that's fine. Really.'

'Rhino Gillis will be looking after you. He won't let anything happen to you. And, besides, it's not a stupid ecological expedition.' There was something in her mother's tone that made Natalie look at her carefully. 'It's actually a well-thought-out scientific expedition that might just pay off in spades.' She glanced over at her daughter. 'And, if it does, I want someone there that I trust who can tell me exactly what happens, as it happens.'

A cold chill ran down Natalie's spine. 'You want me to be your *spy*?'

'I wouldn't put it quite like that.' Gillian Livingstone smiled, but there was something in that smile which wasn't in the least humorous. 'It's just that Calum doesn't think about business opportunities the way I do, and if I'm going to be contributing my technical expertise to this expedition, then I want to make sure that it's worth my while.'

'Please, come this way,' Brad Chesterson said to the group of observers in the Maryland forest clearing. He led the way into a prefab hut, where a large plasma screen was attached to a computer. Over to one side, a second computer was displaying fluctuating graphs. A technician sat in front of it, monitoring the graphs and occasionally typing instructions into the keyboard.

Brad Chesterson pressed a key on the computer keyboard, and the screen sprang to life. On it, Tara could clearly see the back of Corporal Higgs as he moved through the forest. The picture was obviously being relayed from the video cameras and sensor systems that made up ARLENE's 'head'.

'We can watch from here as ARLENE follows Corporal Higgs on his mission. Notice that it maintains a constant distance from him, as ordered. If he stops, it stops. If he speeds up, it speeds up.' His gaze scanned the group. 'Does anybody have any questions?'

Tara surprised herself by raising a hand. 'Yeah – I

notice that you're monitoring ARLENE's performance parameters over there.' She pointed to the computer that the technician was using. 'Information is obviously being passed from Arlene to here, and it might be going the other way. Can you prove that you're not actually steering ARLENE around by remote control – that it's actually making its own decisions about which route to take?'

'Of course,' Chesterson said. He glanced at the technician. 'Bob, step away from the PC for a moment.' As the technician complied, Chesterson took a small radio system from his pocket. 'Corporal Higgs, can you change ARLENE's orders please? Over.'

'Affirmative.' Higgs's voice crackled from the radio and from the plasma TV. Seconds later Tara heard him say: 'ARLENE, wait for one minute, then locate me and resume mission profile.' He moved off through the trees. Within a few moments, he had vanished into the shadows. ARLENE stopped and waited patiently, as ordered. After sixty seconds, it started to move after the corporal. It seemed to be moving more slowly now that it couldn't see the man it was supposed to be following. Its sensor 'head' scanned back and forth, looking for some sign of Higgs.

The picture on the screen suddenly changed from a straightforward camera view to a split screen. One side of the screen was the camera view as before, while the other side was an infrared view of the same scene. Most of the picture was cool and dark, but the body heat of the occasional small animal or bird stood out as a blotch of orange and yellow. ARLENE's head continued scanning, and suddenly a bigger blotch of bright colour appeared. It was vaguely man-shaped, and it was moving away. ARLENE immediately started moving faster to try to catch up with the corporal.

'You'll notice,' Chesterson said, 'that ARLENE followed Corporal Higgs's instructions directly, and then made its own choice of switching to infrared vision to locate him again. Now that it has located him, it will catch up and then resume following him.'

'How does ARLENE know that she's locked on to Corporal Higgs, and not someone else?' Tara asked.

'*She?*' Chesterson said, amused. '*It* has exceedingly sensitive audio receivers. It matches the sound of the target's heartbeat with previous readings it has taken of Corporal Higgs. If the two match, then it knows that it has found the right target.'

'And what happens if *it* finds the wrong target?' Tara persisted.

'It will quietly back away and continue to seek the corporal.'

'And if *it* can't find him?'

'Eventually it will make a decision either to try to locate the corporal by emitting an audio signal, or to terminate the mission and return here, to base. That decision will be made by balancing the importance of completing the mission with the importance of maintaining a stealthy presence.'

'How have you implemented the artificial intelligence?'

Chesterson nodded. 'An excellent question. As you'll appreciate, a great deal of the programming is covered by commercial confidentiality, but what I can say is that her thought processes are based on a complex set of heuristic algorithms supported by a complex neural net.' He smiled. 'Does that make sense?'

'You said "*her*",' Tara pointed out. 'And, yes, it does make sense. I presume there's a Bayesian statistical database underlying the whole thing.'

'Indeed,' Chesterson answered, the smile sliding from his face. 'Does anyone *else* have any questions?'

'*Can* ARLENE be run on remote control?' Rhino asked. 'You know, like a remotely piloted drone?'

'There is, of course, a reversionary remote-control mode,' Chesterson admitted.

'But that will be highly dependent on available bandwidth, surely,' Tara pointed out. She was pleased to see Chesterson scowl. A couple of the other men in the group turned to look at her with interest. 'I would imagine,' she continued, 'that you could only remotely control three or four of these things in the same area, and that's only if there aren't any other remotely controlled things, like reconnaissance drones, around.'

'That is . . . a limitation,' Chesterson admitted, 'but not a serious one. The intent, obviously, is that ARLENE works in robotic mode, making its own decisions in accordance with the orders it is given by the operator – in this case, Corporal Higgs.'

Tara decided that she didn't like Chesterson. He was too officious, too smoothly corporate. She didn't trust him. 'It just occurred to me that this kind of technology would be ideal for all the generals who are sitting in their comfortable offices a long way from the fighting. They can get to see everything that's going on, just as it happens, and they can give orders directly to the troops on the ground. And not just the generals – politicians could get involved as well. They could all sit around a set of TV screens and fight the whole war by remote control.'

A couple of the men in the group – mainly the ones without uniforms, Tara noticed – typed notes into their tablet computers and their mobile phones. Maybe she'd given them some ideas.

'We provide the technology,' Chesterson said smoothly. 'It's up to the buyer how it's used.'

'Could ARLENE be fitted with a weapon?' Tara persisted. 'Could it become a soldier in its own right?'

'As I said, it's not up to us what the user decides to do with the technology.' Chesterson's face was creased into an unhappy mask.

'We'll take that as a "yes",' Rhino said. He quickly asked another question, an innocuous one, and Tara could tell that he was trying to defuse the tension that her pointed questions had caused. She was uneasy though. The use of a robot that carried bags and rucksacks was difficult to deny, but a robot that carried a gun – that was another kettle of fish entirely.

Rhino's question had calmed the situation down. Chesterson was smiling, and demonstrating something else to the group.

'Corporal Higgs,' he said into the radio, 'please instruct ARLENE to remain where it is for ten minutes while you return to base, then to retrace its path and find its own way back.'

'Affirmative,' Higgs's voice said. Moments later, Tara heard him relay the orders to the robot.

She wandered outside, and stared across at the trees on the far side of the clearing. The sun was higher in the sky now, and she could feel its heat like a weight pressing down on her. She wondered in what range of temperatures ARLENE could work, but decided not to ask the question. Chesterson had obviously already decided that she was trouble. It was the same with her tutors back at college. Tara had yet to find a way of asking questions that didn't make it sound like she was being confrontational.

A movement in the trees attracted her attention. It was Corporal Higgs. He exited the treeline and marched rapidly across the clearing. As he got to her, he nodded.

'Ma'am,' he said. She smiled at him.

The group inside started asking Higgs questions about ARLENE as soon as he got inside, but Tara stayed where she was. She was waiting for ARLENE to appear.

And she wasn't disappointed. The robot bag-carrier appeared from the shadows between the trees and started walking across the clearing towards her with its scuttling, insect-like gait. She found herself wondering just how fast it could go. Could it outrun a man?

As it got closer, she walked out to meet it. She stopped about six metres away, directly in the path that it was taking back to the hut.

ARLENE continued walking towards her.

Tara folded her arms and stared at it.

The robot continued moving. If it didn't stop, it was going to walk right over her.

Or through her.

CHAPTER

nine

Tara stood her ground and waited. The robot got closer and closer, its neck and sensor package looming above her. She felt a flutter of nervousness but she wanted to check something. She wanted to check that it had enough awareness to notice her and avoid her.

ARLENE stopped about two metres away from her. Its sensor package stared down at her, then moved first to one side and then to the other. Tara was the focus of its attention as it tried to work out what she was and what to do about her.

She let out a breath of relief as ARLENE scuttled to one side and then walked past her. At least it hadn't tried to go over her.

She turned to walk back just as ARLENE reached the hut and as the group of observers, led by Brad Chesterson, emerged. Rhino was talking to Chesterson. She heard him saying, 'As far as I know, it's already been accepted. An ARLENE system is going to be boxed up and sent to us for evaluation. Professor Livingstone has already agreed it with your board of directors. What we need from you is all the technical documentation you can provide, and some personal tuition if at all possible.'

Tara watched as ARLENE stopped by the hut. The robot settled down on its mechanical haunches, more like a horse than an insect, making it easy to take the bags and rucksacks off it. The observers clustered around it, making appreciative noises about its design and its ruggedness. Tara was impressed as well, but she could see the dark side as well as the light side. She could see how the robot could be abused.

She walked over to the hut to join Rhino and Brad Chesterson. Maybe she should apologize to the man. She hadn't intended to irritate him – not much, anyway.

A movement caught her attention, and she looked sideways to where ARLENE was sitting.

The robot's sensor-package head was swivelling to follow her as she moved. It was *watching* her.

She stared into the darkness of the hut, in case someone was using the remote-control software to track her as she moved, but both the computers were sitting by themselves, unused. Yet on the plasma screen she could see a close-up image of her head.

She turned back to ARLENE and stared straight at its camera. ARLENE stared back at her for a long moment, and then looked away, almost dismissively.

It was morning, and Gecko was crouching on a rooftop overlooking his flat.

He didn't like what he was seeing.

Two men were standing in his room. They weren't the same two men that he had talked to a few days ago, but they had been poured from the same mould: high cheekbones, shaven heads, scars, leather jackets. They were Eastern European gangsters.

It looked as if they had been waiting for him for a while, then got bored and started searching his flat for some clue as to where he had gone. He could see clothes and books scattered around the floor, and the drawers had been pulled out of his bedside cabinet and turned upside down, presumably on the off-chance that he had taped some incriminating evidence underneath. As if he would do anything that stupid. He'd decided a long time ago that if he ever *had* anything incriminating then he would wrap it in a waterproof wrapper and leave it on a rooftop somewhere, where only he and a handful of others could get to it. Hiding something in his room would just be stupid.

One of the gangsters walked over to the window and looked out. Luckily he didn't look up.

Gecko sighed. Turning round, he slumped down with his back against the low wall that ran along the edge of the building. Pigeons stuttered back and forth on stubby little legs over by the trapdoor that led down into the top floor of the building, watching him out of the corners of their eyes. He envied the way that they could fly from roof to roof, not having to worry about planning the routes and taking the chance that muscular strength and speed would win out over gravity. On the other hand, most of them had malformed, twisted feet from where cuts had become infected from the dirt and pollution that coated the rooftops and windowsills. Cuts and grazes were a common problem for free-runners, but they all knew that hands and other exposed areas needed to be kept scrupulously clean, and they all carried little bottles of antiseptic spray just for that purpose.

On a whim, he pulled his mobile phone from the secure pocket in which he kept it. There was a message from Tara – they had exchanged mobile phone numbers before she had flown to America. She had left it about half an hour ago.

'*Hi*,' her voice said. '*We've just landed at Heathrow. Had a great trip. Rhino's a good guy – I think you'll like him. He's a bit like you, I guess – small and muscular.*' There was a pause while Tara realized the implications of what she had said. '*Not that I've been looking at you. Or him. Not in that way.*' She was getting more and more flustered now, and Gecko started grinning. '*Anyway*,' she said, trying to regain her composure, '*we're getting a taxi back to Calum's place once we've got our baggage sorted out. Apparently Calum wants us all to get together for a final briefing. So I guess I'll see you there.*'

Gecko slid his mobile phone back into his pocket and fastened the flap across it. He stood up and stretched, preparing himself for the run across the rooftops back to Calum's apartment. He turned round to take a last look down into his flat – and felt a shiver go down his spine.

The two gangsters were gone.

Had they given up for the day, or . . . ?

The trapdoor in the centre of the roof burst upward. One of the shaven-headed men erupted from the space like a jack-in-the-box.

Calum suppressed a frustrated sigh. He didn't seem to be getting through to Professor Livingstone.

'I don't think you understand,' he said as patiently as he could. 'The intention isn't to go in with nets and cattle prods and anaesthetic darts. This isn't like *King Kong*, where we bring the last survivor of an unknown race of creatures back to civilization and exhibit it in a carnival for entertainment. If we get even a scrap of hair I'll be happy. Anything that we can get a DNA sample from.'

'You're missing the big picture,' Gillian said, shaking her head. '*If* the Almasti exist, and that's a big *if*, then bringing one back would be –' she paused, searching for the right word – 'a *phenomenon*. Newspapers from here to China and back would put two photographs on their front page and their home page – one of the Almast and one of the person who captured it. This might be the missing link between apes and humans – a living example of where we have descended from. We're talking worldwide exposure!'

'I'm not missing the big picture,' Calum said testily. 'I'm ignoring it. I don't *like* the big picture. I don't *want* to be on the front page or the home page of *anything*. I just want to bring back enough viable genetic material so that the Almasti's entire genome can be sequenced. After that, I would rather they were left in peace.'

'You're being naive, Calum.'

'Maybe I am,' he said. He glanced at the professor. She had a frustrated scowl on her face. 'Look, I understand where you're coming from. You're a businesswoman, and you have been for as long as I've known you. If *your* photograph is on every front page and home page, then the business opportunities flood in, don't they? *Everyone* will know who you are.'

'You think I'm treating this as an advertising opportunity?' she asked with quiet intensity.

'I think you're treating it as a number of things, including an advertising opportunity, but you're forgetting – this is *my* expedition. I'm the one setting it up and financing it. Whatever comes out of it gets used in the ways that *I* decide.'

Gillian just shook her head. 'You're very like your father, you know?'

'Thank you,' he said, feeling the sad tug of memories.

'I didn't mean it as a compliment. He was an idealist, and so are you. He could never see the complexity of problems, or the implications of the various answers. To him, and to your mother, the world was a very simple place, but it *isn't*, Calum. It really isn't.'

'*My* world is that simple, and my world exists for about as far as I can reach. Which, in this instance, is all the way to Georgia.'

She put her hands up defensively. 'OK. All right. Just promise me that you'll think about what I've said.'

He recognized her words as a typical negotiating ploy to get out of a dead-end situation, and he responded in a like manner. 'Yes, I promise I'll think about it,' he said with as much conviction as he could force into his voice.

'Right,' Professor Livingstone said, clapping her hands together, 'on to the next point – someone in your party needs to be armed.'

Calum felt his skin crawl at the very thought of weapons. He didn't like violence. He didn't even like thinking about the *possibility* of violence.

Gillian noticed his reluctance. She raised a hand to forestall his response. 'Don't worry – I'm thinking of something less lethal than it sounds.' She reached down to a case that she'd brought in with her, and which was resting by her feet. 'This is a new thing that's been developed by one of the laboratories I do consulting work for. They've given me one of the first off the production line.' She put the case on the counter and flipped the catches. Calum watched edgily as she opened it and took out something that looked like a lot of black metal tubes strapped together, with a shoulder stock at one end, a handle and trigger in the middle and a wide barrel at the other end.

'What the hell is that?' he asked. 'Some kind of multi-barrelled shotgun? If the Almasti are alive, then I want them to stay that way.'

'It's a non-lethal weapon.' She patted the middle of the gun where all the tubes seemed to be part of a rotating mechanism. 'It's a rapid-fire taser shotgun. There's no gunpowder inside – it works on compressed air. The munitions it fires are mainly lithium-ion batteries, with two sharp prongs at the far end. When they hit something, the prongs touch the skin and complete a circuit, and the battery delivers a charge of several thousand volts. It's not enough to kill anyone or anything – except maybe a mouse – but it'll knock a man or a wolf or a bear out for quite a while. It's yours for as long as you need it. It's certified flight safe, as long as it's in the cargo hold with the appropriate documentation – which is already in the case.'

'No,' he said forcefully, pushing it back. 'No, no, no, no, no. You're trying to drag this expedition in a direction in which it will not go – not for as long as I have a say. No weapons, no exploitation, no advertising opportunities, *nothing*! Is that clear?'

She shook her head sadly. 'It's clear, but it's short-sighted and it's wrong. Look, I'll leave the taser shotgun here. Think about it.'

Another negotiating tactic. 'OK, I'll think about it,' he said softly. 'But the answer will still be "no".'

'Family quarrel?' a voice asked from the doorway. 'Should I back away and leave you to it?'

'Come in, Natalie,' Gillian said, waving a hand, 'and discover the reason why you never had a brother.'

'Eeuw!' Natalie exclaimed as she pushed the door open and entered the apartment. 'I don't even want to think about it.'

Calum watched as she walked across to the table.

Realizing that he was watching, and realizing that Natalie had noticed that he was watching, he looked away. And felt himself flush with embarrassment.

The thug looked around the rooftop, caught sight of Gecko and started moving towards him. He obviously wasn't a free-runner – he was too bulky – but he moved like a freight train, big and unstoppable.

The second gangster emerged from the trapdoor more carefully, but then he was carrying a gun.

Gecko knew immediately that they had seen him from the window, pretended not to and had set out to ambush him unawares. He wasn't sure if they were out to catch him and make their boss's offer more forcefully, or whether they had been sent to punish him for not saying yes by breaking his arms and legs, but frankly he wasn't going to hang around to find out.

His best route off the roof was straight ahead, but that would mean going through the two gangsters. That was out of the question. There was only one alternative.

Gecko jumped up on to the waist-high rim that bordered the roof area and started to run. Within less than a second, he was sprinting at full speed. The far edge of the building seemed to rush towards him. He was pretty sure he knew what lay beyond it, but it had been a long while since he had done that particular jump and he was a little fuzzy about the details. He seemed to remember that it was a tricky one, with a high element of risk. Not the kind of run he would normally choose. The problem was, he had no time for a calm, considered reconnaissance.

He reached the end of the small wall and jumped blindly into space, arms extended for balance, legs bent slightly to absorb the impact of landing – assuming he didn't plummet all the way to the ground.

He quickly evaluated the situation as he fell. It wasn't good. The roof ahead of him was further than was comfortable – or even achievable without having the wind at his back. Worse, it was a pitched roof, built as a triangle. It would have been bad enough if he'd been falling towards one of the pitched sides, but he was end-on to the building. If he didn't land exactly on the peak where the two sides met, then he would hit either the left or the right side. Unable to get a purchase on the slope, his feet would slip and he would fall, rolling down the roof until he hit the guttering and fell off.

Just to make it worse, the end of the roof peak had a decoration on it, a little curlicue that probably looked really quaint from the street but which at his level looked more like a major obstacle to landing. He had to hope that his momentum carried him *over* the decoration and on to the ten-centimetre-wide peak.

This was not looking like a successful jump.

All of these thoughts flashed through his mind in the time it took him to cover about five metres horizontally and drop two metres vertically. The roof of the building he was aiming for rushed towards him, growing larger and larger in his field of vision. He wasn't going to make it! He was dropping too fast! He was heading straight for the triangular wall between the sloping roofs!

The little plaster curlicue seemed to rise past his eyes as he dropped. Desperately he reached out for it, hands scrabbling for a grip. His fingers closed over it just as he slammed into the wall. The impact drove the breath from his body and sent a pulse of pain through every bone and every muscle he had. Instead of dropping like a stone he just hung there, hands clamped on a fragile plaster decoration that had endured God knows how many years of rain, snow and baking sun.

He brought his legs up and braced himself against the wall. A quick glance over his shoulder showed him that the two thugs hadn't yet made it to their side of the chasm. That was a relief – they were probably in a mood to use that gun by now.

He heaved himself up with his arms, while at the same time trying to walk up the wall with his feet.

His arms were burning as they took his entire weight. He could feel them trembling with the stress he was putting on them. His fingers felt as if their joints were coming apart, the skin and tissue stretching like elastic.

He hauled as hard as he could, edging his feet higher, small step after small step. He couldn't let it all end here.

The plaster decoration was level with his eyes. He lunged upward and wrapped his right arm round it. That gave him enough purchase to pull himself inelegantly up, scrabbling with his feet to maintain the momentum. Within moments he was folded over the roof: legs hanging on one side, torso and arms and head on the other.

He felt like he was going to be sick.

Glancing over at where he had come from, he saw the two thugs staring at him. One of them raised his gun. The other slapped it down with a curse. Maybe they didn't want to draw attention to themselves. They were both looking hard at the roof that Gecko was folded across, trying to work out if there was a way across there for them, or maybe trying to work out where to go next to intercept him.

He wanted to stay there and catch his breath, but he didn't have the luxury of time. He climbed to his feet and painfully started to walk along the ridge where the two slanted roofs met, balancing like a circus wire-walker.

At the other end of the roof he looked around to get his bearings. If he slid down to the guttering on the right-hand side, then he could shin down a drainpipe to where he could then launch himself across empty space to another, flatter roof. From there he knew a route that would get him to Calum Challenger's apartment.

He glanced backwards. The two Eastern Europeans were gone. The problem was that he knew he would see them again, unless he got away from London in a hurry.

Tbilisi was looking more and more like a good thing to him.

*

Sitting cross-legged on the ground, Rhino glanced around at Tara, Natalie and Gecko. They were sprawled out in a rough circle on the grass, obviously exhausted, tucking into sandwiches and drinks from a cool box that he had brought with him. Behind them lay the wooden aerial pathways, ropes, climbing frames and zip-wires of the adventure playground that extended for several acres through the forest, and off to one side, near the cars, were Gillian Livingstone and Calum Challenger.

It was two days since he and Tara had arrived back from America. Rhino let them all rest and relax while they were eating. They'd already been through an intensive morning of running, climbing and various other kinds of exercise. They had benefited, toning their muscles and learning how to work together, and he had got the chance to see them in action and get some idea of how they were going to function as a team.

Gecko, the Brazilian lad, had been fastest and most confident, just as Rhino had expected. The rope ladders, rope bridges and thick branches that formed the woodland assault course were like home to him. If he could survive up on London's rooftops, jumping from roof to roof, then this was just a walk in the park for him.

Natalie Livingstone – Professor Gillian Livingstone's daughter – was adequate. She obviously had quite a degree of athletic ability, and Rhino remembered her mother saying once that Natalie was on the track-and-field team at her school, but she was held back by the simple fact that she so obviously *hated* doing the assault course. She tottered primly along the aerial walkways as though she was on a catwalk wearing high heels, and she seemed determined not to get a single speck of dirt on her hands. Every so often she would look down at Rhino with daggers in her eyes.

Tara Flynn was the worst, of course. Still wearing her hoodie and black jeans, she showed no natural grace or skill at all, but where Natalie was spending every moment wishing she wasn't there, Tara was grimly focused on finishing. Rhino wasn't sure if she was trying to impress him, or the lad Gecko, or just trying to prove something to herself, but he was proud of the effort she was making. He'd got to quite like her in America, on their trip to the Aberdeen Proving Ground. She was tough and resilient, which counted for a lot in Rhino's book.

As he sat there, watching them eat, he could see that Natalie was actually the weak link. Tara and Gecko had thrown themselves into the idea of the expedition – he suspected that both of them were running away from something – but Natalie was effectively being forced to go along. That would breed resentment, and resentment would breed anger. And that could tear the team apart.

The next few weeks were going to be interesting.

Calum wheeled himself forward, interrupting Rhino's thoughts. 'Can I have everyone's attention? I'd like to test out something that could potentially help all of us during the expedition.'

Rooting around in a box on his lap, he brought out

something that looked like a towelling headband – the kind of thing middle-aged men wore to keep the sweat out of their eyes when they were playing squash. There was something attached to it, and Rhino shifted position to get a better look.

'It's a communications system,' Calum said, holding it up. 'There are miniature loudspeakers and a microphone woven into the headband itself, along with a long-life battery. But the important part is this.' He turned the headband to show a small metal tube stitched to the side. 'It's a high-definition digital camera that's positioned so that it's looking along the line of sight of the person who's wearing it.'

Rhino frowned. He didn't like being surprised by the sudden addition of kit to the expedition he was supposed to be organizing. 'I can't see the point,' he said. 'We're not intending to split up, but if we do then Georgia has a good mobile-phone network that covers most of the country. We can keep in contact with each other if there's a problem. And why would we want to see what the others are seeing?'

Calum stared at him for a moment. 'It's not for you to keep in contact with each other,' he said slowly, as if explaining something to an idiot. 'It's so that I can see what's going on and give you instructions. There's an antenna in the headband that sends the audio and visual signals straight to my computer via whatever geostationary communications satellites are available.'

Rhino felt a small, cold ball of anger forming

somewhere near his heart. He stood. 'Calum, we need to talk.'

'That's exactly why I got hold of these things.'

Tara, Gecko and Natalie tensed. Rhino could sense it from the corner of his eye, although he kept his attention focused on Calum.

'Is there a problem?' asked Calum.

'I'm supposed to be in charge of this expedition. I'm supposed to be the one who makes the decisions and gets everyone in and out in one piece. Now I find that you're going to be watching us every second of the way and giving us "advice" whenever you feel like it. Who is in charge of this mission, Calum? What's my role, if you're going to be looking over my shoulder and countermanding my orders?'

Calum put his hands up. 'Hey, sorry. I didn't realize you were so touchy about this kind of thing.'

'Yes,' Rhino said patiently, 'I *am* touchy about this kind of thing. Confusion over who is giving orders leads to problems, and problems lead to someone getting hurt. In the military we call it the "long screwdriver" effect.'

Calum frowned. Rhino went on to explain: 'Imagine you're working on defusing a bomb, an improvised explosive device, and suddenly your boss reaches in over your shoulder with a long screwdriver and starts poking around in the guts of the bomb. It could be disastrous. In military terms, that might lead to politicians watching military operations as they unfold and throwing in orders that just serve to confuse things. We need to be very clear about who has authority out in the field, and as far as I am concerned it's *me*.'

'OK,' Calum said slowly. 'I'm sorry. I just wanted to make sure that I could see what was going on. I had no intention of leading the expedition by remote control.'

Calum seemed genuinely contrite, but Rhino wasn't so sure that he was telling the truth. Maybe he was lying to himself. He gestured to Calum to join him, walked over to the minibus and sat on the footplate at the back. Calum wheeled himself over.

Calum started to say something, but Rhino raised a hand to stop him.

'I don't mean to embarrass you, or contradict you,' Rhino started, 'but I've seen this happen so often on military missions, and it always ends badly. There has to be a clear chain of command, and it has to be headed up by the commanding officer on the ground, not the general back in his office.'

Rhino could see the emotional struggle playing out across Calum's face. 'You don't know how much I want to go on this expedition,' he whispered.

'I do.' Rhino shrugged. 'Look, six years ago I was looking like a potential Olympic team member. I was a long-distance runner. I broke my leg in three places in a car accident. By the time I came out of physiotherapy and rehabilitation, it was too late. I missed my chance. I realize it's not quite the same situation as yours, but I had to watch other people go off and do the thing that I had spent years building up to.'

Calum nodded. 'OK,' he conceded, 'maybe you do know.'

'I know it's tough being in a wheelchair. I know you try not to think about it. It's obvious from your apartment that you don't want to make any concessions to your problems, and I admire that. But you have to take a step back. You've set all this up – and it's a big, ambitious undertaking – and you're funding the whole thing, which means you're pretty much my boss in all of this, but you can't lead the expedition from five hundred miles away. You have to trust me.'

Calum nodded.

'Good.' Time to give Calum some concession in return, so that he didn't feel completely ousted. 'Look, we'll take the headbands. You can watch what we do to your heart's content. If we have any questions, or need support, we'll tell you. If you want to direct our attention to a particular thing that we might otherwise miss, that's fine. But you don't get to give orders, OK?'

'OK.'

'Right.' Rhino leaned forward and clapped Calum on the shoulder. 'Glad we could sort that out.'

'I never got a chance to ask,' Calum said, changing the subject, 'but how did the ARLENE work out?'

'I was impressed.' Rhino nodded towards Tara and the others. 'And by Tara as well. She asked some very direct questions. Got some backs up. But yes. I think the ARLENE could be very useful to us.'

'The company is cooperating?'

'They are. They've promised to have one of their demonstration models shipped directly to Tbilisi for us to pick up when we arrive. Professor Livingstone must have some friends in high places.'

Calum glanced over at her. 'Yes,' he said thoughtfully. 'She does tend to spring the occasional surprise.'

'What, like her daughter coming on the expedition?'

'Yes.' Calum grimaced. 'I must admit I wasn't expecting that. I tried arguing with her, but . . .' He trailed off, shrugging.

'She's very determined that Natalie is part of the team,' Rhino said. 'Do you believe the story she gave you?'

'What, about her setting up business meetings in Tbilisi so that she could check that the ARLENE was working OK and not likely to be damaged, and her not wanting to leave Natalie alone in London or send her back to America?'

Rhino nodded. At least Gillian had given Calum the same story as she had given him, but it didn't quite make sense. 'I wonder. Heading out into the foothills of the Caucasus Mountains isn't exactly a walk in the park. Things can go wrong, even in the best-planned expeditions.'

'Why – what do you think she's up to?' Calum asked, intrigued.

'I'm not sure. At first I thought she wanted someone

on the team who could be her eyes and ears. Like a human version of that headband of yours.'

'Funny,' said Calum quietly. 'I originally thought that was why she had suggested *you*.'

Rhino smiled. Calum obviously wasn't stupid. 'But I dismissed that argument, on the basis that nobody would willingly send their own daughter into danger.'

'So what other reason could there be?'

Rhino glanced at Natalie. 'I think this is like an outward-bound course. I think Gillian expects this expedition to toughen her daughter up and make her more . . .' He trailed off, unsure what the word was.

'Human?' Calum suggested.

Rhino laughed. 'That's cruel,' he said, 'but entirely fair, as far as I can see from my short experience. She's difficult, isn't she?'

'She is,' Calum agreed, but the way his gaze lingered on Natalie's face indicated to Rhino that the boy was thinking about Natalie as more than just an extra and unwelcome addition to his expedition.

CHAPTER

ten

Tara Flynn was heavily jet-lagged. This was the fourth time zone she had experienced in four days, and her body had given up trying to tell what time it was. Somewhere in her head, a little part of her brain had thrown up its hands and said, 'You know what? – I can't do this! Just tell me when time starts behaving itself again!'

It was some hideously early hour of the morning, although as far as her body was concerned it might just as well have been mid-afternoon. Tara glanced around. Gecko was beside her, sleeping like a baby. Natalie was next to Gecko, on the aisle seat. She had earplugs in and a padded blindfold across her eyes, but Tara didn't think she was sleeping. She kept drumming her fingers and making unhappy shapes with her mouth.

Rhino was across the aisle. He was reading a travel book about Georgia that he had picked up at Heathrow. It was difficult to tell from where Tara was sitting, but she thought he was trying to memorize some phrases in Georgian. Not that standard phrases were going to come in useful. *Can you direct me to the British embassy?* was all very well, but what was Georgian for *Have you seen a thing that's a cross between a man and an ape anywhere around here?*

Rhino seemed to sense her gaze. He glanced up, and smiled at her. *Are you OK?* he mouthed. She gave him a thumbs up as the plane descended smoothly towards Tbilisi airport.

The aircraft's tyres hit the runway and it rolled towards the terminal building.

Gazing out of the window, Tara was strangely impressed. She hadn't quite known what to expect, but she'd had a feeling that any country that had spent so long as part of the monolithic, communist Soviet Union would be dull, drab and grey. That wasn't the immediate impression she got. The terminal building looked new, and designed to impress. It was also a mass of blazing lights, sending out a welcoming signal to arriving travellers.

Inside the aeroplane, all the lights went on. Natalie pulled off her blindfold and gazed around unhappily. She did not look like she wanted to be there.

Gecko was already texting on his mobile. He glanced at Tara and smiled. 'Just letting Calum know we have arrived,' he said.

'You've got a signal already?'

'Yeah, the phone locked straight on to a local mobile service. This is civilization!'

Across the aisle, Rhino put his book down. 'Time to disembark,' he said. 'Customs and immigration should be a doddle. Just present your passports, smile and don't cause any trouble. I'd hate to have to bail any of you out of jail this early in the expedition. Then we have to pick up our luggage from the reclaim area. We'll get a taxi from the airport to the centre of Tbilisi – it's about a thirty-minute drive. We're staying in a hotel in the city centre. Given that it's still stupid o'clock in the morning, I suggest you all get your heads down and get a few hours' rest. We'll meet at lunchtime, get some food inside us and decide on our next move. Everyone OK with that?'

They all nodded.

'What about the ARLENE system?' Tara asked. 'Isn't it supposed to be here with us?'

Rhino nodded. 'Good point. The crates should have been loaded on the aircraft as cargo – along with our tents and other camping supplies. First thing in the morning I'll arrange to hire a van, then Gecko and I will come back and pick all the crates up. When we head off into the Caucasus foothills, we'll take the van along as far as we can, then unload ARLENE and construct the beast. It's modular, and it was designed to slot together easily. We'll load it up with our tents and supplies, and it can follow us and take the strain.'

'I don't suppose it comes with a saddle?' Natalie asked.

Rhino raised an eyebrow. 'Worried about a little exercise, Natalie?'

'Not worried.' She pouted. 'I just don't like it.'

Gecko raised a hand. 'While we are here, should we

check that the crates have made it off the aircraft OK? I mean, if there is a problem it is best that we find out now, rather than tomorrow.'

'Good point.' Rhino nodded. 'OK, change of plan. Tara and Natalie, when we've got our luggage, you two stay in the arrivals hall. Gecko and I will go and check the crates.'

Natalie groaned, but stopped when Rhino glanced over at her.

Passengers were disembarking from the aircraft now, and Rhino gestured to Natalie, Gecko and Tara to go ahead of him.

'Can you believe this is happening?' Gecko said over his shoulder to Tara.

'I stopped believing in what's happening a few days ago,' she replied. 'I just keep going so I can find out what's going to happen next.'

Leaving the girls in the arrivals hall with the suitcases and bags, Rhino and Gecko headed towards the cargo unloading area. Glancing over his shoulder, Gecko noticed that Natalie had pulled her blindfold on again and was stretched out across a trio of seats. Tara had slipped her tablet out of her rucksack and was searching for a free Wi-Fi service.

'Are they going to be OK by themselves?' he asked Rhino.

'If anyone tries to mess with them, Natalie can freeze them out with her withering stare and Tara will kick them in the nuts,' Rhino replied. 'They'll be fine. Besides, there's a visible police presence at the airport, and the Georgian police force is very good.'

They headed down a side corridor. Rhino stopped a passing uniformed security guard and asked him something. The man pointed at a swing door.

'This way.' Rhino pushed the door open and went through into a featureless, utilitarian corridor. Gecko followed. A sign hanging from the ceiling was labelled in flowing Georgian script and also in English. It said *Cargo pickup – straight ahead.*

'Is there not supposed to be some kind of customs demarcation between passenger areas and the runway side of things?' Gecko asked as they walked.

'In theory, yes,' Rhino said over his shoulder. 'In practice, not so much. Besides, we're customers, which means that we're always in the right. Just keep with me and you'll be fine.'

Gecko wasn't reassured. The corridor led them to a stairway, and the stairway led out into the open air. Gecko could smell the sweet aroma of the aviation fuel drifting across the tarmac. The air was cold, but dry.

An airport cargo vehicle went past them, the orange light on its roof flashing. Behind it, like carriages on a kids' toy train, followed a series of wheeled wire cages all connected together. They were piled up with wooden crates.

'That's probably the cargo from our flight,' Rhino observed. 'I don't think there is any other aircraft scheduled for a bit.'

Rhino and Gecko followed the airport cargo vehicle and its train of cages. It headed across a stretch of tarmac towards a hangar. The hangar's doors were wide open and its interior was brightly lit. There were men inside, working on a set of crates that had already been delivered by another airport cargo vehicle, which was just pulling away. At the back of the hangar Gecko noticed a parked black van. Two men in dark windcheaters were taking crates from nearby wire cages and putting them into the back of the van. They didn't look like normal airport personnel: they weren't wearing brightly coloured overalls, or carrying ear defenders, like the other people Gecko had seen around.

Rhino waved at the nearest overalled man. 'Excuse me!' he called. 'Do you speak English?'

'Yes, a little,' the man said in a thickly accented voice. He was burly and hadn't shaved for a couple of days. He was carrying a clipboard holding several sheets of paper.

'I'm looking for my cargo.'

'Cannot take cargo now,' the man said, shaking his head. 'It needs to be processed. Customs, you know? Paperwork needs to be checked.'

'I just want to make sure that it's made it from London all right. We had a change of planes at Frankfurt. I guess there's a chance it got left behind.' Rhino took a sheet of paper from his pocket, unfolded it and held it in front of the airport worker's face. 'Here's the reference number.'

The man glanced at it, and frowned. He checked the

number against one on the clipboard he was carrying. 'That cargo is not yours,' he said, glancing suspiciously at the two of them.

'I've got the paperwork,' Rhino said, frowning. 'That proves it's mine.'

'The cargo is not yours,' the cargo worker insisted.

'Then whose is it?'

He pointed across to the back of the hangar, where the two men in dark windcheaters were loading the last of their crates into their van. 'Is theirs,' the cargo worker said. 'They have customs exemption form. They have reference number. They take crates now.'

Rhino reached out and grabbed the man by the front of his overalls. 'You gave *them* my cargo? How much did they pay you?'

'They had paperwork!' the man protested. He shrugged, avoiding Rhino's fierce gaze. 'And they paid me five hundred American dollars.'

Rhino released him, pushing him away. The man staggered back a few paces. Rhino turned towards where the two men with the van were just sliding the last crate in place. 'Excuse me – can I have a word?'

The men looked at each other, slammed the back door down and ran for the front of the van.

'Hey!' Rhino shouted. He broke into a run.

The van's engine started. Tyres smoking as they spun against the tarmac, the van accelerated. There was no direct route to the exit – the van would have to manoeuvre around several obstructions, and that meant they might just have a chance of stopping it.

Gecko glanced around, wondering what to do. He felt suddenly helpless.

The van slowed down to get past one of the airport cargo vehicles, almost giving Rhino time to catch up with it before it accelerated away from him again.

Gecko saw that there was an empty lone wire cage over near the hangar doors. It must have become detached from its cargo vehicle. Between him and it was a pyramidal pile of differently sized crates that had been stacked up higgledy-piggledy, like a gigantic Tetris game gone wrong. The pile was four crates high. Without quite knowing what he was going to do, Gecko sprinted towards the pile. As he was running, he was calculating angles and speeds in his mind. There was no time to go around the pile – the van would be out of the hangar by the time he got to the doors. He had to go over.

Gecko vaulted on to the first crate and scrambled up on top of the second one. He could feel rough wood and splinters beneath his hands. Regardless, he pulled himself up on top of the third crate. He could hear the van on the other side of the crates now, its engine revving hard as it tried to build up speed and drive out of the warehouse. He thudded his shoulder against the topmost crate and pushed hard.

For a moment he thought the crate was going to stay exactly where it was, but then he felt it move. He pushed harder. With a grating of wood on wood, the crate slid forward.

Somewhere behind him, Gecko could hear the cargo workers shouting. Ignoring them, he put his entire weight into pushing the crate.

It got to the edge of the crate on which it was resting, teetered for a moment and then fell. Gecko's momentum almost carried him with it. He flailed his arms, trying to shift his centre of gravity backwards.

The crate toppled almost in slow motion. It hit the corner of a lower crate and spun. With it out of the way, Gecko was now on top of the pile. He saw the van heading towards the hangar doors with Rhino in pursuit, and saw the crate fall directly in its path.

The driver spun his steering wheel at the last moment, and the van skidded into a turn. The crate hit the ground and smashed, spilling its contents all over the place. They looked like parts for some industrial machine.

Rhino got to the van just as it was turning, but he was on the passenger side, not the driver's side. He wrenched the door open and grabbed the passenger. The man lashed out with his hand, catching Rhino on the forehead, but Rhino's left hand was pulling the man out while his right hand was reaching across to slam down on the seat-belt release. The release gave way and the man seemed to fly out of the van.

The driver must have put his foot on the accelerator because the van suddenly sprang forward, leaving Rhino behind but letting the unlocked rear door fly up. The vehicle skidded around the fallen crate, straightened up and headed directly for the hangar doors.

Gecko glanced around, sizing up his options. Without really thinking, he leaped from the pile of crates to the cab of a stationary airport cargo vehicle. His foot caught on the orange roof light, and he almost fell, but he leaped from the top of the cab to the bonnet and from the bonnet to the ground.

He was almost at the hangar's exit now. The van was heading towards him from his left. He grabbed at the lone empty wire cage he had seen a few seconds ago. It was on wheels, and he pushed it as hard as he could.

The wire cage rolled into the path of the van. Gecko leaped back out of the way as the van smashed into it. The driver threw his hands up to protect his face as the cage flipped into the air and hit the windscreen. The van braked hard, the wire cage rolled past it and out of the way, and the driver pressed his foot on the accelerator again to send the vehicle springing forward. Gecko swore in Brazilian, thinking that he had failed in his attempt to stop it from driving out of the hangar, but he had delayed it just long enough for Rhino to get to the back of the van. The door was still hanging open, and Rhino jumped inside. As the van zoomed past Gecko, the Brazilian boy saw Rhino pulling himself hand over hand into the back. Rhino was trying to avoid the cargo crates as they slid around and threatened to crush him.

Gecko watched in amazement as Rhino clambered over the last crate and got to the back of the driver's seat. It was difficult to tell at that distance, but Gecko thought he saw Rhino lock his right arm round the driver's neck. The van slewed left, slowed down and came to a stop with its rear doors and passenger door flapping.

Gecko glanccd back into the hangar. The cargo workers were watching in dumbfounded amazement. Fortunately, none of them were phoning for help.

He looked back towards the van just in time to see Rhino fly out of the open passenger door. There must have been some kind of fight going on in the cab, because the driver jumped out of the other side and sprinted across the tarmac towards darkness and safety. He had blood on his face.

Gecko ran towards where Rhino was lying on the ground. 'Are you OK?'

'Strong punch,' Rhino said as Gecko got to him. 'I think he had a knuckleduster or something.' He put a hand up to his forehead and touched it gingerly. When he took it away, there was blood on his fingers. 'Ouch.'

'Stay there,' Gecko said. 'I'll get medical help.'

'Don't do that,' Rhino said. He climbed to his feet. 'I'm just bruised and battered, not seriously injured. I've got worse injuries than this on a Friday night in Hereford town centre.' He glanced back into the warehouse. 'What happened to the other guy?'

Gecko shrugged. 'I did not see.'

'OK.' Rhino handed over the paper he had taken from his pocket earlier on and showed it to the cargo handler. 'This is the cargo manifest for our stuff. You check the crates in the back. I want to know if anything is missing. I'll go and check on the passenger, and sort things out with the cargo guys.'

As Rhino limped off, Gecko climbed into the back of the van. It looked like a cross between a minibus and a cargo shifter.

He stared at the crates. Each one had a stencilled reference number on it, and – wonder of wonders – the crates had all been stacked with their reference numbers the right way up. He set about cross-referencing the numbers on the crates with the numbers on the manifest.

He was just finishing when Rhino returned.

'What's the story?' Rhino asked.

'There are two crates missing, I think,' Gecko replied.

'It's OK – I know where they are. The two thieves left them behind when they realized we'd rumbled them. They're sitting back there in the hangar.'

Gecko glanced into the brightly lit interior of the hangar. 'What about the second man?'

'No sign of him. I think he decided that discretion was the better part of valour, and legged it as fast as he could.'

'And the cargo handlers?'

'I've explained the way things are to them. They'll forget about everything they've seen if we don't report to their superiors that they took a bribe to turn a blind eye while someone tried to steal our stuff.'

'Which does raise the question,' Gecko said, 'why were they stealing our stuff?'

Rhino shrugged. 'Two options – either they didn't know what it was and just decided to take a pile of crates away and see what they'd got, or they deliberately stole our stuff *because* it was ours.'

'They had a fake manifest with our reference number,' Gecko pointed out, 'and they had already faked a customs exemption form. They *knew* that our crates were going to be there, and they deliberately chose to take them.'

Rhino nodded. 'That's right. And it does raise the question – why us?'

Gecko looked around. 'We are not going to report this to the police, are we?'

'That would cause more trouble than it would solve. We'd get tied up in witness statements and all kinds of paperwork that would just slow us down. Best thing is to just accept it and move on.' He patted the side of the van. 'But look on the bright side – we don't have to hire a van tomorrow. We've already got one!'

Gecko stared at the van, then at Rhino. 'But it is not ours!'

'Do you really think the current owners are going to come back for it?'

'But – what if they stole it, and the police arrest us for stealing?'

'Those two took the trouble to fake our manifest and a customs exemption form. That shows forethought and planning. They wouldn't have done anything as stupid as to drive around in a stolen van. No, this will have been purchased on the quiet, from some small second-hand dealership. It'll be legitimate. And we won't need it for more than a few days.' He glanced at it appreciatively. 'Mitsubishi Delica, diesel engine, four-wheel drive. Engine beneath the front passenger seat. Rails so that you can fit anything up to six extra seats in the back, so they're surprisingly versatile as well as being powerful. I've seen these things used to pull Land Rovers out of mud. They're nippy, they're strong and they're surprisingly comfortable. I might just keep this thing, if I can work out a way to get it back to England.' He smiled. 'And the thieves have packed all but two crates already for us. That was considerate.'

Gecko still had an uncomfortable feeling in his chest. 'I would still like to know what they were doing, stealing our equipment.'

'If I had to make a guess,' Rhino answered thoughtfully, 'I'd say that they somehow heard about ARLENE and decided that they wanted to get hold of some semi-secret US government equipment. They could probably sell it on the black market for millions of dollars. The Chinese or the North Koreans would sell their own honourable ancestors to get hold of it.'

'There is another possibility,' Gecko pointed out.

'What's that?'

'They might have been targeting us, rather than the equipment. They might have found out about the expedition and they are trying to stop us.'

'Why would anyone want to stop an expedition to find a possible ape-man creature that probably doesn't exist anyway?'

'I do not know.' Gecko shrugged, then caught up with Rhino's last statement. 'What, you do not think we're going to find this Almast thing?'

'I have to say, it's possibly the most unlikely thing I've heard apart from the Loch Ness Monster. I mean, what are the odds of there being a missing link, a real Neanderthal, living quietly here in the foothills? Surely someone would have spotted these Almasti creatures before now.'

'Not if they are avoiding humans. So, if you do not believe in the Almasti, what are you doing here?'

'I'm earning money, and keeping my head down,' Rhino replied brutally. 'What's your excuse? Are you going along with it because you have a desperate desire to find new species and expand the frontiers of biology?'

Gecko opened his mouth to answer, then realized that he didn't know what to say. Did he *really* believe in the Almasti, or was he just going along on the expedition to get away from the men who wanted him to be their pet thief?

Rhino had been watching Gecko's face. 'OK, you're here because you're running away from something, not because you believe in Calum Challenger's cause. Natalie we already know about – she's only here because her mother ordered her to come along. So what about Tara? I get the impression that unknown animals aren't exactly her cup of tea. I suspect she prefers circuit boards and computer code to mythical ape-men.'

'She is . . . trying to avoid getting involved with a company that . . . that wants to use her skills,' Gecko explained haltingly. He wasn't sure how much Tara would want Rhino to know about Nemor, or how much she had already told him when they were in America.

'OK, so she's been pushed on to the expedition by circumstances, not pulled on by a love of extinct animals and dubious DNA benefits.' Rhino sighed. 'So the only person who really believes in the purpose of this expedition is the one who's not here. Great.' He thumped the side of the van. 'Normally I love a challenge, but this is going too far. Come on, let's get back to the others and drive them into town. We still have an expedition to plan and execute, even if nobody actually believes in it.'

Gecko climbed into the passenger seat, shocked by Rhino's attitude. Maybe he'd been guilty himself of not thinking too much about what the four of them were doing, or how quickly they had been pulled together by Calum's enthusiasm, but the thought that none of them actually wanted to be there was surprisingly hurtful.

How, he wondered, could they possibly pull this expedition off successfully if none of them believed in it?

CHAPTER eleven

'Watch out!' Natalie shouted.

The taxi driver didn't seem to hear her. He just headed straight for the cars ahead. He even seemed to accelerate.

Her mother put her hand reassuringly on Natalie's knee. 'Don't worry, darling – he knows what he's doing.'

'I don't care whether he *knows* what he's doing or not,' Natalie snapped, hearing the edge of panic in her voice. 'What he's doing is going to get us killed!'

As the car hurtled towards the line of traffic, a gap appeared at the last minute. The driver spun the steering wheel and the car slewed right, slotting neatly into the gap. Matching speeds with precision, he joined the flow. There wasn't even a blare of horns to mark his sudden arrival. It seemed as if the other drivers regarded it is something normal.

'There are only a couple of rules of driving in Georgia, as far as I can tell,' Gillian Livingstone said calmly. 'The first is that if there's a gap, your car can fit into it. The second is that there's always a gap, even if you have to make it yourself. Oh, and the third is that nobody has priority at junctions, which means in practice that everyone has priority, and uses it.'

Natalie shivered. 'I hate this place.'

'You hate everywhere that isn't Los Angeles. And when you're in Los Angeles you hate it there as well.'

Natalie didn't rise to the bait. Instead, she looked out of the car's window at the sights of Tbilisi, capital of Georgia.

The city was, she had to admit, striking. It was a riot of bright colours. The buildings were not just painted in different colours, but designed in different styles as well. Some were tall and thin, some short and wide; some had complicated rooflines and some were flat; some had lots of small windows and some had a handful of big ones. There was no pattern, no uniformity, apart from the fact that all the buildings had balconies beneath their windows, usually with vases, a cat and some washing. People seemed to have just built what they liked where they liked, but rather than being a mess the results were surprisingly attractive.

And there were no gaps, Natalie noticed. In New York it seemed as if every big building was separated from its neighbours by sidewalks, alleyways or stretches of grass, but here the buildings all ran together into a continuous frontage. Looking closer, Natalie could see where there might have *been* gaps, at one time, but someone had come along and built thin buildings in the gaps, or linked the two sides with a stretch of differently coloured wall with a gateway in it.

It was chaotic, but at the same time it was charming.

'This city is a mess,' she said dismissively. After all, she didn't want to give her mother the idea that she had anything but contempt for the places to which she was taken.

It was the day after she had arrived with Rhino Gillis, Gecko and Tara. Rhino had managed to get hold of some crummy second-hand van, and they'd had a bumpy half-hour drive into the centre of Tbilisi, where their hotel was located. It was OK, she supposed. It was more of a managed apartment than a hotel, with four bedrooms leading off a central living room. There was even a small kitchen area, which had filled Natalie with horror. She hoped that they wouldn't be expected to cook their own food. If it came to that, she was going to phone out for pizza.

Her mother had called the next morning. She'd arrived on an earlier flight, and was intending to head into the American embassy to chat to the ambassador. And Natalie, of course, was expected to go with her. Rhino had agreed – not that it was his place to agree. Gillian Livingstone pretty much did what she wanted.

The car swerved out of the flow of traffic and darted across a road towards a side street. The driver parked the car diagonally. 'Embassy up there,' he grunted, gesturing along the side street. It sloped upward, of course. Nothing was ever easy in Natalie's life, not even short walks.

'Can't you get any closer?' her mother asked.

He shook his head. 'Security. Best for me to park here and you to walk. Not too far.'

Gillian shrugged. 'When in Rome . . .' she murmured. She waited for a moment, expecting the driver to get out and open her door for her. When he didn't, she opened it herself and stepped out. 'Come on, Natalie – it looks like we're slumming it.'

As the two of them walked uphill, her mother confided, 'I don't expect to be in there more than an hour – the ambassador is a busy man. We'll swap pleasantries, he'll offer us a cup of coffee, I'll talk a little bit about the business meetings I've got planned and he'll try to give me a steer on how to deal with Georgian businessmen, as if I need it. At the end I'll just drop in the fact that Rhino Gillis is here with the three of you, and you're all going to be heading out into the foothills of the Caucasus Mountains. I'll mention these stupid Almast creatures, and he'll laugh. He won't take it seriously, of course, but he might have heard a rumour, or know someone that you can talk to. It's worth asking, and at least we can alert him to your presence, just in case there's any trouble. Apart from saying "Hello", "No sugar, thank you", and "Goodbye", I don't expect you to say anything.'

'As if.' Natalie had no intention of adding anything to the conversation between her mother and the ambassador.

'Actually,' she said, surprising herself, 'I don't think it *is* stupid.'

'You don't think *what* is stupid?'

'This Almast thing.'

Her mother turned to glance at her, eyes hidden behind dark glasses. 'Don't tell me that Calum has persuaded you? Look, if there was really a tribe of Neanderthals running around anywhere in the civilized world, then we would know about it. Given the number of TV documentary teams criss-crossing the world in search of something unique to film, I'd be surprised if there's anything larger than a beetle that hasn't had a zoom lens pointed at it.'

'Then why did you agree to Calum setting up this expedition? And why are you making me go along with it?'

'Calum is a . . . unique child,' Gillian said quietly. 'He's fantastically intelligent, but he's not got much perspective. Because he doesn't get out much, he spends a lot of time propping up his own obsessions by hunting around the internet. The trouble is that he's got access to a large pot of money, and his Great-Aunt Merrily doesn't pull as hard on the purse strings as she should. Calum is free to explore those obsessions, and if he's not carefully controlled then he'll end up frittering away his inheritance. It's my job, as I see it, to keep him relatively sane and focused, and make sure there's still a comfortable amount of money left in his trust fund when he reaches maturity.' She sighed. 'That means I have to sometimes pander to his weird obsessions in order to stop him going mad, but it also means that I get to temper his enthusiasm and make sure he thinks about all those little things, like, oh, I don't know, health and safety, and cost-effectiveness.' She sighed. 'Look, I'm not saying that the Almasti *don't* exist. I'm just saying that it's unlikely that they do and, even *if* they do, I'm sorry, but three teenagers and a former soldier who can't adjust to life in the civilian world aren't going to be the ones to accidentally stumble across them.'

'But if we do,' Natalie said, equally quietly, 'you want dibs on the intellectual-property rights.'

'Hey,' her mother said casually, 'I'm an entrepreneur. It's my ability to take advantage of unlikely business opportunities that keeps you in designer shoes.'

'The thing is,' Natalie explained, unsure why she was bothering but somehow knowing that it was important, 'Calum gave us all some material to read over on the flight. It was kinda interesting. We think the world's a really small place, and there's nothing left to be discovered, but apparently naturalists are finding new species, like, every *day* almost – not just beetles and stuff, but big things, like deer and new types of wild cat. A new type of lizard has only just been discovered on an island off the coast of New Guinea – it's been called the bumblebee gecko. There was this naturalist who decided to catalogue the bees and wasps in his back garden in England, and he, like, found that there were things flying around there that hadn't been catalogued – ever – by scientists. There're literally things right under our noses that we haven't discovered, and when you think that there's still sixty per cent of the Earth's land surface and ninety-nine per cent of the ocean that hasn't been properly explored, then it makes you think that maybe we *don't* know it all. Calum told me that there have been two new species a month discovered around deep-sea volcanic vents for the past twenty-five years. That's over six hundred new species! There *are* things out there that we haven't come across yet, and Calum's right – there may be things that can help with medicine and stuff. After all, penicillin came from a fungus that was growing on someone's Petri dish, and aspirin was developed when biologists realized that animals were chewing the bark of willow trees when they were in pain. There's so much tropical rainforest out there, with so many unknown plants, that there might be cures for cancer, and tuberculosis, and cholera, and typhoid, and all those diseases that kill so many babies every year.' She paused to take a breath. 'Do you even *know* how many babies die of typhoid every year?'

'As it happens,' her mother said, staring at Natalie with a strange expression on her face, 'I do. But do *you* know how many types of virus or bacteria have been sitting around in the rainforest for hundreds of thousands of years, infecting the local wildlife with nothing worse than a slight sniffle and a headache, just waiting for humans to come along and act as a host? HIV, Ebola, haemorrhagic fever . . . When they're transferred from animals to humans, they suddenly become fatal, and worse – easily transmissible. There are things out there that should probably be left well alone,

Natalie.' She stopped walking, and Natalie stopped too. 'You actually care about this, don't you?'

Natalie shrugged. 'It makes sense,' she said. 'It *does* make sense. There are all these problems in the world that we know about, but there're all these potential solutions out there in the world we *don't* know about. We need to connect them together somehow.'

Gillian smiled, but there was little humour in the smile. 'Strange – I've been waiting for a while to see what it was that was going to snag your attention, apart from shoes and boys. I thought for a while it was going to be athletics, or swimming, and I had dreams about you competing in the Olympics. But you've wrong-footed me. I think you may have found your vocation, and it's the last thing I would have predicted.' She reached out and touched Natalie's cheek. 'You've surprised me, and you've made me strangely proud. Good on you.'

Natalie found herself suddenly unable to say anything. She felt her cheeks going red, and she had a horrible feeling that there might be tears bubbling up beneath her ice-cold exterior.

'Don't worry,' her mother said. 'I won't tell anyone.'

'This doesn't mean I've gone off shoes,' Natalie managed to say.

Tara gazed around the bookshop with a smile on her face. 'Now *this*,' she said, 'is more like it.'

Beside her, Gecko sighed. 'Do we *have* to?' he asked.

Bookshops weren't really his thing. Shops in general weren't really his thing.

'We have to,' she confirmed. 'We need maps, and guidebooks, and whatever else we can find.'

'Haven't you got a computer for that?'

'Ever heard of low battery power?'

He watched as she walked up to the cash desk. 'I'm sorry – do you speak English?' she asked the girl who looked up at her.

'I do,' the girl said with an accent. 'Can I help you?'

'I'm looking for maps of Georgia.'

'City maps?' the girl asked.

'No – maps of the area around the Caucasus Mountains.' She glanced at Gecko. 'I know Rhino brought some with him,' she explained, 'but those were just what he could find in London in the days before we flew out. I think he called in some favours from army friends of his, but even so, there might be something more detailed locally. You never know.'

The girl behind the cash desk had been waiting patiently while Tara spoke. 'We have *some* maps,' she said carefully, 'but I do not think they are the kind of thing you want to take with you if you are camping. They are more like tourist maps. I can recommend a camping shop just a short walk away, yes? They have maps.'

'Yes, please,' Tara said gratefully.

'I will write the name of the place, and how to get there,' the girl said. She picked up a pen and scribbled something on a piece of paper she'd pulled from beneath the till.

Gecko got bored, and started looking along the shelves nearest to the till. His gaze skimmed across various covers without stopping until he found a large hardback book with a red cover, highlighted with golden patterns. It caught his eye, at least in part because it was larger and more colourful than the books around it. Picking it up, he flicked through it. Each page contained a mass of text in the flowing Georgian script with which he was gradually becoming familiar – script that was almost like artwork in its own right – but there were also illustrations of men in armour, and animals, and forests. The illustrations were dark, and modern, and quite fantastical.

'It is called *Knight in a Leopard's Skin*,' the girl at the till said, noticing his interest. 'It is a classical tale in Georgian literature.' She smiled shyly. 'We publish it ourselves. This bookshop is part of Georgia's largest publishing house.'

'It is . . . lovely,' Gecko said, and he meant it.

'It is quite controversial,' the girl continued. 'We chose to make the illustrations modern, rather than . . . how would you say it? . . . antique. A lot of people argued with us, but the book has sold very well.'

'If I had any money, I would buy it,' Gecko said.

She smiled. 'If I could, I would give you a copy for free.'

Gecko smiled back, unsure what to say. He was saved from embarrassment when his mobile rang. He answered it with an apologetic shrug at the girl behind the till.

'Yeah, Gecko?'

'Hi, yeah,' a voice said, 'this is Natalie. I'm phoning from the US embassy.'

'Great,' said Gecko. 'I am answering from a bookshop.'

'Oh. OK. Well, my mother's been talking to the ambassador, and he's made some calls and stuff, and he's come up with the name of a guide here in Tbilisi who's familiar with the Caucasus Mountains. His name is Levan Ketsbaia. He speaks good English, charges reasonable rates and can be trusted. Apparently the embassy staff use him from time to time if they have to leave the city for any reason. I thought you might get in contact with him or something.'

'Did you try phoning him direct?' Gecko asked.

'Eeuw, no!' Natalie responded. 'I don't talk to strangers if I can possibly help it. Besides, it's more your thing.'

'OK – text his number through.'

'I will. Later.' She rang off, leaving Gecko wondering if she was saying she'd text the number through later or was just indicating that she would see him later. He spoke five languages, but he found Natalie very difficult to understand. She seemed to have a language all her own.

'That was Natalie,' he said to Tara as his phone pinged to indicate an incoming text message. 'She has got a lead on a possible local guide.'

'Better pass it on to Rhino. He'll be better at working out whether a tour guide knows his stuff than we will.'

'Hey,' Gecko protested, 'I know about human nature

and stuff. I have knocked around. I can tell whether a man is trustworthy or not!'

'No offence,' Tara said, 'but I think we should leave it to the professionals.' She held up the piece of paper that the girl behind the till had been working on. 'Meantime, you and I can go and check out this camping shop. With a bit of luck they'll have maps of the area, and they might also be able to help fill some of the gaps in our kit that Rhino couldn't get hold of back in England before we left.'

'Kendal Mint Cake,' Gecko said suddenly as a thought struck him.

'What?'

'That stuff you can only get in camping shops. It is like a slab of pure sugar, flavoured with peppermint oil. It is supposed to be some kind of high-energy food supply for hikers, but there is so much sugar in there that hummingbirds would get hyper on it. I used to love the stuff. I could eat an entire bar in one go.'

Tara looked Gecko up and down. 'If I did that, it would go straight to my hips and thighs. Where does it go on you?'

'Charm and charisma,' he replied with a smile.

Calum sat in darkness, his face lit only by his computer screens.

Six of them were blank – waiting for the streaming video that would be sent back, via satellite, from the cameras on the headbands he'd given the four members of the expedition and from the visual and infrared sensors of the ARLENE robot. The team was still in Tbilisi, according to the schedule, and he wouldn't expect them to wear the headbands until they set out for the Caucasus foothills. They weren't doing anything in Georgia's capital city apart from allowing their body clocks time to adjust, finding a guide and picking up whatever items they needed to complete their supplies. If they wore the camera headbands for that, then they would get some strange looks from the locals. Much as Calum wanted to know what they were doing, what was happening to them, every second of the day, he knew he had to wait.

It was difficult for him though. He so desperately wanted to be a part of the expedition. He so desperately wanted to be *there* with them.

Maybe, one day, he would be able to. If this expedition, or the next one, or the one after that, was successful.

The seventh screen showed a Google Maps view of Tbilisi with the locations of Rhino, Tara, Gecko and Natalie displayed in different colours. Calum had hacked into their mobile-phone accounts while they were on the flight and set their phones to send him GPS coordinates every fifteen minutes. He hadn't told them. He had a suspicion that they would have objected, but he had to know where they were, just in case something happened. At least, that's what he told himself.

Tara and Gecko were off in one location, Rhino was a mile or so away from them, and Natalie was across the other side of the city. Her GPS location coincided with that of her mother. When Gilliam had told him that she was heading to Tbilisi as well, Calum had hacked her phone too. If she was taking an interest in the expedition, then he was going to take an interest in her. He didn't want her to know more about what was going on than he did. When and if Rhino managed to employ a guide, Calum was going to have to do the same with his mobile phone – assuming he had one.

The eighth and ninth screens were running continual search-engine sweeps of the internet, looking for any mentions of the Almasti. If there was any fresh information, then he wanted to know about it straight away so he could pass it on to the team.

He checked his watch. Four o'clock in the afternoon UK time – or eight o'clock in the evening in Tbilisi. The team was probably making arrangements for dinner. Rhino would almost certainly take the opportunity to brief them on the plans for the next few days. He and Rhino had agreed that the best thing was for them to head for the village nearest to the location where the photograph of the possible Almast had been taken. It was as good a starting point as any. The village was called Ruspiri, and it was a small place in the back end of nowhere, occupied by farmers, hunters and the occasional daring backpacker.

The tenth screen showed a mosaic of photographs of Natalie Livingstone. Some were things he'd found on the internet – high-school yearbook stuff, things from the Facebook and Flickr accounts of friends, and a few were candid snaps he'd pulled off his security systems from the two occasions she'd visited the apartment. He felt a bit like a stalker, putting the photographs together and displaying them – no, that wasn't true, he felt a *lot* like a stalker – but there was something about her that made his heart feel like it was tearing in two every time he saw her. What *was* it? She wasn't exactly the kind of girl he usually went for – she was arrogant, shallow and vain – but he couldn't get her beautiful tanned skin and her violet eyes out of his mind.

That was another reason why he so desperately wanted to be on the expedition.

He was just reaching forward to type some instructions into his keyboard when the lights went out.

Calum froze. Power cut? Unusual, in the centre of London. Fuse blown in the fuse box? Possible – the warehouse was old, and the wiring wasn't as up to date as it could be, especially downstairs in the area where his great-grandfather's samples and exhibits were stored. He sighed. He supposed that he'd have to go and check, difficult though it might be. The alternative would be to phone his great-aunt's chauffeur and general handyman, Mr Macfarlane, and ask him to come over, and Calum would rather cut his own right hand off than do that.

He was just about to turn away from the computer and swing his way towards the door when he heard movement outside. Scuffling at the door. Scratching.

The sound of the lock being forced.

A feeling of disbelief swept over him. His warehouse,

his *apartment*, being burgled? While he was *inside*? Unbe*liev*able.

His brain raced, trying to work out what to do, which of the various options that presented themselves would be best. He'd always relied on the security system to deter thieves and intruders, but with the power off it was no more use than a chocolate teapot. He could call the police, in fact he probably *should* call the police, but it would take them at least ten minutes to get to him, more if they were busy or thought he was a hoax call. He could phone Mr Macfarlane – the man had hidden depths, and might be able to help – but he was miles away. And, apart from his great-aunt, everyone else he knew was several hundred miles away in Georgia.

He picked up his mobile phone from beside the keyboard. At least if he phoned the police he'd know that help was on its way.

The words on the screen were brutally plain. *No signal.*

He'd always had a mobile-phone signal in the apartment. The intruders were jamming the frequencies, not letting anything in or out.

He was going to have to deal with this himself.

Somehow.

CHAPTER

twelve

It was early the next day that the expedition rolled out of Tbilisi.

Rhino glanced at their driver. Levan Ketsbaia was a burly man with a mass of unruly black hair, thick eyebrows and a few days' stubble around his cheeks, chin and neck. His eyes were a faded green, quite startling in his swarthy face, and he had a gold stud in his right earlobe.

Rhino had found Levan in a coffee shop in the centre of Tbilisi. They had arranged a meeting there via phone calls, as Rhino had wanted to spend some time in the man's company, weigh him up, look for signs that he was reliable, honest and knowledgeable.

The first thing Rhino noticed as he sat down was that Levan was drinking mineral water. That was a good sign. A man who drank beer or wine at lunchtime was probably not to be trusted. He might take his own supply of alcohol with him on the expedition, and get drunk at the wrong moment – the wrong moment on an expedition being virtually any moment, of course.

Levan looked up at Rhino. 'Please, join me.' He waved at the food in front of him – circles of some doughy substance that filled the plate. 'Georgian food – please help yourself. It is bread stuffed with local cheese. People call it "Georgian pizza".'

Another good sign – Levan wasn't immediately trying to get Rhino to buy drinks and food for him, even before they had agreed on his fees and terms of employment. That suggested he wasn't a chancer, looking to exploit his employers.

They talked for a couple of hours, and by the end of it Rhino was convinced that they had found their guide. Levan spoke openly and honestly about his life – including service in the army during the era when Russia had controlled the country – and his love for the countryside. Rhino asked him searching questions on survival skills, mountaineering and camping, and he answered them all in detail and with humour. Rhino decided that he trusted Levan and, more than that, he *liked* him too.

Now, as Levan drove through Tbilisi towards the countryside, Tara leaned forward from her seat in the back.

'Mr Ketsbaia . . .'

'Levan,' he called back over his shoulder. 'I insist – it is Levan. And you are . . . Tara?'

'That's right.' She seemed to glow slightly with pleasure at the fact that he had remembered, despite their brief introduction earlier. 'Can I ask you a question?'

'Of course. Any question you like – apart from mathematics. I do not like mathematics.'

'No, it's not mathematics.' She waved a hand at the scene beyond the windscreen. 'I can't help but notice that wherever you look there are signs for art shops, art galleries or art exhibitions. They all look handmade. Is *everyone* in Tbilisi an artist?'

'Very much so,' he replied. 'Georgians are a very artistic people. If we are not painters, then we are writers. If we are not writers, then we are poets.'

'What about you?' Tara asked. 'When you're not doing this, what do *you* do?'

'I am sculptor,' he said proudly. 'I carve stone.'

'How long until we get to where we're going?' Natalie called, removing her headphones.

'To the Caucasus Mountains? Six hours, I think.'

'You *think*?' Natalie questioned. 'I thought you were some kind of super-guide or something.'

'Is depending on traffic, and weather, and state of roads,' he explained patiently. 'Never trust a man who gives you an absolute answer to a question like that. He is usually guessing.'

Within fifteen minutes they had got to a point where the city of Tbilisi gave way to rolling countryside – bare earth interrupted by patches of vegetation, outcrops of rock and the occasional shack. To their right the ground rose up into a series of sharp-edged hills that looked like miniature mountain ranges. The highest peaks all seemed to have churches built on them – closer to God, Rhino assumed, but a hell of a walk for the parishioners.

The road curved around the hills and through a pass that led to the other side. As they emerged from the shelter of the hills, and the road dipped away in front of them, the Georgian countryside was exposed in all its glory. Rhino could see small villages, ploughed fields, rivers carving their way through the landscape. On his right was a collection of several houses, all clustered together. They had the same colour walls and the same colour roofs. An attempt by the Soviets to build some kind of collective village, he assumed.

The van rolled on, covering the miles with ease. The engine maintained a constant tone, and Rhino was pleased to see that the fuel gauge was barely moving. That was a relief – he'd had a worry that they were going to have to refuel on a regular basis, which might be difficult in the mountains. In the back, Tara, Natalie and Gecko were all sleeping. That wasn't a surprise – their body clocks still hadn't adapted to the new time zone, and he suspected that they weren't sleeping very well at night. He found that he couldn't sleep. The passing countryside held too much interest for him.

The road rolled on ahead of them, with the occasional car or truck passing them by. A side road led away to the right. Levan indicated it with a wave of his hand. 'Down there is village where Stalin was born,' he said darkly. 'A son of Georgia, but not one we are proud of.'

Stalin. The man in charge of the Soviet Union for over

twenty years until 1953. A brutal dictator who had been responsible for the deaths of millions of Soviet citizens over the course of his bloody reign. And this was where he had been born?

Rhino shook his head in wry surprise. How exactly had he ended up here? he asked himself.

Calum listened, helpless, as the intruders forced the door open.

They were using brute force, rather than finesse, but paradoxically that was worse – it told him they were sophisticated, rather than amateurs. The lock was a state-of-the-art eight-tumbler option with steel deadbolts. Anybody trying to pick it with the high-tech equivalent of a hairpin was going to have their work cut out for them. On the other hand, anyone trying to force it with a crowbar, backed up with a hydraulic jack, wouldn't have much trouble *if* the security system was down. Which it was.

The door squeaked and groaned as the intruders put it under more and more pressure. Calum's heart raced. Maybe someone had broken in downstairs for a look around and was now trying to get in upstairs. Maybe they hadn't found whatever they were looking for downstairs. Perhaps they didn't *know* what they were looking for, but wanted to rifle through everything he possessed to see what came up.

Calum frantically searched his mind for options, and came up blank. If they made it in – and frankly that was looking like a certainty in the next few minutes – then he was toast. He had no defences, nothing with which to fight them off.

Or did he?

He suddenly remembered the weapon that he and Professor Livingstone had argued about – the multi-shot taser gun. He'd stored it in a cupboard on the other side of the room. If he could just get to it in time . . .

Before the thought was finished he was swinging across the room as fast as he could, holding tight to the leather straps that hung from the ceiling.

When he was halfway across, the door burst open, sending splinters of wood flying.

Beyond the threshold was darkness, but the intruders had flashlights. They shone them into the room, scanning from side to side to pick up anyone who happened to be there.

Before the light touched him, Calum used his overdeveloped upper-body strength to pull himself up to the ceiling. The strain on his arms and his back was incredible. It felt like acid burning through his muscles. His biceps started to shake with the strain, but he was up high enough that the flashlights were panning beneath him, not picking up on anything.

'It's clear,' came a whispered voice – female.

Another voice, this one male: 'You sure?'

'Yeah. Computer's on though. Must be someone around.'

'Not necessarily. Some people never turn their computers off.'

A pause. 'We were told this kid never goes out. Maybe he's in the toilet.'

'All right – you head over to the computer. Remember what we're looking for. I'll check the other rooms.'

'What are you going to do if you find him?' the man asked.

'Make sure he can't call for help,' the woman said grimly. 'Ever.'

Two dark shapes entered the room. Calum couldn't see more than their vague outlines, but he could hear them. And he could smell them – a rancid mix of sweat and tobacco smoke.

One of them headed across to where the computer screens glowed. The other headed straight ahead, beneath Calum, to where the bedrooms and the bathroom were located.

When he judged that both the intruders had their backs to him, Calum silently lowered himself down from the ceiling. He was facing the open door, away from them both. Resisting the urge to look over his shoulder, he swung as quietly as he could across to the other side of the room.

The cupboard where he had left the taser gun was a black shape in the darkness. Still hanging by one hand, he used the other to gently pull out the drawer where the weapon lay.

Wood grated against wood, and he paused, holding his breath.

'What was that?'

A pause, then the woman answered: 'Probably the floorboards shifting. This place is *old*. And it smells.'

Calum counted to five, then eased the drawer further open. Reaching inside he felt the cold metal curves of the taser gun. The hand that was holding on to the leather strap and taking all his weight began to cramp. Sharp pains ran up his wrist like little electric eels. He could feel his fingers trembling. He couldn't hold on for much longer.

He gripped the butt of the gun and pulled it out of the drawer. The extra weight dragged at his other hand, pulling the tendons in his shoulders tight.

The gun hit the drawer as he pulled it out, making a dull *thud*.

'What the . . . ?' The two flashlights converged on him, catching him like a moth fluttering in car headlamps. 'It's the kid!'

'Get him!' the woman snapped. '*Hurt* him!'

Calum brought the weapon up, pointed it towards one of the flashlights and pulled the trigger. The barrel rotated and the weapon fired with a dull *crack*! Something flew out of the barrel and across the intervening space, hitting a patch of darkness just above the flashlight's glare. Calum was startled to see a blue spark light up a shocked face from beneath, as a rapid clicking sound echoed around the apartment. The man's mouth dropped open in a surprised exclamation and his eyes widened as the electrical current coursed through his body. Moments later Calum heard the sound of a body dropping heavily to the wooden floor.

'Giggs?' the woman shouted. *'Giggs?'*

'He's sparked out,' Calum said, turning the gun towards the sound of the woman's voice and firing again. Another *crack!* and another dark shape flew from the rotating barrel of the gun. The woman thrashed around with her flashlight, knocking the projectile away but smashing her lens at the same time. The apartment was suddenly plunged into darkness, apart from the pool of light cast by the fallen man's torch.

Calum heard footsteps rushing across the wooden floor, then the sound of something being dragged. Pulled down by the weight of his body and the weight of the gun, his straining hand finally slipped off the leather strap. He fell heavily to the floor. The impact momentarily stunned him. For a moment he lay there, head ringing like a bell, knowing that he was helpless if the intruders decided to attack him, but the scuffling sounds he heard suggested that the woman was dragging her colleague towards the open door. It slammed shut, and then there was silence.

Calum counted to sixty, then pulled himself across the floor to where the electrocuted man's flashlight was still pointed off to one side. He grabbed it and scanned the apartment with it.

There was nobody there but him. The intruders had gone.

*

The drive from Tbilisi to the village of Ruspiri had become a monotonous endurance test. Tara's head kept on dropping lower and lower, as she slipped into sleep, only for her forehead to hit the headrest of the seat in front of her and send her jerking back into wakefulness. She didn't know how long they'd been driving, but it seemed longer than the entire time they'd spent in the aircraft flying over to Tbilisi from Heathrow.

The landscape of scrub, open ground and distant hills didn't do much to help. Nor did the road, which pretty much kept on going in a dead straight line. A hot sun shone down from a blue bowl of a sky, and only the shifting shadows marked the passage of time. Otherwise they might have been suspended in purgatory, for all the progress they seemed to be making.

Tara glanced sideways. Gecko was asleep. Behind her, Natalie was slumped with her headphones on. She might have been asleep, or she might have been listening to music. Tara tried to guess what kind of music Natalie liked. The most likely things were Rihanna and Britney Spears. Tara was thankful for the headphones.

She turned back to stare out of the windscreen. They seemed to be leaving civilization behind. Any villages they passed through were small, weather-beaten and apparently inhabited only by women in shawls sitting by the side of the road, men bent over the open bonnets of battered old cars and scruffy dogs looking for scraps of food.

They had stopped for lunch at a small roadside restaurant. They were the only people there, but even so, the waitress didn't seem pleased to see them. Levan had ordered for them – dishes of unidentifiable meat, flat bread stuffed with salty cheese, small pasta dumplings. Natalie had turned her nose up at it and asked if there was any chance of an apple.

Ahead and to her right Rhino was awake, but he wasn't moving much. Conserving energy, she supposed. Every now and then he would ask their guide a question about the kind of weather they could expect or the types of animals that lived in the Caucasus Mountains. To his left, Levan was driving with fixed concentration, his dark eyebrows low over his green eyes.

'Does the whole country look like this?' Tara asked, in an attempt to make conversation.

'Not at all,' Levan said without turning his head. 'Georgia is the point where Eastern Europe meets Western Asia. If you take that set of borders where Russia, Turkey, Armenia and Azerbaijan would otherwise meet, and draw a circle round it, that is Georgia, and so in different parts of the country we have different –' he struggled for the right word – '*environments*. Different climates. To the south is beaches and blue oceans. The people there are quick-witted and like to play practical jokes. To the east is verging on desert – very dry. The people there have most patience of all Georgians. To the west is forests, and to the north, where we are going, is mountains. Georgia is a very complicated country. Lots of things to see, lots of things to do.'

They passed over a bridge that carried them across a wide ravine. Somewhere down at the bottom was a river, glinting like silver in the sunlight. Tara glanced along the length of the ravine to where it opened out into what looked like a descending series of flat plateaux, like plates that had been carelessly stacked.

She must have slept again without noticing, because the next time she looked out of the window the sun was low in the sky, casting long shadows across the landscape, and her head was muzzy. Her forehead was sore as well, which meant she had probably woken herself up again by slowly pitching forward on to Rhino's seat back.

There were mountains in the distance ahead. Not hills, as before, but actual mountains. They had craggy tops, like broken teeth, and they were topped with stark white snow. There were patches of snow on the ground by the road as well, but this snow appeared dirty and old, and gave the impression that it hadn't melted only because it couldn't be bothered. Around the snow was scrubby grass, and the occasional stunted tree. The road ahead of them meandered with the undulations of the terrain. Rather than being covered with tarmac, it was more like a dirt track that had been defined and compacted by generations of vehicles driving on more or less the same line.

'We are near Ruspiri,' Levan announced. 'That is where we will base ourselves, ready for an expedition into the mountains in the next day or two.' He glanced quickly back over his shoulder to see whether anybody apart from Rhino was awake and listening. 'Georgia has a tradition of hospitality,' he said. 'The villagers will take us in and look after us, but remember that they are poor by your standards and most of them will not speak any language apart from their own. Be friendly, and smile, and everything will be all right. A word of caution – do not talk about Russia, or Soviet Union, or times when Georgia was under their control. People have long memories, and there is much bitterness and disagreement. Most families will have scars caused by Soviet army occupation. Best to avoid whole subject.'

The village gradually appeared ahead of the van – a collection of wooden houses and barns. Old, rusty cars were parked by the side of the road, and dogs and chickens wandered freely around. As the van arrived in the village, and Levan steered it off the dirt road and parked it under the spreading branches of a tree, people began to emerge from the shadows.

Tara gazed around, taking it all in. The villagers were all dressed in clothes that had once been brightly coloured – reds and greens predominated – but were now faded by years of sunshine and washing. The skin of anyone under thirty was smooth but tanned a deep brown; the skin of anyone over that age was like leather that had been crumpled up and smoothed out many times. The eyes of the children and teenagers were wide and wary; the eyes of their parents and grandparents were almost invisible in the wrinkled skin.

She had a feeling that she was an awfully long way away from a Wi-Fi hotspot.

Levan stepped out of the van. Smiling broadly, he said something in Georgian to the assembled villagers. His hands were spread out to either side to indicate peaceful intent.

Rhino opened the passenger door and stepped out. He removed his sunglasses as he joined Levan – Tara assumed that he was deliberately making eye contact rather than hiding behind the dark lenses. The villagers stared at him, obviously knowing straight away that he was a foreigner. Fingers were pointed, and whispered conversations were held.

A man stepped forward from the crowd that had gathered. His hair was dark, streaked with grey, and he had a full beard. His eyes, which hadn't quite vanished in the creases of his face, were startlingly blue, like chips of seawater turned to ice. He said something to Levan, and the guide responded with another flood of Georgian. The man, who seemed to be acting as a spokesman, asked another question, and Levan answered again. The spokesman nodded, opening his arms wide to encompass the village and the crowd. Something seemed to pass through the assembled villagers, some ripple of emotion. Tara could feel things relax. Whatever had been said, it had apparently led to their acceptance.

Levan turned round and gestured to the three of them to join him and Rhino. Tara led the way, with Gecko next and Natalie reluctantly third.

'This is the village of Ruspiri,' Levan pronounced, 'and this is the head man of the village, Shota Gigauri.' The head man nodded, grinning, when Levan mentioned his name. His teeth were stained brown, probably by tobacco, and five or six of them were missing. Tara assumed that dentists were hard to find all the way out in the wilds. 'We are welcomed to the village as honoured guests. There is an inn with rooms where we can stay, and the people of Ruspiri will do whatever they can to help us.'

'Do they know what we are looking for?' Rhino asked.

'I have not said definitely – only that you are in search of animals that live in the mountains.'

Shota Gigauri said something, and the villagers laughed.

'He says,' Levan said, flashing his teeth in a smile, 'that you are all very young and very small to be looking for wild animals. He thinks the wild animals will end up looking for you!'

Rhino glanced over at the three of them. 'Gecko – you think you can show them some of your stuff?'

Gecko nodded. 'I have had a look around. I think I have got some routes worked out. What is the state of the roofs – am I likely to fall through?'

'They will be firm,' Levan promised. 'They have to stand up to regular storms.'

From a standing start, Gecko suddenly burst into a full run, taking the villagers by surprise. He headed for a pile of wood that had been stacked and corded, running up it as if it was a set of steps. From there he launched himself into the air, reaching up for the edge of a roof. He pulled himself up to the roof so smoothly that it seemed effortless, and ran along its edge like a man running along a tightrope. At the end of the roof he leaped across to the next one, hitting it and tucking himself into a forward roll that Tara suspected was more for show than for balance.

The head man put his head back and laughed hugely. He clapped his hands together, and said something to Levan.

'He says maybe you *can* outrun the wolves and the bears,' Levan translated.

'I do not need to outrun the wolves and the bears,' Gecko called back with a cheeky smile. He pointed at Natalie. 'I just need to outrun *her*.'

The villagers seemed to understand what he was saying without the need for any translation. They all laughed. Suddenly it seemed as if the five of them had been accepted into the village.

CHAPTER

thirteen

Gecko was sweating, and not because he was free-running across the rooftops of the village of Ruspiri. No, he was sweating because he was unloading boxes and crates from the back of the Mitsubishi Delica that he and Rhino has managed to steal from the thugs who'd tried to steal their cargo.

Rhino had moved the van to a patch of open ground just behind the inn where they were staying. The accommodation was basic – beds made of unpainted wood, rough sheets, woollen blankets woven in many colours – but they had all slept for ten hours straight. Natalie had claimed she hadn't slept a wink, of course, but Gecko had heard the snores coming from behind the closed door of her room. He smiled, remembering. She may have been as beautiful, skinny and long-legged as a fashion model, but she snored like a bull.

He hoisted the last crate in his arms and carried it to the cleared area where Rhino and Tara were opening them up with crowbars.

Between them, Rhino and Tara had managed to

pile up a whole heap of mechanical components, boxes of electronics, pistons, wires and thicker cables. Already they had assembled something about the size of a child's bed out of sections of steel that had circular holes punched through them to reduce the weight. Tara was working on one side and Rhino the other, bolting what looked like metallic shoulder joints to the corners. The boxes of electronics had already been fitted inside and linked together by cables, and a rudimentary neck was beginning to form at one end.

'Can you tell what it is yet?' Tara asked.

'I think I saw something like that in a sci-fi film once,' Gecko replied. 'It did not end well for humanity.'

Rhino looked up and raised an eyebrow. 'Believe me, when we're out in the open and this thing is hauling our rucksacks around for us, we'll be grateful.'

'But we are going into the mountains,' Gecko pointed out. 'This thing cannot climb – can it?'

Tara looked up in alarm from where she was plugging a series of cables into sockets. 'Neither can I! I don't have to, do I? That wasn't in the brochure!'

Rhino shook his head. 'We're looking for things that are like us, remember? Two legs, two arms, roughly the same body mass. They aren't going to live up on the higher parts of the mountains like goats. If they exist, they'll be lower down, where they can build a community, grow food and hunt. No climbing required.'

'Thank heavens for that!'

Rhino glanced across at her. 'Do you think you can

finish this thing off? I need to ask the head man some questions.'

She nodded. 'Leave it to me – I'm good at high-tech jigsaw puzzles.' As Rhino stood up, she gestured to Gecko. 'OK, hand me a cross-head screwdriver.'

'A *what*?'

Rhino glanced from the one to the other. 'Right – I'll leave this in your expert hands, then.'

Rhino found the head man and Levan sharing a bottle of some dark liquid in the shade of a walnut tree.

'Georgian wine,' Levan said, indicating the bottle. 'Locally produced. It is . . . diplomatic . . . to drink. Will you join us?'

'Happy to,' Rhino said. He sat down.

Shota Gigauri produced a glass from somewhere, wiped it with a cloth, set it in front of Rhino and poured a glass of wine for him.

'Have you asked our host about the Almasti?' Rhino asked. As Levan opened his mouth to answer, Rhino raised his glass to the head man and took a sip. The wine was thin, vinegary, but he could drink it.

'I have mentioned it,' Levan answered. 'I hope you do not mind? No? Well, he says that there have been stories in Ruspiri for many generations of a tribe of people who live further up the mountain. They do not come down this far, and they do not trade with the villagers here, but sometimes, perhaps once every few years, one is glimpsed by hunters in the bushes, or silhouetted against the skyline on a ridge. He says that the people of this tribe are small, and they are hairy.'

The head man seemed to be following the conversation. He tapped his forehead several times and said something in Georgian.

'He also says that they have thick foreheads that hang over their eyes, although he probably says that about the members of any village apart from his own.'

'It sounds like there might be something up there after all,' Rhino mused.

Shota Gigauri raised a hand, as if he had just remembered something. He delved into first one pocket and then another, looking for something. Eventually he pulled out an object, which he held out to Rhino for inspection.

'What's this?' Rhino asked, staring at the object. It was a turquoise stone that had been carved into a shape that might have been a bird, or a snake, or something abstract. 'I'm not in the market for trinkets.'

Shota spoke for a while. Eventually Levan had to hold a hand up to stop him so that he could translate. 'He says that the villagers sometimes find things like this near the mountains, as if they have been dropped. They sell them for a lot of money in the markets closer to Tbilisi. Apparently the stone is quite rare. They believe that the Almasti make them, but they are not sure.'

'The trouble is, if they are that hard to meet, I'm not sure we'll ever get close,' Rhino said regretfully.

Levan said something to the head man, and he answered with a long sentence involving much arm-waving.

'He says,' Levan relayed to Rhino, 'that you may be in luck. He says that for the past few months something has been taking their chickens and raiding their grain supplies. For a while they thought it was wild dogs or mountain foxes, but the village dogs seem to be scared of it, whatever it is, and stay away from it, where they would normally bark at a wild dog or a fox. The villagers have set traps, and watched from hidden places, but the thief, whoever or whatever it is, is too cautious for them. They have never seen it. The older villagers say that it is an Almast that has come down from the mountains, possibly thrown out of its own tribe, but the younger villagers just laugh at them.'

'Ask him,' Rhino said carefully, 'if he would accept our help in finding out who or what this thief is. We have cameras, and traps that we can set.'

Levan relayed the message. Shota Gigauri nodded emphatically, and said something directly to Rhino.

'He says that he would be very grateful,' Levan translated. 'The harvest has been poor this year, thanks to the weather, and they cannot afford to lose any food. He says that the village cannot repay you except in gratitude.'

'Tell him that their gratitude, and their friendship, is all that we need.'

Tara tensed herself and stabbed the spear-like metal shaft into the ground. She twisted it a couple of times, feeling stones grind and move beneath the sharp tip as it penetrated further into the ground. When the sphere on top of the shaft was level with her eyes, she stepped back and admired her handiwork.

The shaft and the apple-sized sphere were both coloured a neutral grey-green. Only the band of shiny glass that ran round the circumference of the sphere made it at all obvious to anyone who might have been looking out for it.

The thing she had just planted like a high-tech sunflower was one of a bunch of twenty that had been packed together in one of the boxes that had come with them from England. Tara wasn't sure whether they had been Calum's idea or Rhino's, but she had to admit they were a stroke of genius. Inside the sphere that sat on top of the shaft was a low-light camera and a vibration sensor. Thanks to the transparent lens that ran all the way round the sphere, the camera could take a single digital photograph of everything around it, but it would only take that photograph if triggered by the vibration sensor. That sensor was connected to the shaft, so it could feel any vibration in the ground for a radius of fifteen feet or so around it. The shaft also doubled as a Wi-Fi antenna, so that the photograph could be transmitted instantly to Tara's tablet.

This was the final sensor in the package. Like the rest, it had been planted in a ring just outside the boundary of the village. When Tara activated them at sunset, the sensors would form a net all around the village. Anything that touched the ground around the sensors would trigger a photograph to be taken, and an alarm would sound on her tablet. Fair enough, some of the images would be village dogs, or maybe some of the locals themselves, but if something was sneaking into the village to steal supplies then she was sure she would capture its picture.

Tara was exhausted. She wasn't used to this much physical effort. She had walked around the village twice now: once to check out the best locations and the second time to plant the sensors. The ground was stony, and some of the shafts had required a lot of pushing. As far as Tara was concerned, her role should be to sit somewhere comfortable and use her computing skills, not install a comprehensive sensor network by hand, but everybody else had something to do. Well, apart from Natalie. Nobody was quite sure where Natalie had gone.

Once she had got her breath back, Tara reached out and twisted the sphere ninety degrees clockwise. That switched it on. The tiny battery inside would keep it working for a week or so before it needed to be recharged.

She glanced around. It was lunchtime, and she could see villagers returning from the fields and the hills for food. She realized that she was hungry as well. She hadn't eaten since breakfast, and she'd been working hard. Time for lunch, she decided. Sensor network testing could wait until later. It wasn't as if they'd be using the sensors until sunset, at least.

*

Gecko stood in the central area of the village – not quite a square, but the junction of several paths and the nearest thing to a middle that the village had. The inn where the five of them were staying stood on one side, and a sort of village hall on the other.

Five of the local boys and girls stood in front of him, hands by their sides as if they were in the army and on parade. They had all seen his exhibition of free-running skills earlier on, and Rhino had decided that it might make the team more accepted in the village if Gecko could give the kids some training. He'd run it past the head man, through Levan's translation skills, and the head man had enthusiastically agreed.

'Right,' he said, clapping his hands. 'Time to put some of these moves together.' He knew that they didn't know what he was saying, but at least he was attracting their attention. And they'd already got the hang of 'Yes', 'No' and 'Stop, you'll hurt yourself!'.

He gestured to the improvised training course that he had set up. First was a two-metre-high pile of oil-stained wooden blocks that looked like railway sleepers. Second, a couple of metres away, was a wooden pole set up parallel to the ground about a metre and a half up and running between two trestles. Third, he'd used some of the railway sleepers to build a rough set of steps that finished in mid-air at about head height. Jumping distance from the top of the stairs was a thick wooden table whose rough surface was about waist height. All in all it was a neat little improvised free-running course.

He pointed at the first kid – a small, cheeky boy with a wide, gap-toothed grin. 'You – go!'

The boy ran towards the pile of wooden blocks and stopped when he got to the flat side. Gecko wasn't sure he'd be able to make it, but the kid jumped as high as he could. His fingers clamped on the top sleeper and his feet scrabbled to push him up. It wasn't elegant, but it worked. Once on top he jumped down on the other side and ran at the suspended pole. He pulled himself up and walked precariously along, using his arms for balance. At the other end he jumped back to the ground and made for the wooden steps. He was up them in a flash. He hesitated on the top, judging the gap to the table, then leaped for it. He hit just millimetres from the edge, and converted his forward momentum into a clumsy roll, which took him to the other side. He sprang back to his feet, grinning from ear to ear, and turned to look triumphantly at his friends.

'Good!' Gecko called. He pointed to the next kid – a girl who was a few centimetres taller and a few years older. 'Now you.'

The girl was more thoughtful, less impulsive. She considered for a moment before sprinting at the pile of sleepers, calculating her best approach. Just before she got to them she leaped like a hurdler. Her foot hit the middle sleeper at the same time as her hands caught the top, and she pulled herself smoothly up. Instead of climbing down the other side, she jumped straight for the horizontal pole. Gecko held his breath, but she landed with perfect balance on the end of the pole and before he knew it she had run delicately along like a gymnast on a beam and leaped down from the other end. She took the wooden steps two at a time, then jumped for the table. She landed right in the middle, absorbing the impact by bending her knees, then converted her forward motion into a perfect handstand at the far end of the table, hands clamping round the edge, before toppling forward and landing on her feet with a gymnastic flourish.

'Now that,' Gecko called admiringly, 'is just showing off.'

She turned and flashed him a smile before scampering back to her friends.

The next kid looked like he wanted to back out now, before he hurt himself. Gecko smiled reassuringly at him. He still remembered the time it had taken him to learn how to free-run, and the bruises, scrapes and sprains he'd picked up in the process. It was a matter of faith – starting a run knowing that you were going to get hurt, not knowing how you were going to get through to the end, but doing it anyway, hoping it would all turn out OK in the end and the hurt wouldn't be too bad. After all, it was only pain.

'Come on,' he said gently, 'give it a go.'

Rhino's phone vibrated in his pocket.

He was sitting in the village hall with a map spread out

on the table in front of him. Shota Gigauri and two of the locals were standing around the table, also looking at the map. The villagers were burly men, both hunters who had spent a lot of time up in the Caucasus foothills. They knew the lie of the land. Levan Ketsbaia stood off to one side, ready to interpret as necessary.

Rhino had been asking the villagers about things that weren't shown on the map – where was the going best, where were patches of vegetation that were too difficult to get through, where were gullies or defiles too wide to cross easily, where might a tribe of people who didn't want to be discovered build their village? The men were proving very helpful on the first three questions but a bit vague on the fourth. There was a lot of open terrain out there, but most of it had been covered by the hunters over the years when they were searching for small game – rabbits, deer and so on. They were stumped when it came to guessing where a whole village – even a small one – might be hidden.

Rhino raised his hands in apology as the phone continued to buzz. Levan said something in a quiet voice, and the three villagers laughed.

Walking outside, Rhino pulled the mobile from his pocket and pressed the *Accept* key. He was surprised that he could get any mobile coverage at all that far in the wilds of Tbilisi, but thank heavens for small mercies.

'Hello,' he said cautiously, neutrally, not giving his name.

'Is that Rhino?'

He recognized the voice, despite the fact that it was faint and almost inaudible over the static. 'Professor Livingstone?'

'Yes, it's me. How's Natalie?'

'She's fine. She managed the journey OK, and she got a good night's sleep. I'm not sure the food is up to her standards, and her greatest concern at the moment is working out how to recharge her MP3 player, but apart from that she's doing well.'

'Good. A little discomfort will do her the world of good. Her father and I are guilty of protecting her from reality, I'm afraid. She needs to discover that things won't always go the way she wants them to.'

'And this is the perfect place to learn that lesson,' Rhino said, smiling.

'How's the expedition coming along? Any sign of the elusive Almasti?'

'Not so far, but it's early days.' He paused for a second. 'What about you – getting anywhere with your business meetings?'

'Some positive signs,' Gillian said non-committally. 'But that's the other reason I wanted to talk to you. I've heard from some of my contacts here that there's another expedition heading out from Tbilisi roughly in your direction.'

'Another expedition?' Rhino felt a cold bud of concern start to unfurl in his chest. 'What exactly are they looking for – or are they just tourists?'

'They're not tourists. From what I've heard they're a well-equipped team of men and women in their twenties and thirties. All of them appear to be fit and tanned, which suggests they've done this kind of thing before. I'm told they looked like a military unit on manoeuvres. They left Tbilisi this morning in three Humvees, having spent most of the past two days trying to get hold of a guide to the local area.' She paused, and Rhino could hear the smile in her voice. 'Apparently you made off with the best one before they could get to him.'

'And there's no word on the object of their expedition?'

'Nothing. Whatever it is they're looking for, they're serious about it.' She paused. 'The rumour is that they're armed. Nothing definite, but someone said that someone else had seen one of them checking over a handgun. Are *you* armed?'

'No,' he said, grimacing. 'I couldn't get a weapon through airport security, for obvious reasons, and I haven't got the contacts here to be able to get hold of a gun easily.' He thought for a moment. 'Maybe they're looking for bears or wolves in the mountains – something to stuff and mount on the wall so they can brag to their friends.'

'Just as long as it's not your head that ends up on their wall,' Gillian said darkly. 'Or Natalie's.'

'I'll be careful – you can count on it.'

'I already am,' she said, and rang off.

Another expedition? It might be a coincidence – they might be heading somewhere else entirely – but Rhino didn't believe in coincidences. He had a bad feeling that someone else had decided to go looking for the Almasti.

Or someone had decided to go looking for Calum's expedition. That, he thought, was even more worrying. He needed to talk to Calum and make him aware of what was going on.

Every light in the apartmentwas on. There were no shadows, nowhere that anybody could hide. The apartment's security systems had been checked over and enhanced by a company that Calum knew and trusted, and the security-system diagnostics were now permanently displayed on one of his ten LCD computer screens – histograms showing power levels and little inset windows showing the output from the various infra-red and low-light cameras that had been fitted to the outside of the building.

Calum wasn't taking any chances of there being another break-in.

He'd upgraded the locks on all the doors as well, upstairs and at street level, and had an uninterruptible power supply fitted.

Now he sat in front of his computer screens like a spider at the centre of its web, secure in the knowledge that he was safe.

But he didn't feel safe. He didn't feel safe at all.

He knew what the problem was. He didn't just *live* in his apartment the way that other people lived in their apartments, flats or houses. His apartment was his *shell*, the barrier between him and a hostile world. It was his second skin.

And someone had broken through that skin.

He was worried that it was going to happen again, despite all his precautions. He now jumped at the slightest sound in the apartment – the creaking of old wood and old bricks, the pigeons on the roof, the muffled horns from taxis passing by outside. He was unsettled, nervous, jittery.

He'd wondered whether to inform the police about the break-in, but he had decided in the end that he shouldn't. He couldn't stand the idea of a bunch of people invading his privacy to take fingerprints and photographs and statements.

You head over to the computer. Remember what we're looking for. That's what the woman had said. He could feel a red tide of anger rising within him as he recalled the words. They had come into his apartment with an objective in mind. They hadn't just been looking for things to steal – they had been looking for *information*. For something on his computer. And they'd been prepared to kill him if he'd tried to stop them from getting it.

Surely it had to be connected to this new expedition that Rhino had told him about. Was this part of a two-pronged approach – infiltrate his apartment looking for information while at the same time sending a team out to follow his team? But why? He felt his right hand clench as he considered the thought. What was there about the existence of the Almasti that meant people would break the law, commit breaking and entering and theft and possibly even murder, to find out? As committed as Calum was to tracking and discovering the Almasti – assuming they were there to begin with – he knew that their existence was more of an academic issue than anything that could lead to lawbreaking and extreme violence. What could possibly lead a competitor to resort to criminal activity to beat him?

As he sat at his computer, his gaze switching from one computer screen to another but not really registering the images on any of them, Calum found his mind wandering. He remembered Tara mentioning the international industrial consortium that had targeted her and forced her to hack into his Lost Worlds website. Nemor Incorporated certainly seemed interested in what he was doing – was this new expedition in Georgia something that they had arranged? Could they also have tried to break into his apartment when their efforts to hack his website had been blocked? Calum was a big fan of logic, and it certainly seemed logical that Nemor Inc. would escalate their attempts to find out what he was doing once their initial approaches had failed.

Another thought struck him – one that was a lot darker and less welcome. He had asked Professor Livingstone if she had ever heard of, or worked with, Nemor Incorporated. She had, as far as he could remember, ducked the question.

Was that, he wondered bleakly, something he ought to be worried about?

CHAPTER

fourteen

Tara adjusted the headband over her forehead, nestling the twin loudspeakers above each ear. She was surprised that the headband didn't seem too heavy, considering the amount of technology it contained.

She was sitting on a bench at a heavy wooden table outside the inn in Ruspiri where they were staying. The sun had just dipped below the rounded shapes of the Caucasus Mountains, outlining them in orange and purple. It was probably less than an hour before sunset, which meant that it was mid-afternoon in England.

She reached up to touch the high-definition video camera that was attached to the headband just above the left speaker. She had a horrible feeling that the headband made her look like a refugee from a 1980s fitness video, but she supposed that was a price she had to pay.

Right. Time to check that the connection actually worked, otherwise they'd brought the headbands all this way for nothing.

Her mobile phone and her tablet were sitting on the table in front of her. She reached out and tapped a message – *Ready to synchronize?* – into her mobile and texted it straight to Calum in England. Thanks to the magic of wireless technology, the message took longer to type than it took to wing its way via radio waves and satellite communications several thousand miles away. Within a few seconds Calum's response was displayed on her screen – *Let's go!*

She reached up and pressed a button behind the tiny camera 'Can you hear me?' she asked.

Calum's reply was so clear that it sounded as if he was standing right behind her. She had to fight the urge to turn around and look for him. 'Not only can I hear you, but I can see what you're seeing as well.'

'Remind me not to wear this thing into the bathroom,' Tara murmured, then said, more loudly, 'OK, let's check the basics. Audio first.' She counted to ten slowly. 'Did you get all that?'

'Everything was loud and clear apart from "three". That was a little fuzzy. Can you do "three" again?'

'I see that sarcasm gets transmitted clearly as well,' she said. 'OK, video now. I'm going to look left and right. Let me know if there are any digital artefacts or any obvious buffering.'

She glanced left to where a group of local kids was climbing up a pile of lumber that had been stacked there and jumping off from the top. They looked like smaller versions of Gecko. As her gaze tracked back past the inn, she automatically focused on the window of her bedroom on the first floor. To her right was an area of cleared ground where the Delica van was parked.

'All video is clear,' Calum's ghostly voice said. 'Is that the famous van I've heard about?'

'It is.'

'No clues inside as to who hired it or bought it?'

She shook her head. 'Nothing.'

'Ouch – don't do that!'

'What?'

'Shake your head. The way the picture goes makes me feel suddenly nauseous.'

'Take a pill,' she said. 'You think you're nauseous now, you wait until you've got all four of us walking over rough ground.'

'Fair point.'

'Do you want to check that the satellite bandwidth can cope with video and audio together?' Tara asked.

'Not much point,' he said. 'I can hear you fine, and the video doesn't seem to be dropping out. All in all, this is a neat little piece of technology. I feel like I'm almost there with you.'

'But you're not – you're somewhere the beds are more comfortable and the food is better.' She paused, considering. 'How *are* things back in England?'

'As usual, the newspapers and news channels report lots of activity but very little change,' Calum replied.

'And what about Nemor Incorporated?' Tara asked carefully.

'What about them?'

'Have they been in contact – about me?'

Calum didn't reply for a moment. When he did finally say something, his tone was as carefully composed as hers had been. 'I've not heard anything from them.'

'Are you sure?' Tara pressed. 'If anything's happened, I can take it. I don't like being kept in the dark.'

Calum sighed. 'Look, someone tried to break into my apartment. It might have been burglars, it might have been Nemor Incorporated or it might have been those Russian gangsters who were targeting Gecko. I don't know for sure, but I've upgraded my security to the point where a mosquito would need a photopass and a set of references to get in here.'

'Are you OK?' Tara asked, concerned. 'Have you told the police?'

'I thought about it, but decided not to. They can't tell me anything I don't already know.' He took a deep breath. 'Enough of this – what's happening out there? Do the villagers know anything about the Almasti?'

'They say that something's been sneaking around the village at night and stealing their food, but nobody's seen it. The older villagers claim it's an Almast, but the younger ones think it's a wolf, or maybe someone from a nearby village.'

'Well,' Calum said, 'it's a start. Now, what about my pet?'

'What, Natalie? She's OK.'

'I see the sarcasm works in both directions,' he said, his voice sounding like he was smiling. 'You know what I mean.'

'I know.' Tara twisted on her bench to look directly behind her. There, in an open area of ground, stood ARLENE. The robot mule looked like some futuristic metal sculpture of a horse. A six-legged horse.

'Very nice,' Calum said appreciatively. 'You've run all the self-test routines?'

'Every single one.'

'Then let's see what it can do.'

Tara turned back and tapped instructions into the application that was open on her tablet. Wireless connections carried her instructions to ARLENE. The robot's head perked up, and a blue LED lit up on the side of its head.

'Oh, wow, that's bizarre,' Calum murmured. 'Through your camera I can see ARLENE looking at you, and through ARLENE's camera I can see *you* looking at *it*. Very disturbing.'

Tara held up her left hand. 'How many fingers am I holding up?'

'Technically, two fingers and a thumb.'

'And do my lips move in synchronization with what I'm saying?'

'As far as I can tell, yes.' Tara heard him take a breath. 'I think we have ourselves an expedition.'

'I think you're right,' she said, pleased with herself.

*

The sun had dropped way behind the mountains when Natalie left the inn.

The sky was the purple colour of an old bruise, and the stars were beginning to come out. Fortunately there was an almost full moon in the sky, because Ruspiri, as she had discovered, didn't have any street lights. *Un*fortunately there were rag-like skeins of cloud being blown by the wind all across the sky, which meant that the moon kept vanishing and then reappearing.

Not only did Ruspiri not have any street lights – it didn't have a lot of other things as well. There was no pharmacy, no shoe shop, no gymnasium or swimming pool and no sauna. And, judging from the bright, smiling faces of the villagers she'd encountered so far, it didn't have any dentists either.

This was the very definition of hell, she decided.

She held her mobile phone up and checked the screen. Several of her friends had sent her emails and texts, wondering where she was and what she was doing. Part of her wanted to look through them all and find out what was going on back home, but another part of her didn't want to know how epic Savannah's pool party had turned out to be, or how Bryce – whom she was kinda supposed to be dating – had made out with Deanna, or how the latest handbags had just arrived in Madison's and were, like, really *unbelievable*.

On the other hand, she supposed that she could message *them* and let them know how she was, what she was doing. Yeah, that would *really* work. They'd be all *But who is doing your manicures for you?* and *How can you survive without MTV?* and she'd feel sad, and there would be tears. The world was passing her by while she was stuck in a backward village in a backward country that didn't even appear on any maps that she'd ever seen. Or, if it had, she hadn't noticed it.

Natalie was so wrapped up in her thoughts that by the time she came back to reality she had wandered into a part of the village that she didn't recognize. The buildings were mainly barns and stuff, and there was nobody around. The sky was completely black now, apart from the scattering of stars and the tattered grey scarves of cloud that moved across the face of the moon.

Natalie muttered a word under her breath that her mother would have disapproved of. Who would have thought that this place was even big enough to get lost in? She supposed she could pull the headband and camera thing from the pocket where she'd screwed it up and ask Calum for help, but she really didn't like the idea of people always keeping tabs on her. She'd had enough of that with her mother and the security firms she had hired over the years. No, that camera was staying in her pocket for as long as she could manage it.

She turned round, intending to retrace her steps to the inn.

Someone was standing in the shadows of the nearest building.

'Hi!' she said brightly, feeling her heart speed up. She

was beginning to regret listening to Rhino when he'd told her that there was no chance of her getting her Mace spray through customs. 'Can you direct me back to the centre of the village? I'm kinda displaced from where I should be.'

That's right, a little voice in the back of her mind said. *Tell the creepy man that you're lost. That'll engage his sympathy.*

'You know what – don't worry,' she said. 'I'll just walk back the way I came.'

The shadowy figure didn't move, and didn't say anything. Natalie almost convinced herself that it was a trick of the light, maybe a tree or something that looked like a person, but she could suddenly smell something really pungent, like the kind of smell you got in the elephant house at the zoo. Despite herself, she winced and waved a hand across her nose. Before she could stop herself, she said, 'Did you get that aftershave for Christmas?' Even as she heard the words come out of her mouth she wished she hadn't said them. The only thing that was likely to save her from violence was the fact that the person she faced probably didn't understand English.

The figure in the shadows made a strange *snuffling* sound and took a step backwards. As it did so, a sudden strong waft of that zoo smell made Natalie cough and nearly retch.

The wind chose that moment to push away the rag-like clouds covering the moon. Strong, bright moonlight illuminated the village like a stage spotlight, banishing the shadows for a few seconds.

Natalie found herself face to face with something from a nightmare.

It was halfway between a chimpanzee and a man. Its arms were hairy and longer than they should feasibly have been, and it stood in a half-crouch, but it was the face that made her gasp and clutch a hand over her mouth. The face was grey and wizened, like that of an old man, but fringed in wild black hair. The forehead jutted out sharply, casting the eyes in shadow. The thing had a distinct but flattened nose. Its teeth, revealed as it snarled at her, were massive slabs of yellow ivory.

Natalie backed away, hand still over her mouth. Her heart was pounding.

The creature – the *Almast?* – stepped forward. Its back was curved, giving it a hunched look. Its shoulders were almost level with its ears. Its hands were large, and tipped with thick, dirty nails that looked like they could disembowel a pig.

It was only when she saw its body clearly that Natalie realized *why* this wasn't a chimpanzee, or a gorilla, or some other kind of monkey that had somehow ended up in a small village in the wilds of Georgia.

It was wearing a rough linen shirt and something that looked like a kilt. A turquoise pebble with a hole drilled through it dangled from a leather thong round its neck.

The Almast took a step towards her, holding out its hand. Was it trying to make friends, or was it reaching for her throat?

She made a quick decision, and screamed.

The creature stepped backwards, shocked. Its eyes opened wide. They were startlingly brown and mild. It raised its hand in a *stop* kind of gesture. Natalie noticed that its other hand was holding a bag, little more than a long length of cloth that had been wrapped round something – probably meat, or grain, or a chicken that the Almast had stolen from the village.

The ape-like Almast glanced left and right, looking for any sign that Natalie's scream had alerted anyone to its presence. Nobody else appeared. Natalie couldn't hear anyone shouting or running towards them.

The Almast turned back to Natalie. With incredible speed it reached out and clamped its right hand across her mouth. Its skin was dry and hard, like leather, and she could feel the prickle of hairs on its palm sticking into her lips. Her heart was racing so fast that she was worried it was going to burst under the strain.

Bizarrely, she became fixated with the hairs on its chest, and the polished turquoise stone that hung from its neck.

The Almast moved closer to her. Tucking the raggedy bag it was holding beneath its right elbow, it raised its left hand to its mouth and pinched its lips together. It stared at Natalie meaningfully. It was trying to tell her to shut up! It was *communicating*!

If Natalie wouldn't take orders from her own mother and father, then she was damned if she was going to take orders from a dirty ape. She wrenched herself free from its grip and shouted at the top of her voice, 'Help! Anyone, please help!'

The Almast snarled at her, teeth bared in obvious anger.

'Hey!' a deep voice shouted. 'Get off that woman!'

Natalie turned her head to see Levan Ketsbaia running along the path towards her. He came to a stop a few metres away, mouth open to say something else, but his eyes widened in shock as he suddenly realized exactly what was standing in front of him.

The Almast dropped the bundle it was holding beneath its right elbow. It stepped forward, arms reaching out for the guide.

Levan took a step towards the Almast, bringing himself within the circle of its arms. He pushed it hard in the chest. The creature staggered backwards, arms flailing wildly.

'Are you OK, girl?' Levan asked breathlessly. 'I heard you scream.'

Natalie nodded, unable to form words.

'What *is* this thing?' he continued.

'It's the thing we're looking for,' she finally managed to say.

'It seems to have found you first,' he said, but he had taken his eyes off the Almast, and while he was distracted the creature took its chance to spring at him, teeth bared. It was going for his throat!

Levan grabbed the Almast's head in both hands and tried to keep its teeth from fastening about his throat, but its hands were scrabbling at his chest. Natalie could see the material of his shirt shredding beneath its nails, and blood begin to splatter across his chest as the nails grazed his skin. His face was creased in pain and exertion.

The Georgian guide fell backwards. Natalie thought for a second that he had been pushed, but he brought his right leg up, bent tight, and pushed his foot into the Almast's stomach. As Levan's back hit the ground, he rolled, still holding on to the creature's head but pushing up with all the power of his right leg. The Almast flew over him and he let go of its head. It flipped through the air, grunting in fury, and hit the side of a barn. Natalie heard its head connect with a solid *thud.* It slid down the side of the barn, but, amazingly, when it crumpled to the ground in a heap of tangled limbs, it immediately tried to stand up again.

'Stay back,' Levan cautioned as he rolled on to his stomach and pushed himself to his feet. His chest was a mass of ripped fabric and bright red blood. He staggered over to where the Almast was holding on to the barn wall in an effort to stay upright. Levan lashed out with his right fist, catching the Almast on the chin. Its head snapped to one side, but it remained upright and conscious. Natalie had a feeling that Levan's blow would have paralysed an ox, but the Almast seemed to just shake it off.

Levan tried to bring his left fist up in a hard uppercut that surely would have knocked the creature out, but it grabbed his hand and squeezed. Levan's expression changed from one of concentrated anger to one of shock as the Almast ground the bones of his hand together, knuckle against knuckle. Natalie braced herself for the cracking sound of something breaking in Levan's hand, but before things went too far Levan stepped forward and brought his knee up into the Almast's groin. The creature let go of his hand and squealed. Protecting itself from another attack with its left hand, it swept its right fist sideways across Levan's face. The guide flew through the air and hit the ground with an audible grunt. Rolling over on to his back, he clutched at his shoulder in agony.

The Almast glanced from Levan to Natalie and back again, and then at the bag that it had dropped. It seemed uncertain what to do. For a long moment the three of them waited, each for the other to make a move. Eventually the Almast snarled. It took a step towards Natalie, hands outstretched and claw-like. For a second she thought it was going to rush at her again, but the sound of shouts from the direction of the village centre distracted its attention. It darted towards the bag, snatched it up and loped towards the edge of the village.

There was some kind of disturbance behind Natalie: she could hear voices calling, and torches appeared to be pointed her way, making her shadow flicker in front of her. In the distance the Almast was running past the final building and towards the scrubby bushes that marked the place where the local countryside began. A sudden flash of bright white light made Natalie blink. The Almast lurched to one side, throwing an arm up to protect its eyes and almost letting go of its stolen bag. The source of the light seemed to be an apple-sized sphere that had been planted on top of a metal pole just past the final building.

The light vanished, leaving a green, blobby afterglow in the centre of Natalie's vision. By the time the blob had faded away, the Almast had vanished into the bushes.

Someone grabbed her shoulder. She turned to find Rhino and Gecko standing beside her, poised for action. A handful of villagers were bent over Levan Ketsbaia, talking to him in rapid Georgian.

'Are you OK?' Gecko asked, pulling Natalie's attention back.

'You shouldn't have wandered off by yourself,' Rhino said in an irritated tone.

'It was one of those things we're looking for,' Natalie gasped. 'And, by the way – you're not my father. Or my mother.'

'For which I'm sure we're all equally grateful,' Rhino murmured. He glanced towards the village boundary. 'Are you sure it was an Almast?'

'Either that or they're making a horror movie around here and they're doing some late-night filming.' She sighed. 'Yes, it was an Almast, not a villager, or a dog, or anything like that. I know what I saw.'

Rhino looked at Gecko, then out into the darkness.

Gecko nodded and ran forward to where the buildings ended and the bushes began. He stopped and stared out into the darkness, pointing his torch in various directions.

Rhino bent down and examined the ground. 'The earth's too hard to take any tracks,' he said to himself. 'No rain for a while. We won't be able to follow it.'

Gecko walked back more slowly than he had gone out. He was shaking his head. 'I cannot see anything. It has run away.'

Rhino crossed over to where the villagers were clustered around Levan. He bent down and talked to the injured guide for a few moments before returning to Natalie and Gecko. He looked angry and frustrated.

Before he could say anything, Tara arrived. She was breathless from running. 'I got a signal from one of the sensors. What happened? What did I miss?' She glanced at Levan, who was being helped to his feet. 'My God – is he OK?'

'Fortunately, he's going to live,' Rhino said. 'His chest is a mess, and his shoulder appears to be dislocated. There's some discussion about whether he should be put in the back of a car and driven straight to hospital, or whether a local doctor ought to be called out, or whether the villagers can reset the shoulder themselves. Apart from giving him a tetanus shot I can't really help.'

'What did that to him?' Tara breathed, wide-eyed.

'Natalie had a close encounter with one of the Almasti,' Rhino explained.

'And she survived?' Tara gave Natalie a thumbs-up. 'Well done, you.'

'Is that thing something to do with you?' Natalie asked, indicating the globe on a stick that had given out that bright white flash of light. 'It's just that it looks kinda geeky.'

'Yeah, that's one of our sensors.' She frowned. 'Don't you remember me talking about them on the flight out?'

'Sorry.' Natalie shrugged. 'I must have been asleep.'

'I only got one signal.' Tara looked at Rhino. 'That means it's still in the village. If it had come in and then left again there would have been two signals.'

Rhino shook his head. 'Natalie said she saw it leaving the village. That means it must have been here before you put the sensors up and activated them.'

'Here in the village?' Tara repeated. 'You mean, while I was wandering around alone, that thing might have been *watching* me? *Following* me?'

'And you survived?' Natalie said brightly. She gave Tara a sarcastic thumbs-up. 'Well done, you!'

Tara narrowed her eyes and stared directly at Natalie, but Natalie had been stared at by experts – not least, her mother – without being fazed. She just smiled back innocently.

'Well, at least we've got a photograph of Natalie's latest boyfriend,' Tara said, looking away. 'Let's go and take a look at it.'

Tara led the way back through the village to the

inn. Some of the villagers were around, disturbed by the commotion, but the guide, Levan, told them that there was nothing to worry about and encouraged them to go back to bed. There being no street lights to speak of, and no electricity in the houses, Natalie got the impression that they pretty much went to bed when the sun went down and got up when it rose.

Back in the inn, Tara led them all to her room, which was, Natalie noticed, just as rough as her own.

Tara's tablet was on the bed. She flung herself down in front of it and typed some instructions into the keyboard. The screen flashed to life with a photograph.

Natalie shuddered.

It was the thing she had seen, captured in mid-stride. Its mouth was open, revealing its yellow, tombstone-like teeth, and its eyes were wide. It definitely wasn't a villager – not unless they'd been keeping some deformed monster-child hidden away. The picture looked like a brighter, sharper image of the photograph that Calum had found on the internet, the one that had sparked off this whole crazy expedition.

'The hunt is on,' Rhino murmured.

'The question is,' Tara added, 'who is hunting whom?'

CHAPTER

fifteen

Calum sat in front of his computer screens, staring at the image that Tara had emailed through from the village of Ruspiri.

He couldn't quite believe it. The picture taken of the Almast by the backpacker had been blurry and difficult to make out. This one was perfectly sharp. There was no doubt this time, no ambiguity. The Almasti existed.

As well as the image on his central screen, three of the surrounding screens were all showing grainier versions of the same image but seen from various directions, transmitted from the headbands of Tara, Gecko and Rhino. He'd insisted that they all wear the headbands every moment they were awake, now that they were sure they were on the right track. As Natalie's experience had proved, anything could happen without warning. He was pleased to see that she was wearing hers now, although she kept pulling at it as if she really wanted to take it off.

'Calum, are you listening to this?' Rhino said.

'I am.' He quickly flicked his gaze across the screens. 'Gecko, can you turn round and face Rhino? I want to see him speak.'

One of the screens displayed a blur for a moment, and then Rhino's face appeared.

'I'm not sure we can track the creature very well – certainly not now, at night, but even when the sun's up I doubt that it's left much of a track. The ground is too hard to retain any imprints, and the vegetation is too dry. It's going to be difficult to work out where it went. Our best bet is to fall back on the original plan – look for likely areas in the foothills where a village or a settlement might be hidden.'

'I understand what you're saying.' Calum sighed. 'But I wish there was some way of capitalizing on the fact that you've actually had a face-to-face experience.'

'Actually,' a voice said, 'I think there's a way you might be able to track it.'

It took Calum a couple of moments to identify the voice, and just as he did so all but one of the headband cameras suddenly slewed round to focus on Natalie's face.

'What do you mean?' Rhino's voice asked.

Natalie looked uncomfortable at being the focus of so much attention. Her gaze flickered from side to side, as if she was looking for some way out, and there were spots of colour in her cheeks. 'Well,' she said, 'I kinda slipped my mobile phone into one of the pockets on its shirt-thing.'

There was silence in the room in Ruspiri. As far

away as England, Calum could have heard a pin drop. 'You did *what*?' he asked eventually, if only to break the silence.

'I slipped my mobile into its shirt pocket.'

Rhino had found his voice by now. 'Why did you do that?' he asked mildly.

'Well, it wasn't like I was getting much of a signal, and I didn't want to talk to any of my friends because it would just make me sad. And it occurred to me that you guys might be able to track my mobile's signal.' She looked concerned. 'You can do that, can't you? I mean, I've seen it on *CSI*.'

'Yes,' Calum said, 'we can do that. Or, rather, *I* can do that from here. But, Natalie, that was a brilliant idea.'

'Don't sound so surprised,' she said.

'Won't the Almast feel the weight of the phone in its pocket?' Tara's voice asked.

Natalie shook her head. 'It's a really lightweight mobile. I keep forgetting I've got it with me.' She paused, and smiled brightly. 'And it's pink!'

'Battery life?' Gecko asked.

'I charged it yesterday from the lighter socket in the van. It's got pretty much a full charge.'

'Let's hope your mother doesn't ring it,' Gecko's voice said.

Natalie flinched. 'Actually, what worries me is: what happens if she rings and that creature answers?'

There was silence for a few moments as the group

tried to imagine the consequences, and then tried not to.

'I'll start the tracking programs,' Calum said. 'If I get a location, I'll let you know.'

Rhino started to say something, then paused as the sound of raised voices from outside intruded on the conversation. 'Hang on a sec,' he said. 'I'm going to check on what's going on out there.'

'Tara,' Calum said, 'while I'm booting up the tracking programs and Rhino is talking to the villagers, can you run a check on the boundary sensors? I'd hate to have something sneak past them while we were distracted.'

'Will do, boss.'

'I'll go with her,' Natalie offered.

The team in Georgia fragmented as each of them went different ways, and the computer screens in Calum's apartment started to display different pictures rather than different versions of the same one. Calum switched his attention to a screen where he could flash up the apps that he could use to track mobile-phone locations. It wasn't *entirely* legal, but then it wasn't entirely *illegal* either. It was a grey area of law. It took him less than five minutes to call up a Google Earth map of northern Georgia with the position of Natalie's phone on it. The accuracy wasn't perfect – the cell size was pretty huge that far into the wilds of the country – but it was enough to work out the location of the Almast to within a mile or so. It was heading roughly north-west, away from the village and into the mountains.

He could feel his heart beating faster than usual. He felt breathless, excited.

The chase was on.

'He says that this is an insult, and it must be punished.' Levan levered himself up on one elbow. His chest was swaddled in bandages that looked like they were left over from the Second World War, and he was lying on a makeshift camp bed at the back of the village hall where his wounds had been treated and his dislocated shoulder had been popped back into place.

Rhino nodded. 'I can understand his point. There's only so much food theft that a small community like this can tolerate.'

He glanced at the front of the hall where a villager with a long grey-and-black beard and a scar across his right eye was gesticulating to a crowd of his friends. Adjusting the band that encircled his head, he murmured, 'Are you getting all this?'

'Getting it,' Calum's voice whispered in his ear from several thousand miles away, 'but not understanding it.'

'He says,' Levan continued, translating, 'that if someone wants to come and trade with them, then that is acceptable, but to sneak around and steal from the storage barns is wrong under all circumstances.' He paused, letting the bearded man say something else. 'He says that any male villager over the age of sixteen and under the age of fifty should take up a rifle and join him in tracking this thief into the mountains, where they will get their food back and take revenge.'

'At night?' Rhino asked.

'He says that they can take torches.'

Someone in the crowd asked a question. The bearded villager tried to answer, but someone else got in first and the debate quickly disintegrated into a series of shouted diatribes. Fists were shaken and it looked as if fights might break out.

'There appears to be some debate over whether or not they should wait for the morning,' Levan said drily. 'There is also a small but vocal minority who say that the thief is an Almast, which is a supernatural creature, and that hunting a supernatural creature will bring death and devastation to the village. Others want to see this thing's head stuffed and mounted on the wall of the inn, regardless of whether or not it is supernatural.'

'We have to delay them,' Calum's voice said via the headband. 'Can you do anything, Rhino?'

As the village head man walked to the front of the crowd and raised his hands, trying to exert some measure of control, Rhino's mind raced, evaluating the various possibilities that might spin out from this moment, depending on how the arguments went. 'They're an angry lot,' he said, crouching down closer to where Levan was half lying, 'and that's not a good thing. When tempers get frayed, the wrong decisions get made, and that can lead to trouble. The last thing we want is a gang of armed villagers with flaming torches and pitchforks roaming the countryside looking for a monster.' He looked at Levan and shrugged. 'No offence,' he added.

'None taken,' Levan said. 'I too have seen *Frankenstein*, and it does not end well, either for the monster or for several of the villagers.'

'Can you interrupt?'

'What do I say?'

'Point out that there may not be just one Almast – there may be a whole village or tribe of them. Point out that if one Almast can rip your chest like it did, then ten or twenty of them could cause a lot more damage, and a hundred of them could kill every man in Ruspiri. Tell them that our expedition can leave quickly and hunt the creature down using our electronic devices without giving ourselves away, and that we can come back and tell them where the Almasti are based and how many of them there are.'

'You would do that?'

Rhino shrugged. 'I work for Calum Challenger, not for them – but they don't need to know that. I just want to avoid them going out mob-handed and kicking off some kind of riot.'

Levan extended a bandaged hand and Rhino pulled him up off the camp bed. 'I should have gone into diplomatic corps,' he muttered, then stumbled to the front of the crowd. He got control of the argument simply by shouting louder than any of the others. Maybe it was his force of personality, maybe it was just that the villagers felt sorry for him because of his injuries, but they let him talk. He spoke rapidly in Georgian, emphasizing his words with dramatic hand gestures. At one point he indicated the bandages on his chest, and Rhino assumed he was talking about his own recent fight with the Almast. A few questions were thrown at him, and he bounced the answers back without hesitation. Eventually the crowd quietened down. Some kind of agreement seemed to have been reached.

Levan returned to where Rhino stood. He was looking white and drained. 'They will agree not to set out to hunt this thing down until tomorrow lunchtime,' he said. 'If you wish to leave before then to find the Almast, then that is your affair.' He shrugged. 'I think they are beginning to realize the dangers of what they are doing, and they want to get a priest in to bless them before they start.' He shrugged. 'Sorry – best I could do.'

'I only hope it's enough,' Calum's voice said in Rhino's ear as Rhino scanned the crowd. 'It would be a tragedy if this tribe of Neanderthals, or whatever they are, got wiped out before the world even knew they were there.'

Natalie stared down at the ground, hoping against hope that a flash of colour would attract her attention. She was retracing her steps through the village, as best she could. Somewhere out here was her headband, which she had slipped back into her pocket as soon as the group meeting had finished. Forgetting the fact that it was a complete fashion disaster: Calum had made it clear that there was a lot of expensive technology in those headbands, and he wouldn't be pleased if she had lost one before the expedition had really got under way. He had already emphasized – more than once – that he was annoyed with her for not wearing hers at all times.

'Damn it,' she muttered, 'why can't it have a flashing light or something?'

It occurred to her that if she told Rhino she'd lost the headband then he could get Calum to do something, like shout loudly through her loudspeakers, or set off some kind of alarm or something. But that would mean admitting she'd made a mistake, and that was the last thing she intended doing. No, she would find it herself.

She looked around, making sure she knew where she was and, more importantly, where the others were in relation to her. The centre of the village wasn't in sight, but she knew that it was just round two corners. She could retrace her steps pretty quickly if she needed to, and she'd swapped her shoes for trainers back at the inn so she could run quickly if anything happened. Not that she was expecting anything to happen. Surely her share of bad luck had been exhausted for the day?

Just as the thought crossed her mind, she heard a noise behind her. She turned round. Part of her expected it to be Rhino or Gecko looking for her, but part of her was worried it was the Almast again. Her heart skipped a beat, then seemed to go to double time.

It wasn't Rhino. It wasn't Gecko. It wasn't even the Almast. It was a man she didn't recognize. He looked more Norwegian than Georgian, with fine, blond hair and pale skin. He was thin, almost bony, and he was wearing similar camouflage fatigues to Rhino's. On Rhino they looked functional, but on this man they almost looked like high fashion.

Oh, and he had a gun strapped to his hip. She felt her stomach lurch as she noticed that.

'Hello,' he said. 'You must be Natalie Livingstone. I have seen your photograph.'

'Who are you?' she asked, tensing, ready to run.

'Don't worry – there will be time enough for introductions later.' He smiled, but there was no humour in the expression. 'For now we need you to come with us.'

'Us?' she parroted, wondering who else there was. As a hand clamped itself across her mouth and pulled her backwards, she decided that there were some questions it was best not to ask.

When Rhino appeared from the village hall, marching towards the van as if he was on a parade ground, Gecko stepped forward to intercept him.

'Everyone's collecting their stuff,' he said. 'I've checked the fuel, oil and water, just in case, and we're all right. We're just about ready to go when you are.'

'All of the supplies and provisions loaded in the van?'

Gecko nodded.

'What about ARLENE?' a voice said. Gecko looked around for a few moments before realizing that it was Calum, speaking through the headband loudspeakers.

'We've put ARLENE together,' he replied, 'which means that it won't fit into the van. The idea is that ARLENE keeps pace with the van until we run out of road, then we leave the van, load ARLENE up and head off into the mountains.'

'Sounds like a plan,' Calum said. 'As far as I can tell from the digital maps and satellite photos, you'll only be able to go ten miles or so before the gradient becomes too steep for the van, and, frankly, I can't see you making more than ten miles an hour for that first section, even with four-wheel drive.'

Rhino nodded. 'Agreed, but it's ten miles that we don't have to walk, and it gets us further ahead. The villagers are holding off on any hunt until tomorrow afternoon. We need to get significantly ahead of them in that time.'

'It should be possible,' Gecko said. 'They don't have the advantage of Calum tracking Natalie's mobile phone.'

'For as long as that advantage lasts. The phone might fall out of the Almast's pocket, or it might discover it and throw it away,' Calum said.

Gecko shrugged. 'We will have to take our chances.

What about our guide – is he coming with us?'

'No, he's too badly injured. If those cuts open up and start bleeding while we're in the Caucasus Mountains, we'll never be able to get help to him. I know about first aid, but I'm not a surgeon. Best we leave him behind.' Rhino laughed humourlessly. 'It's not as if we're expecting the Almasti to speak Georgian. I doubt that a translator would be much use.'

'If this thing *is* an Almast,' Gecko pointed out. 'It might still be someone from an unknown village in the mountains.'

A voice came from the direction of the inn. 'Hi – are we ready to go?'

Rhino and Gecko turned to see Tara walking towards them. She had a rucksack slung over her shoulder.

'Just about,' Rhino said. 'Where's Natalie?'

Tara shrugged. 'No idea. I thought she was with you guys.'

'I haven't seen her since our meeting,' Gecko said. 'Maybe she's gone back to her room for a lie-down.' He paused. 'Calum – can you see from her headband where she is?'

'She's not wearing her headband.' Calum's voice echoed in Gecko's ear, and presumably in Tara's and Rhino's ears as well. He sounded annoyed. 'I think she's got privacy issues. I think she's also a spoilt brat. She knows how much those headbands cost.'

'What about her mobile phone – can you track it?'

Tara asked. She caught herself straight away. 'Oh, right. She gave it to the Almast.'

Rhino looked around decisively. 'Right – Tara, you search the inn. Gecko – you take the village hall. I'll walk around the village. First one to find her gets to tell her how stupid it is to wander off when there's an Almast somewhere in the vicinity, not to mention a whole lot of excitable villagers.'

Everyone headed off in different directions, all aiming to do the same thing – find Natalie. Following instructions, Gecko headed for the village hall. It seemed like most of the men above the age of fifteen were streaming out of the place following the meeting about the Almast. There were beards and moustaches on display that Gecko found almost frightening. He slipped past them and checked out the hall from front to back. It smelt of tobacco, alcohol and lots of people wearing wool clothing. He made sure he checked every nook and cranny of the place, just in case Natalie was hiding away somewhere, but there was no sign of her anywhere.

He emerged into daylight to find Tara coming out of the inn. She shook her head before Gecko could say anything. 'No luck – I looked everywhere I could. Unless she's booked a different room under a false name, she's not in there.'

'What do you think has happened to her?' Gecko asked.

She shrugged casually, but there was worry written

across her face. 'No idea. Maybe the Almast came back to get the one person who's seen it. Or maybe one of the younger villagers took a shine to her.'

'I doubt he'd be able to keep her in shoes for more than a week,' Gecko said drily. He shook his head. '*Este é louco*,' he muttered. 'This is mad.'

'Tell me about it,' Rhino called as he strode back. 'I've checked the whole village, and I've got nothing.'

'Tara thought that maybe the Almast had got her,' Gecko suggested.

'It's as good as explanation as any.'

'So what do we do?'

'We do what we were going to do – follow Natalie's mobile signal. We thought we'd be following the Almast, but we might be following her as well. I'll make sure Levan keeps an eye out for her here, just in case she comes back.' He clapped his hands together. 'Right – everyone in the van. Gecko – you're navigating. Tara – you're making sure that ARLENE keeps up. I'll just go and tell Levan about Natalie and let him know that we're off.'

Within minutes, they were leaving the village and heading towards the mountains. Rhino was driving, Tara was sitting beside him and Gecko was in the back. ARLENE trotted like a pony by the side of the van. Some of the villagers stopped what they were doing to watch them leave – probably more because of ARLENE than anything else. Gecko wasn't sure whether he liked the place or not – the villagers had seemed pleasant enough, but they didn't go out of their way to be friendly.

He glanced sideways, expecting to see Natalie on the seat beside him, looking bored, but the seat was empty. He felt a jolt of concern run through his heart.

Wherever she was, he hoped she was OK.

Natalie's captors manhandled her through the village and out into the countryside without being observed by anything larger than a dog. They were professional and economical in their movements, responding silently to hand signals given by the man who had originally confronted her.

Natalie couldn't help but notice that, when they got to the sensor systems round the border of the village, four of the men opened up what looked like blankets of thin metallic foil. With a man on each side, they manoeuvred the blankets so that they formed a tunnel between two of the sensors. The remaining men took Natalie out between the blankets without, presumably, triggering any reaction.

A quarter of a mile or so from Ruspiri, the men pushed her towards a clump of trees and scrubby bushes that were big enough to hide a couple of elephants. The men didn't have any elephants – or, if they did, they were hidden somewhere else – but they did have three Humvees – wide, squat, four-wheeled vehicles that looked like a cross between an SUV and a Transformer. Natalie recognized them: the vehicles were something of a fashion accessory around Los Angeles.

These three were painted a matt black, and bristled with antennae of various types.

The blond-haired man steered Natalie towards the passenger side of the lead Humvee. He held the door open while she entered and then, slamming her door, moved round to the driver's side and got in.

He stared at her for a few long moments with his pale blue eyes.

'What am I doing here?' she snapped as angrily as she could manage. 'I know this is a foreign country, but I am an American citizen and the US embassy will be very concerned to know that I have been kidnapped.'

'Let's dispense with the theatrics,' the man said. 'You must know that we won't be scared by mention of the US embassy, and you must know that there is no task force ready to set out and rescue you. You are on your own, and your safety and survival depend *only* on the decisions that you make. Clear? Now, there are certain things I want to know. They include the commitment of your various friends to this expedition they are on, the nature of the supplies you have brought with you and whether Captain Gillis and your guide, Levan Ketsbaia, are armed.'

'I'm not going to tell you anything.' Natalie folded her arms defiantly and looked away, but her heart was beating fast.

'You will,' he said calmly. 'I deplore the use of unnecessary violence, although I will countenance it if required, but there are easier ways to get the information

I need. I could tie your hands together, attach them to a long leash, fix the leash to the rear bumper of this Humvee and drive off, leaving you to either keep up or tell me what I want to know. I understand you are a long-distance runner, back in the USA. You might be able to keep up for a while, but one misstep would lead to you being dragged along the ground, scraping the flesh from your legs and arms and back. But that is a crude, unpleasant way of getting information. My preference is for a drug that, within a few moments, will cause you to feel unbearable thirst. I have a can of soda here with me, fresh from the cool box. I will hold it up in front of your eyes, with the condensation misting on its surface, and you will tell me everything and anything I want, just to get hold of it. I have seen experienced soldiers break down within ten minutes just to get a sip from the can. You will not be a challenge. Now, it should be obvious to you that you will tell me everything. The only choice you have is whether you do so quickly, without pain and suffering, or slowly.'

Natalie sighed, and closed her eyes momentarily. This was a nightmare, but she wasn't waking up.

'Who *are* you?' she asked quietly.

'My name is Craig Roxton,' he said, in exactly the same tone of voice that he had used to terrify her, 'and I work for a company named Nemor Incorporated. Now that we have introduced ourselves, let us begin . . .'

CHAPTER

sixteen

They had to abandon the van just over two hours after leaving the village.

The ground had mainly sloped upward all the way, but the Delica's four-wheel drive had managed admirably, and its heavy-duty tyres had bitten into the ground and pulled them onward with barely any sign of strain in the engine noise. The road they had taken from the village had petered out into a track after a while, then into a path, then into a slightly different-coloured line in the long grass. Gravel scattered across the ground became small stones, then larger stones, then boulders. Presumably, Tara thought, the next step would be the mountains themselves.

Naively, Tara had expected the ground to just head up and up and up until they arrived at the mountains, but there were unexpected dips on the way – areas of ground out of sight until they crested the tops of the ridges that hid them, large enough in which to hide entire villages. Not that they had found any villages on the way. Ruspiri seemed to be the last outpost of civilization.

ARLENE had kept up with no problems. For the first hour or so Tara had been paranoid about checking that the robot hadn't fallen over and been left behind, or that the supplies and luggage hadn't fallen off it, and about monitoring its power levels and vital signs using the software on her tablet, but after an hour had passed with no accidents she had relaxed. It really was an autonomous system. Now the robot's presence was just something in the corner of her eye, something reassuring on which she didn't feel she had to keep tabs.

They had crossed several streams along the way. The first two had been little more than shallow trickles of ice-cold water heading down from the mountains that hardly got the underside of the van wet, but the third had been wider and deeper, and Rhino had decided that the risk of flooding the engine was greater than the risk that they wouldn't be able to find a ford or a bridge if they turned off the path, and so he drove along the side of the river for a while until he found an area where they could cross. Tara had been pretty sure that she could have got ARLENE to cross the stream, picking its way carefully over, and got it to wait for them to find their way back to it, but Rhino had insisted that the robot stay with them.

Rhino had driven all the way, concentrating on the route and on making sure that the van's tyres didn't get bogged down anywhere. Gecko was in the back with a map and a compass, trying to make sure that they knew where they were. Tara was in the passenger seat with a tablet computer on her lap. It was her job to liaise with Calum back in London, who was watching the map displays on his ten-screen computer and tracking the progress of the Almast with Natalie's mobile phone in its pocket. Or, Tara was beginning to think, the rabbit whose neck the Almast had tied the mobile round and then set running in a different direction. She supposed it depended on how intelligent the Almast was, and whether or not it had discovered the mobile yet and wondered what it was.

The Almast had maintained a reasonably straight route towards the mountains after leaving the village. It had wandered back and forth a little bit, presumably taking advantage of areas of flatter terrain, but it had gone straight across all the streams. On an open road the van would have been able to catch up with no problems, but on rolling terrain littered with rocks and crossed by the occasional stream the Almast was actually making better time. The only way the expedition was keeping up was because the Almast had taken a break for a while, resting and perhaps eating some of the grain it had stolen to keep its energy up. Or maybe it had been busy catching that rabbit and tying Natalie's mobile round its neck.

'Where do you think it's heading?' Tara asked the absent Calum after a while.

'Not sure,' his voice said over the headband loudspeakers. 'I've tried extrapolating the line it's been taking further into the mountains on Google Earth, but I can't see any signs of habitation – no villages, no buildings, nothing. I just hope it isn't heading through a mountain pass and across to the other side of the Caucasus. That would be annoying.'

'Very,' she agreed. 'Look on the bright side – maybe the Almasti live in caves.'

'Let's hope,' Calum said darkly.

Tara had found herself captivated by the scenery as they drove. She was a city girl, used to having buildings huddled around her, and the vast open spaces were making her dizzy. The mountain peaks were a jagged line high above them, like the sharp edge of a carving knife: not as rough as other mountain ranges she had seen in photographs, like the Alps or the Himalayas, but still impressive. The sky behind the peaks was the deepest blue, and the wisps of cloud that were blown past by the wind seemed to catch on the mountain tops, like chiffon scarves, and flutter gently.

'Time to stop,' Rhino said regretfully as the Delica had climbed slowly up a particularly sharp slope. 'If I push this thing any further, I'll risk overheating the engine, or stripping the gearbox.' He brought the van to a halt and turned the engine off. Tara started to type instructions into her tablet to bring ARLENE to a halt, but the robot had already detected that the van had stopped and had come to a halt itself, like a patient donkey.

Gecko slid open the side door and jumped to the ground. He glanced around. 'Everyone, make sure you remember where we parked,' he said, grinning.

'We're on a schedule,' Rhino pointed out. 'Let's get the supplies out of the van and load ARLENE up.'

'It could have carried them all the way from Ruspiri,' Tara pointed out. 'I said so back there. We didn't need to load the van up, only to unload it again now.'

'I wanted to make sure that ARLENE could keep up unloaded,' Rhino said. 'I didn't want to put too much weight on it to start off with. Standard military technique – do things incrementally, rather than all at once, just in case there's a problem.' He opened up the back of the van and began to haul out cases and boxes.

'Speaking of problems,' Gecko said, looking around, 'I need to . . . you know. Go to the bathroom.'

'Just walk round to the other side of the van and go,' Rhino said. 'We're not going to find a washroom out here anywhere.'

Gecko looked as if he was going to argue, but shrugged instead and walked round the corner of the Delica.

'I hadn't thought about that,' Tara said loudly to cover any sounds that might be coming from behind the van. She started pulling the boxes across to ARLENE. 'If I had, I would have brought some chemical toilets with us, and a small tent. ARLENE could have carried them all.'

'Let me tell you something,' Rhino said, hauling a particularly large box out of the back of the van. 'A few years ago I was on a reconnaissance mission in Afghanistan. I spent three days lying on a hilltop observing a Taliban encampment. There were guards all around the camp, and if I'd moved I would have been seen. Do you want to know what I did as far as toilet breaks were concerned?'

'Don't tell me – you just didn't drink anything so you became dehydrated and didn't need to go?' Tara replied brightly.

'No, I—'

'I said don't tell me,' she protested, hands raised. 'I really don't want to know, and I'm trying not to work it out myself.'

Gecko arrived back a few minutes later. He was moving fast, and glancing back over his shoulder.

'What's the matter?' Tara asked.

'I was . . . you know . . . doing my business . . .'

'OK, thanks – move on quickly.'

'And I suddenly realized I was being watched.'

'Not by me,' Tara said.

'No – by something else. I thought it might be the Almast! I looked around and I couldn't see anything at first, but after a few minutes I realized that there was something lying in a dip in the ground about a hundred metres away. When it realized that I had seen it, it stood up. It looked like a dog, an Alsatian, but its pelt was white and grey, and its eyes were a pale blue. It kept on looking at me for a while longer, then it just trotted off.'

'Wolf,' Rhino said succinctly.

'Wolf? Really? Not just a large wild dog?'

'No,' Rhino confirmed, 'it was a wolf. The mountains around here are full of them.'

'Great,' Gecko said. 'I take it you're armed?'

Rhino shrugged. 'On the one hand, I obviously wasn't able to get any weapons through customs, and I didn't want to risk getting in contact with any of the rather more criminal elements in Tbilisi to get my hands on one. On the other hand, you might assume that there were lots of old rifles in Ruspiri, and that I might just have slipped one of the villagers some money and taken one.'

'Well done,' Gecko said in a heartfelt tone of voice.

Tara noticed that he was wiggling his fingers uncomfortably. 'Something wrong?' she asked.

'Got any wet-wipes? Years of my mother telling me to wash my hands are now coming back to haunt me.'

Rhino indicated one of the boxes. 'In there. Just make sure you seal the box up again afterwards.'

'OK.'

It took them twenty minutes to load ARLENE up with all the stuff that had been in the van. Now the robot had things strapped to its back and hanging off both sides, but it didn't seem to be particularly inconvenienced. In fact, Tara was reminded of a game she'd been given one Christmas, where you had to load plastic buckets on the side of a spring-loaded toy donkey, trying not to trigger the spring mechanism. Once or twice, while they had been attaching things, ARLENE had moved its feet wider to maintain stability. Tara had jumped whenever it did so. Any act of apparent intelligence by the robot spooked her.

'Calum – still there?' Rhino asked, slamming the back door closed. He used the remote key to lock the van. Tara wondered against whom he was protecting it, then realized that it was probably more force of habit than anything else.

'Yes, I'm here,' Calum's voice replied from the air. 'I'm not going anywhere.'

'We're going to set off on foot now.'

'Agreed.'

Rhino pointed to two rucksacks on the ground. He was already wearing one, Tara noticed. 'Pick those up and put them on.'

'I thought ARLENE was meant to be carrying all the supplies,' she protested.

'And if ARLENE falls off the side of a mountain path and we lose everything, what are you going to eat and what are you going to sleep on?'

'Good point, well made,' she muttered, bending and picking up the rucksack. It was heavy. She slipped it on to her protesting shoulders.

'OK,' Rhino said grimly. 'Let's go find us an Almast.'

Natalie had run out of things to tell Craig Roxton. In silence she stared out of the passenger window at the passing countryside while he drove and three of his men – his *troops*, she thought – sat in the back and glowered.

The landscape they were driving through was probably the most depressingly flat and boring she had ever seen, and she had lived in El Paso for a while when her mother was working with – never *for*, as she kept pointing out – the US Department of Defence. It consisted entirely of swathes of rocky ground interrupted every now and then by a scraggly bush or a misshaped tree. Life seemed to be just about hanging on in the foothills of the Caucasus Mountains, and it didn't seem too happy about it either.

As the three Humvees had set off from their hiding place and driven off after her friends, Craig Roxton had patiently and politely asked a series of questions that cut right to the heart of what the expedition was doing there, what its plans were and how it was equipped. He seemed to know many of the answers already, and Natalie assumed that he was testing her by asking her things that he already knew. She tried telling him a couple of lies and exaggerations, but he spotted each one and threw it back at her. He didn't seem to mind that she was trying to deceive him – in fact, he almost seemed to be expecting it, and smiled each time he caught her pulling the wool over his eyes. He really was the most exasperatingly patient man she had ever met.

And the scariest. She was pretty sure that he was capable of killing her and leaving her lying in a ditch. The only reason he kept her with him was that she was useful. So she had to keep on being useful.

Inside, Natalie could feel a fluttering sensation, as if butterflies were congregating around her heart like moths around a lamp. She could feel a trembling in her hands. She tried to suppress it – no way was she going to let these gorillas know that she was scared – but the more she suppressed the trembling the more it came out as occasional jerky motions of her hands or arms. Every time she jerked she tried to turn it into a deliberate action, like smoothing her hair down or scratching her nose, but she knew that Roxton realised what she was doing, and was amused by it.

He was very interested in Calum Challenger, she discovered. He kept coming back to questions about him – what was wrong with him, what did he expect to achieve if his expedition found the Almasti, why hadn't he come out to Georgia himself, what was his website actually *for*? He seemed to think that there was a big conspiracy going on somewhere, and that Calum was covering something up – some motive or reason for arranging the expedition. Natalie tried to convince him that Calum was just a teenager exploring his own obsessions with a lot of money behind him, but he obviously didn't believe her.

The other men in the Humvee remained silent and almost immobile, like robots, or statues. They didn't seem to be listening to Roxton and Natalie talking, or looking around them, or doing anything that someone normal would have done. Natalie suspected that they just came alive when Roxton needed them and settled back into suspended animation when he didn't. In a strange way, there were only two personalities in the car.

Roxton was mad. Natalie had spotted it straight away. His faded blue eyes were open too wide and didn't blink, and he could talk calmly about hurting and killing people as if they were nothing more than rabbits or sheep or pigs. There was something deeply wrong with him. Natalie was very, very scared.

There was a device attached to the dashboard of their Humvee. It was something like a large satnav, but as well as showing where they were it also showed the position of something ahead of them. Natalie suspected that it was the van with Rhino, Tara and Gecko inside.

Roxton caught her looking at it. 'You're wondering how I can be following your friends,' he said in a genial tone. 'You assume I have placed a tracking device somewhere on them? In fact, no. I have a *much* cleverer solution.' He smiled. 'Now,' he continued conversationally, 'let us talk about ARLENE.'

'Arlene?' Natalie replied. 'I don't think I've met her.'

'I'm talking about that very clever robot that Captain Gillis is using to transport his equipment. But I think you knew that already. So – tell me all about it.' He paused for a moment, then added quietly, 'You know what will happen if you don't.'

Calum stared at the ten screens of his computer, and swore.

They weren't telling him anything that he wanted to know. Yes, they were full of information, but they didn't contain a single fact that would help him do what he most needed to do – locate Natalie Livingstone.

He slammed his fist on the computer desk. The pile

of pizza boxes stacked on the edge fell off, scattering crusts and splattering *puttanesca* sauce across the floor. He felt so helpless. He knew where Rhino, Gecko and Tara were. He knew where the scavenging Almast was, pretty much. But he didn't have a clue where Natalie was.

If only she had kept her mobile phone on her, he could have tracked her. But then, if she had kept her mobile phone on her, he wouldn't be able to track the Almast, and the whole expedition would have ground to a halt. She'd done something really clever and quick-witted, but the implications of that act were going to come back to haunt her. And him.

How could he tell her mother that he had lost her?

He scanned the screens again, just in case he had missed something. Three of the screens were showing the views from the cameras on the headbands of Rhino, Tara and Gecko. The fourth screen was blank – reserved for the headband camera that Natalie had been wearing but which had disappeared. The fifth screen showed what ARLENE was looking at, while the rest were showing a mixture of maps, Google Earth and various search engines that he'd been using.

Not for the first time, Calum wished he had the computer skills and the nerve to hack into the American reconnaissance-satellite network. The US recon satellites had telescopes so powerful that they could read the headline on a newspaper left on a park bench. The trouble was that none of them were pointed at Georgia, as far as he knew, and he would be risking a lengthy spell in an American prison if he even tried to retask one for his own purposes.

Ironic, he thought. Tara has the skill to do it, Gecko has the nerve and I have the equipment. Between the three of us we make a pretty competent human being.

Or between the four of them, if he included Natalie.

As if prompted by the confusion of his thoughts, Rhino Gillis's voice suddenly spoke in the headphones he was wearing. 'Any news on Natalie, Calum?'

'Nothing yet,' he said as calmly as he could manage.

He typed some instructions into the keyboard. 'Rhino, I've isolated our channel from the others. Tara and Gecko can't hear me – can they hear you?'

'Not if I'm quiet,' Rhino responded. His breath was audible on the loudspeakers as he walked uphill into the Caucasus Mountains. 'They're about six or seven metres in front of me – you can probably see them on my headband camera.'

'OK. Look, I'm worried about her.'

'You and me both, kid.'

'I've been racking my brains, trying to work out what might have happened to her, and I've come up with nothing.' He paused. 'Actually, that's not true. I've come up with everything from her falling down an abandoned mine shaft to being kidnapped by aliens from space. The trouble is that there's no evidence for any of them.'

'I've been thinking as well,' Rhino said. 'You want to know my three top theories, in reverse order?'

'OK.'

'Third – one of the villagers took a fancy to her and has her captive in his house while he tries to persuade her to marry him.'

'Ouch. I don't like that one much.'

'Fortunately for Natalie, I don't think it's what's happened. Before I left I talked to the village head man, Shota Gigauri. He just laughed when I suggested the possibility that she'd been kidnapped by someone in the village. He said, and I quote, that she's too thin, too pale and too talkative to make a good wife for anyone in Ruspiri. Regardless, I've asked Levan Ketsbaia to keep an eye out for her.'

'That's reassuring. So what's the next theory?'

'Second – she decided she doesn't want to be on the expedition and she's paid one of the villagers to drive her back to Mummy in Tbilisi.'

Calum considered the idea for a moment. 'Possible. She certainly didn't want to go to Georgia in the first place. I guess I could phone Gillian to find out if Natalie's been in contact with her, or if she's suddenly appeared back at the hotel, but that would tip her off that something was wrong.'

'Calum, if Natalie suddenly appeared back at the hotel in Tbilisi, Gillian Livingstone would be straight on the phone to *you* to find out what had happened.'

'Good point. We can rule that one out, then. So what's the front runner?'

Rhino paused before answering. When he did speak,

his tone was more serious than before. 'There's a slim chance the Almasti have taken her, but given how timid they are, that's unlikely. What bothers me is the other expedition, the one Gillian warned us about, the one that left Tbilisi shortly after we did . . . If they're looking for the Almasti as well, and if they're unscrupulous enough, they might just decide to take one of our expedition prisoner to find out whether or not we know where the Almasti can be found.'

Calum felt a cold wave wash over his heart. 'You think they would *do* that?'

'Depending on who they're working for, yes.' He paused again. 'It's what I would do.'

'Hmm,' Calum said, not quite sure what the best response was to that admission.

'Did you manage to find out anything about the expedition?'

Calum shook his head, despite the fact that Rhino couldn't see him. 'Nothing. There's no trace of these people going into the country, no trace of them booking into any hotels, no trace of them renting or buying any Humvees or supplies . . . absolutely nothing. Assuming that Gillian's information was correct, of course, and there *is* a second expedition heading out into the Caucasus Mountains. It could just be a mistake, or a misunderstanding.'

'I tend to believe her.'

'So do I,' Calum admitted. 'Look, I've got a suggestion,'

he continued after a few moments. 'You're not going to like it, and Tara and Gecko are going to hate it.'

'Go on.'

'Unpack ARLENE and give it orders to stay back and scout the area behind you. If this second expedition is following you, then ARLENE might be able to find them.'

On the screen showing what Rhino was seeing, the view suddenly slewed around to show ARLENE, lumbering along behind the expedition members. Rhino was obviously looking at the robot, considering.

'Interesting idea. I presume the idea is that we carry what we can ourselves, and leave the rest cached here to recover later.'

'That's right.'

'Is ARLENE up to handling a mission on its own?'

'I think so. Check with Tara. She's read the technical manuals, and she's got the control software on her tablet. She can tell you if ARLENE can be reprogrammed to independently search for a party of people in three vehicles, and she can also tell you if ARLENE's visual sensors and control algorithms are good enough to pick Natalie's face out from a group of others.'

'There's a lot of terrain to cover back there. Just based on probabilities, there's little chance that ARLENE will stumble across this other expedition.'

'You're missing something,' Calum said forcefully. 'Let's assume that this second expedition is following us. Let's also assume that they were responsible for the attempted theft of your equipment back at Tbilisi airport. It makes sense to assume that they have some means of working out where you are. Maybe the Mitsubishi Delica has a tracking device in it, maybe it doesn't, but the terrain being as limited as it is, at some stage that expedition is going to pass through where you left the van. They'll probably have to ditch their vehicles at around the same point. Send ARLENE back to the van, using bushes and trees as cover. If the other expedition isn't there, then ARLENE can wait for them. If they've already got there and moved on, ARLENE can follow their tracks.'

Rhino was silent for a few minutes, thinking. Eventually, he said, 'You're right – it's the only option we have, short of just forgetting about her. I'll tell the others and get started.'

'Keep me in the loop.'

Rhino raised a hand to his headband. His fingers appeared huge in the field of view of the camera. 'Calum, while we're wearing these things you're in the loop whether you want to be or not.' His voice suddenly became louder. 'Tara, Gecko – stop for a minute. I've got something I need to discuss with you . . .'

The Nemor Inc. expedition had got just about as far as it could on wheels – even wheels as wide and robust as those on the Humvees. Ahead of them the ground rose up more steeply than before. It also looked to Natalie as if it was softer, muddier.

The van that Rhino and Gecko had liberated from the thieves at Tbilisi airport sat in the middle of an area of open ground. Seeing it, Natalie felt a momentary pang of loneliness. She was trying not to think too much about what was going on, just living from moment to moment, but knowing that her friends had been there only a little while before made her feel tearful.

Her *friends*? When had that happened? When had they gone from being just people she was stuck with to people she kinda liked being with?

When they had been so concerned for her, back in the village, that was when.

Roxton had stopped the three vehicles and was standing out on the sloping grassland next to the van, obviously making a judgement about what to do next. The wind was ruffling his fine blond hair. Three of his team were standing with him, consulting maps and compasses. Natalie was in the passenger seat of the lead Humvee, where she'd been ordered to stay, watching them all with little interest.

Eventually Roxton left the group and walked back to the Humvee. 'I'm sorry to tell you this, my dear, but I'm afraid we're going to have to abandon the vehicles and carry on by foot.' He smiled. 'In deference to your position as prisoner I have decided that you won't have to carry your fair share of supplies.'

'Gee, thanks,' Natalie said.

'You're going to carry *twice* your fair share.'

'Brilliant – thanks for the consideration.' She paused,

embarrassed. 'Uh, I hate to ask, but is there anywhere I can, like, *pee*?'

'I've got an empty water bottle. Would that do?'

She just stared at him darkly.

Roxton glanced around. 'There are some bushes over there. Would that suit Your Highness's modesty?'

'No,' she said, 'not even close, but I guess it'll have to do.'

'If you're not back in five minutes, I'll send someone to look for you and, believe me, they won't be gentle when they find you.'

'I'll be back,' she said. 'I mean, where else would I go?' As Roxton walked back to his team, she muttered, 'I swear, I'll never again go to anywhere that doesn't have air conditioning, a spa and a decent bathroom.'

She pushed open the passenger-side door and got out of the Humvee. Reluctantly she walked across the marshy ground that lay between her and the clump of bushes that Roxton had indicated. With every step she took, they looked smaller and sparser.

She walked round the bushes, and nearly screamed.

Something dark and huge was towering over her.

CHAPTER

seventeen

Moments passed, during which Natalie was scared rigid and speechless. The late-afternoon sun gleamed off the metal of the creature's legs and neck. The cameras that formed its head were aimed at her, examining her, evaluating her.

It was that thing . . . ARLENE. The load-carrying robot that Tara and Rhino had brought back from America.

The realization that it wasn't the Almast again made her feel weak with relief. She felt her muscles relax. She glanced sideways, but the bushes were thick enough that she couldn't see the Humvees or the Nemor expedition. That meant they couldn't see her or the robot.

She glanced uncertainly at ARLENE again. 'Can you . . . can you hear me?' she asked.

The robot's head bobbed up and down twice.

'Calum – is that you?' she whispered.

The robot nodded again.

'You sent this thing to find me?' A wave of gratitude washed over her, making her feel weak and tearful. 'Thank you. Can you . . . speak? Does this thing have a voice? If it does, be quiet – the people who kidnapped me are only a few yards away.'

The robot's head shook from side to side.

'No loudspeakers, huh? I suppose that makes sense. I mean, who would ARLENE talk to? And what would it need to talk about?'

The robot's head tilted slightly, watching her at an angle. It then pivoted to look at where the Nemor expedition was, if the bushes hadn't been in the way, and back to her again.

'They're following you,' she whispered. 'It's someone called Nemor Incorporated. They want to get to the Almasti before you do.'

ARLENE's head continued to study Natalie. Was Calum really watching her through its lenses? Was Tara watching her too? But what about ARLENE – did the robot have any kind of consciousness? Was *it* watching her as well?

'They'll miss me,' she said eventually. 'I need to get back. And I need to pee.'

She blushed, and suddenly hoped that the robot's sensors couldn't pick up the increased heat from her face.

The robot's head twisted round to stare at its own back, then twisted to look at her again.

'Are you trying to tell me something?'

It nodded again.

'What?'

The head rotated 180 degrees again, so that it

was looking at its own 'spine', and then back to look at Natalie.

'Don't tell me that you want me to climb up on your back. *Please* don't tell me that.'

No movement. The cameras were pointed straight at her eyes.

'That is what you're trying to tell me, isn't it?'

The head nodded.

'Oh heck,' she said in a small voice. 'I really don't want to do that.'

No movement again. Calum wasn't really giving her a choice. Not, she thought, that there was much of a choice anyway. It wasn't like she could stay here with Roxton and his entourage of grim-faced bodyguards.

'OK,' she sighed. 'I don't suppose there's anything as useful as a saddle around?'

Instead of shaking its head, ARLENE bent down, front legs first and then the middle and back legs, so that she could scramble on to its back. There was a curved section of metal like a saddle between its first and second pair of legs, and she found that she could lean forward and sit reasonably comfortably with her legs clutching tightly to the robot's flanks. Her hands gripped two smooth metal projections on its neck that were probably somewhere to attach straps for securing supplies. If ARLENE stopped suddenly, then she would jolt forward, right into the sharp metal staircase of its neck. She grabbed hold extra-tight with her hands and legs, and promised herself that if ARLENE ever did stop suddenly then she would do her best to roll sideways and fall off. It didn't matter how hard the ground was – it would be softer than getting herself impaled on those metal vertebrae.

Quicker than she would have liked, ARLENE levered itself upright. Natalie gasped as her head was suddenly two and a half metres above the ground. She could probably see over the tops of the bushes if she straightened up, so she kept low.

'OK,' she whispered into the robot's microphone ear. 'Let's run like the wind – but safely!'

Calum was confused.

He had been watching what ARLENE had been doing on his computer monitors. The robot had got back to where the van had been left in just half an hour, moving rapidly downhill and using its own programming to work out the best route across the hilly terrain. Once it was there, and once it was obvious that the second expedition hadn't arrived yet, it had selected the best place to hide – a clump of bushes that would completely screen it from sight. It had stayed there, motionless, waiting for something to happen. Fifty minutes later, it did. Three Humvees turned up, circled the van and stopped. Men and women with guns got out and tried the locked doors. A thin man with blond hair had joined them, and they had all talked for a while.

Most importantly, Natalie had been in the front passenger seat of the lead Humvee.

She'd looked bored, and scared. Calum's heart had ached for her, but he knew that there was nothing he could do. He didn't have access to the control functions for the robot. Tara had some of them on her tablet computer, and she had persuaded Calum before leaving England that two of them trying to take control of the robot at the same time would be madness. But even she couldn't take *full* control of the robot – most of its functions were designed to be autonomous. It wasn't a remote-control system – it was a robot that made its own decisions, within broad pre-set mission parameters. And, besides, Calum guessed that Tara was too busy walking uphill with a large rucksack on her back to be monitoring and controlling ARLENE on a moment-by-moment basis. So, now that ARLENE had found Natalie, there wasn't very much they could do. Calum had watched her for a while, wondering if there was any way to attract her attention, but then something strange had happened. Natalie had wandered towards the bushes of her own accord, apparently unaccompanied, and managed to find ARLENE by herself, and she had started talking to it. She had mentioned Nemor Incorporated, which had made Calum suddenly sit up and take notice. And ARLENE had responded to her. Using gestures and movements of its head, the robot had persuaded her to climb on its back. Calum had to admit that it was an innovative solution, but where had it come from? Had ARLENE come up with a plan all by itself?

Whatever the reason, looking at the monitor now, all

Calum could see was grass and bushes and trees hurtling past, and up ahead the increasing slope of the foothills of the Caucasus Mountains. Every now and then, when ARLENE's cameras tipped up far enough, he could see the purple and grey sawtooth peaks of the mountains themselves, with the sun dropping behind them. He couldn't even see if Natalie was still managing to hold on. At first he had been relieved to have found her, but what would happen to her if she slipped off and fell to the ground while ARLENE was travelling so fast? She would almost certainly break a bone, and there would be no way to know where she was or how to get her treated. This was a disaster! He must tell Rhino.

Natalie kept her head down, tucked into her shoulder, as ARLENE raced across the ground. The thudding of ARLENE's six metal feet against soil and rock vibrated up through its metal skeleton and into Natalie's body like continuously rolling thunder, making it difficult to take a breath. Air whistled past her ears and drew her hair out behind her. The metal of the robot's chassis poked her all over.

Moments after she had got on to ARLENE's back, the robot had broken into a lolloping gallop away from the bushes. Somewhere behind them Natalie had heard a shout, and a brief burst of gunfire that had fortunately gone right over her head. She had been missed, and her escape had been seen. Fortunately, ARLENE was making better speed than Roxton's personnel could manage on foot, and they couldn't take the Humvees any further uphill. There was no chance they would catch up.

There was a strong chance, however, that Natalie might end up falling off ARLENE's back if she wasn't careful. The robot wasn't built for passengers – there were no real handholds, and wherever she clamped her thighs to get a grip she felt sharp metal points digging into her skin. It was like trying to find a comfortable spot to perch on a lawnmower, or a clothes horse.

Her hands were damp with sweat, and they kept slipping off the smooth bits of ARLENE's neck on to which she was desperately trying to hold. She wasn't sure she could take more than a few more minutes of this. How far away were Rhino, Tara and Gecko? Surely they couldn't have walked more than a couple of miles from the van in that time?

ARLENE jerked to one side and jumped unexpectedly. Natalie nearly slid sideways off the robot's back, saving herself only by flinging her arms tightly around its neck and holding on for dear life. From the corner of her eye she saw a glittering stream flash beneath them, and then ARLENE's front feet hit the ground on the other side and they were pounding across the ground again. Small stones sprang up from beneath the robot's metal hoofs and clattered against the underside of its body.

This was hell, and it felt like it was never going to end.

The rucksack's straps bit into Gecko's shoulders as he slogged on across the Georgian landscape. His head was low, chin on chest, and all he had seen for the past hour was his feet, repetitively taking steps.

The straps were padded, but they still hurt. He was used to the freedom of free-running with nothing holding him back or weighing him down.

He looked up from the constant hypnotic movement of his feet and stared around. They were higher up now, and the grass and bushes were sparser, interrupted by stretches of bare earth and rock. Ahead of them the ground split apart as if hit by some giant's axe, with steep slopes to the right and the left and a dark ravine or defile directly ahead. Rhino seemed to be aiming them directly for the defile, which made sense. They weren't in any condition to climb the steep slopes to either side, not with the equipment they were carrying on their backs. Presumably Rhino was hoping that the defile opened up into a wider area, like a valley, with a shallower slope upward. Gecko hoped he was right. His experience as a free-runner on London's rooftops had shown him that you couldn't just make assumptions about what was round the corner, or over the edge. You couldn't throw yourself off a roof because you thought there might be a wide ledge underneath.

He glanced over his shoulder. The landscape behind them dropped away, of course, but it was creased and rumpled by millions of years of geological activity. The place where they had left the van was already hidden by several folds in the terrain and various upthrusts of rock. The main feature that he could see was a wide plain off to the west, with the far-off crimson glitter of late-afternoon sunlight on a river bisecting it.

Tara was about six metres behind him, and Rhino three metres behind her, making sure she wasn't being gradually left behind. Despite the massive rucksack on her back, Tara was holding her tablet computer in both hands and staring intently at the screen.

'What's the story?' Gecko called.

'All I can see is the ground rushing past,' she called back. Her face was flushed, and her forehead was glossy with perspiration. 'I can't even tell if Natalie's still on ARLENE's back.'

'Can you recognize the terrain it's running over?' Rhino shouted.

'I keep thinking I see a bush or a tree that looks familiar, but they're gone too fast for me to be sure.'

Rhino glanced back over his shoulder, then ahead to the approaching dark slash in the rocks. 'I hope to God that she makes it before we get in there. I'm not sure that ARLENE can manage the rough terrain inside the defile, and I don't fancy hanging around waiting for her. The Nemor expedition will be moving fast to try and catch up with us.'

Calum's voice suddenly echoed in their headphones: 'Hey, I think I can see you! On ARLENE's camera!'

The three of them glanced down the hill. For a moment there was nothing to see, but then a section of bush pushed apart to reveal the metallic skeleton of ARLENE. The robot stepped through delicately, carefully, then started to move faster up the hill towards them.

For a moment it looked to Gecko as if the robot had nothing on its back. He was convinced that Natalie had fallen off somewhere along the robot's route. But as ARLENE climbed closer and started to slow down again something moved behind its neck, and Gecko suddenly realized that Natalie had been lying flat. She suddenly sat up, and Tara cheered.

Natalie didn't look in the mood for cheering. Her hair was tangled, her face white and strained, and her skin covered in cuts and bruises.

'I need a hairbrush,' she said as ARLENE stopped by Rhino's side.

'You look like you've been through hell and come out the other side,' Tara said as she extended a hand to help Natalie climb down.

'I have. That's why I need a hairbrush.'

Rhino walked forward and took Natalie by the shoulders. 'Are you OK?' he asked. 'Did they hurt you?'

'No,' she replied. 'But I *really* need a hairbrush.'

Rhino smiled, and hugged her. 'You're quite a star, Natalie,' he said. 'I'm proud of you.'

She seemed to collapse against him. 'Am I really safe?'

'Yes.'

'Promise?'

'Promise.'

'Can we go home now?'

He hesitated. 'We still have to find the Almasti.'

'Damn it, I was hoping you might have done that by now.' She looked up into his face. 'You know about the Nemor Incorporated expedition?'

He nodded. 'Yes. Calum said you mentioned it when ARLENE rescued you. It's definitely them, then?'

'It's definitely them. A man named Roxton is in charge. Craig Roxton.'

Rhino's face seemed to Gecko to tighten slightly, as if he had heard the name before, under circumstances that he didn't particularly enjoy remembering. 'They'll have set out after you,' he said. 'And I'm afraid ARLENE leaves some very obvious tracks.' Rhino gestured to the slope ahead of them, and the black crack of the defile. 'At least they won't be able to go past this point except on foot. I'm not even sure ARLENE can get more than a metre or so inside. We're all on the same level now.'

'Yes, but they have guns.'

'We don't need guns,' Calum said in their ears, suddenly reminding them that he was there with them at least in spirit if not in person. 'We're not going to be shooting anything.'

'That's a matter of opinion,' Rhino muttered; then, more loudly, he added, 'Right, let's get a move on. Time is ticking past, and it'll be dark soon. We need to find somewhere to camp, and it's too exposed here. I want to find somewhere more secure – a cave, or something similar. Let's go.'

*

Back in London, Calum kept one eye on the screens showing the headband camera images while he searched on the internet for any details on the name that Natalie had mentioned – Craig Roxton. There appeared to be several Craig Roxtons around the world, including a seller of religious iconography in Texas and a competitive eater in Hawaii, but none of them fitted the profile of a man who might be leading an expedition of trained fighters for a company like Nemor Incorporated.

He switched from basic text search to image search and was presented with a whole screen full of images related to 'Craig Roxton'. Most of them were not relevant, including several showing a row of men at a long table stuffing food into their mouths, but there was one that made Calum lean forward. It showed a thin man with blond hair and washed-out blue eyes. He was wearing military fatigues, and holding a gun. His head was turned to one side and his mouth was open as if he was shouting an order. The background behind him looked like a jungle: vivid green leaves wet with moisture.

Calum stared at the image for a long moment. It was untitled, and when he checked the link it led back to a newspaper archive, just one of a string of photographs that had been used to illustrate an article about mercenary soldiers – fighters who worked for pay rather than belief or honour. If this was the same Craig Roxton Natalie had come up against, then he could be a dangerous man.

Calum turned his attention back to the screens showing the headband images. They were black. For a moment he assumed that the sun had gone down and the team had entered the shadows of the defile, but then he realized that the image intensifier software should have compensated for that. He should have been seeing *something*, even if it was just shades of green.

He typed instructions into his keyboard, cautiously at first and then more frantically, checking the information that was coming from the headbands. They were all online, but they weren't showing anything. Only the ARLENE camera was transmitting an image, and when Calum ordered ARLENE to turn round and scan the area, there was nobody around. The slope was empty.

'Rhino? Tara? Gecko? Is anyone there?'

Nothing at all.

Calum felt a cold chill run through his body. His heart beat twice, three times, quickly. Somewhere out in the wilds of Georgia, while he was distracted, something had gone drastically wrong, and there was nothing he could do about it. Nothing at all.

A hand pushed Tara from behind. It shoved her further down the narrow rocky defile. She turned round to say something snappy, but the sight of the face behind her made her bite her lip. It wasn't human, but it wasn't bestial – quite. It was somewhere disconcertingly in-between.

It was the face of an Almast.

She was finding it difficult to breathe. Partly it was because of the smell – a rank, farm-like odour that hung around the Almasti so thickly that it was almost visible, like fog – but mostly it was because *it was all true*! Somewhere nearby there was an entire *community* of Almasti! Calum would be ecstatic!

If he ever got to find out.

The Almasti had been waiting for them, crouched behind outcrops of leafy bushes and stone. They must have been watching Rhino, Natalie, Gecko and Tara from some vantage point higher up the slope, and arranged an ambush. The four of them had been taken prisoner just after they had left ARLENE behind on the slopes and entered the rocky defile. It had all been over in a flash. They had been grabbed by sinewy, hairy hands and hustled along the floor of the defile before they knew what was happening. Worse, their rucksacks, their headbands and their mobile phones had been torn off them and thrown away, which meant that Calum would have no way of knowing what had happened to them. They were on their own.

Rhino had tried to fight back, of course, but his struggles had been quickly suppressed. Their captors hadn't hit him or hurt him, but they had piled on top of him in what had looked bizarrely like a rugby ruck, and held him down until he stopped struggling. The creatures who had taken them prisoner may have been smaller than all of them apart from Tara, but they were strong. Those thin, hairy limbs hid a lot of muscle.

Physically they were oddly like teenage boys – long limbs, stooped bodies, eyes hidden beneath long fringes of hair – but their skin was strangely *baggy*, hanging loose beneath their arms and under their chins, and it was all lined and wrinkled, as if the Almasti race had mysteriously shrunk from some larger size. Their teeth were big and slab-like, rather than pointed, which was kind of reassuring as it indicated that they were largely vegetarian, but Tara still had a horrible feeling that the four of them were being led along the defile to some kind of communal cooking area where they would be thrown into a large metal pot and boiled alive.

Like the one Natalie had seen back in the village, the Almasti were all wearing clothes: crudely fashioned trousers and sleeveless jerkins that looked as if they had been sewn together from stolen bits of canvas sack. Oddly, they each had a leather thong round their neck with a turquoise stone hanging from it. Decoration, or badges of rank? She wasn't sure, but it meant these creatures weren't just beasts. They had artistic urges. They created jewellery.

Tara caught her breath again. She kept finding herself treating the situation as if it was matter-of-fact, coolly and logically analysing what was going on, and then realizing with a gasp and a skipped heartbeat that it wasn't. It really wasn't. They had been taken captive by a group of half-human, half-ape creatures that were unknown to science! Missing links between humans and their evolutionary past! How incredible was that?

Incredible, yes. Incredible, and incredibly dangerous.

Rhino's mind was racing.

This was a hunting party. He knew that for three reasons. Firstly, most of them were carrying weapons: axes made out of sharpened flints tied to the tops of sticks, knives fashioned from longer sections of flint with dried grass wrapped round the lower third as a handle, and spears constructed from long, straight branches tipped with sharpened stone, or just sharpened to a point and charred by fire to make them hard. Secondly, they moved like a hunting party – cautious, quiet and deferential to the one in charge, the one at the front with a scarred face who was guiding them using hand signals. And, thirdly, they'd already taken a captive before they had attacked Rhino and the rest of the Challenger expedition.

The other captive was another Almast. It was almost indistinguishable from the main group, apart from the fact that it didn't have any weapons and they were pushing it along roughly in front of them. Oh, and every now and then it glanced back at Natalie as if it recognized her, although she hadn't noticed the glances yet. This must be the Almast who had attacked Levan in the village. It seemed to be a runaway, a renegade from the rest of the Almasti, who had been recaptured and was now being taken back to the tribe in disgrace. Maybe its scavenging of the Ruspiri food supplies hadn't been approved by its brethren. So what faced it up ahead? Rhino wondered. Some kind of primitive justice?

More importantly, what faced Rhino and his companions up ahead? Was it the same kind of primitive justice, or was it just a swift execution?

CHAPTER

eighteen

The defile sloped upward, with regular twists to the left and right. Gecko imagined that from above it looked like a crack in a concrete wall. It was wide enough that the party could walk two or three abreast, and its rocky sides towered high above them. Gecko could see enough handholds that he knew he could use to climb up there, if he had to, but what would be the point? Rhino, Natalie and Tara would still be prisoners. Gecko could maybe retrieve the headbands, get in touch with Calum, and get back to the van, but what then? He was hardly in a position to rescue the other three. Not by himself.

Besides, he suspected that the Almasti would be able to scramble up the sides of the defile just as fast as he could. They had the look of free-runners – wiry and lean, but with obvious muscular development. He snatched a look at the hands of the Almast who was walking next to him. They were calloused, and covered with scratches and old scars – the hands of a climber. Or maybe a fighter.

The Almast glanced at him, noticing his interest. It

frowned at him and jerked its head in the direction they were heading. The message was clear – keep walking, and don't get distracted.

This was like a nightmare from which he couldn't wake up.

Gecko's mind churned with half-formed ideas of escape, but none of them led to a place where all four of them ended up safe. For the moment it seemed as if he had no choice apart from to go along with the rest of the party and hope for some better opportunity to come along later.

Ahead of them Gecko noticed that the defile abruptly narrowed so much that they were going to have to go through one at a time. The leader of the Almasti – an older creature with a scar running down the right side of his face – went first, and the three Almasti behind him sorted themselves out into a line. Was Gecko's guard going to go ahead, or did he want Gecko to go first?

The Almast glanced sideways at Gecko. He was presumably wondering the same thing. It was difficult to tell, but he seemed young. His eyes were brown, and Gecko thought he could see humour and a sense of . . . maybe *humanity* in them. It wasn't like looking into the eyes of a dog. It wasn't even like looking into the eyes of a chimpanzee, or a gorilla. It was like looking into the eyes of someone at the next table in a coffee shop or sitting beside you on the bus.

This was incredible. His heart skipped a beat as he realized how amazing this moment was. Gecko was gazing into the eyes of a creature that nobody, apart from the four of them, and Calum, and a handful of people back in Ruspiri, knew existed. They were making history here!

Gecko smiled cautiously, and extended a hand towards the narrow point. The Almast's lips seemed to twitch into what might have been a smile or could have been a snarl – it was difficult to tell – and it extended *it*s hand in the same way.

No, Gecko corrected himself, *he* extended *his* hand. This was a person, not an animal.

Gecko nodded his head, and increased his speed slightly. He went through ahead of the Almast. As soon as he was through, he slowed down slightly, letting his guard catch up. The Almast stared at him, and nodded slightly in what looked like thanks.

Gecko began to smile, and then he noticed that the Almast's arm was extended and he was holding a rough stone knife centimetres from Gecko's back.

They might have been *making* history, but Gecko desperately didn't want to *become* history.

Natalie trudged along with her head bowed, staring at her feet. She was trying not to think. In particular, she was trying not to think about the *hideously* unattractive welts and blisters that were forming on her feet as she walked, about the fact that the Bruno Magli hiking boots that she had forced her mother to buy her were getting scuffed and muddy, or about the way that one particular Almast up ahead, the one who was being pushed along by its companions, kept turning round to look at her. Could life *get* any more horrendous?

She supposed that this was some kind of momentous occasion. After all, they had found the Almasti – or, to be absolutely correct, the Almasti had found them. This was what Calum had wanted. This was what the whole expedition had been about. This could change the world. The trouble was, she couldn't raise much enthusiasm. She was too tired, and too scared, and her feet hurt.

Maybe this was what it was like at any moment when history was made, she thought. Maybe all the observers spent their time standing around and complaining about the weather, or bitching about the fact that they had a headache.

Some kind of commotion was happening in front of her. She looked up, trying to work out what it was. The defile which they had been trudging along for the past hour, and which had led them inexorably and tiringly upward, seemed to be opening out, just as it jinked to the left. The sun had gone down a while ago, and they had been walking by what little moonlight managed to filter from above, but Natalie's dark-adapted eyes were suddenly overwhelmed by the sight of orange firelight flickering on the rocks. She felt her heart leap with a combination of relief and alarm. Relief, because it meant that they might have finally got to where they were going, and she could stop walking. Alarm, because she had a terrible feeling that the end of the walk might just be the end of them.

The Almast ahead of her turned left and vanished from sight. Within a few seconds Natalie was at the point where the defile abruptly turned.

And ended.

She was walking out into a natural arena of rock that seemed to be about the size of a baseball field. It was open to the sky, and the sight of the massed stars and the half-moon that were shining down from above made her catch her breath, but what really caught her attention was the dark spots that seemed to pepper the rising walls of the rocky bowl. They looked like . . . in fact, they *were* . . . caves. But not *just* caves – they were too regular, too rectangular. Natalie realized with a sudden sense of shock that they were doors and windows leading *into* caves. They must have been carved out over thousands upon thousands of years – an entire cave city, deep in the Caucasus Mountains, where the Almasti had lived their lives out of the sight of mankind for as long as mankind had existed. Or longer.

But it was almost entirely deserted. That realization struck Natalie just a few moments later. There were fires burning in a handful of the nearest caves, maybe twenty or so of them, but most of them were black and empty. Hundreds and hundreds of holes in the rock, staring down like empty eye sockets in hundreds and hundreds of skulls, and only a very few were actually occupied by anything alive or intelligent.

Natalie felt suddenly very small, very lost and very scared.

Tara gazed around the prehistoric town in amazement and awe.

This could have been one of the wonders of the world, she thought. In its heyday, when every cave was occupied and had a fire burning in a pit inside, the flood of light down here, at the bottom of the rocky bowl, would have been as bright as daylight. Almasti – males, females, children – would have thronged the area, moving along paths between the caves, climbing up the steeper sides of the bowl, and crossing the open central area, carrying babies and food and all manner of things. There would have been thousands of them.

And now she was looking at the last remnants of them. It was clear that the tribe was dying. They were only occupying a small corner of the town, and they were looking tired. Not personally tired, but tired as a race. As a people. Tara suspected that, each generation, fewer and fewer children were born. Maybe it was because they were finding it increasingly difficult to catch or grow the food they needed, perhaps disease was rife and passed from generation to generation, or perhaps they had just outlived their time. Perhaps the weight of the millennia was bearing down on them, crushing them out of existence.

She felt so sorry for them.

At least, she did until one of them poked her in the back with a spear.

She turned round, ready to make a sarcastic comment that the creature wouldn't understand, but the fierce look on its face made her pause. It gestured for her to move with its spear.

She looked at the others – Rhino, Natalie and Gecko. They were also being herded left, towards one of the openings in the rock. Together the four of them were pushed inside, into the darkness of the cave, lit only by the firelight trickling in from outside. Tara felt her spirits sink. This wasn't good. If there had ever been any doubt that they were captives, rather than honoured guests, this made it clear.

The Almast who had pushed them inside vanished. For a moment Tara had a clear view across the bowl. The momentary hope that the four of them could just walk out was crushed when several Almasti reappeared, straining to push a boulder almost two metres in circumference across the doorway. The stone dragged on the ground, making a grinding sound that Tara could feel through her feet. When it was finally in position, there was barely a hand's breadth of space between it and the edge of the doorway.

They were trapped.

Calum leaned back in his chair, fingers drumming on the desk. Tension flashed through his body like little electric shocks, making him twitch repeatedly. Over the past half-hour he had tried rebooting the system several times, to no effect, and then he had called all four mobile phones belonging to the party. Nobody had answered. He had checked the locations of the mobile phones on his computer using the global positioning software, but, if the signals were to be believed, then all four of them were standing still just inside the opening of the ravine into which they had intended to go. He couldn't control ARLENE – only Tara could do that – but from where the robot stood he could just make out a small pile of things shadowed by the sides of the ravine that might be rucksacks and a couple of mobile phones, carelessly discarded, or might just be some boulders that had fallen from the top. It was difficult to see for sure.

He was going to have to tell someone about this.

He was going to have to tell Natalie's mother, and that was a conversation he really did *not* want to have.

His mouth was dry, and his head was pounding. He needed to get himself a drink from the fridge to steady his nerves and stop his voice from shaking before he made that call.

Things shouldn't have got this far out of control. Even when he'd heard about the second party of explorers setting out from Tbilisi, he'd thought it was exciting. Just a big game. If he had thought that his friends might actually get *hurt*, then he never would have asked them to go.

For the millionth time he wished that he wasn't stuck here in his apartment – just watching, rather than being there with them. Instead of them.

He levered himself up out of his chair and grabbed for the nearest leather ceiling strap. He'd done it a million times before, and the motions were second nature to him now, but his thoughts were a thousand miles away and he wasn't concentrating. His fingers closed over empty air a half-centimetre from the strap. In the split second it took him to realize that he hadn't caught it, momentum carried his body forward past the point of balance. He fell forward, and the only thing he could do was to extend his arms to break his fall.

The impact sent a shockwave of pain all through his body. His headache was suddenly a hundred times worse than it had been. He rolled over on to his back and stared up at the ceiling, and the dangling straps, cursing the accident that had left him so helpless. The only consolation was that nobody was there to see his weakness.

Sighing, he braced himself, ready to try to get back upright.

He glanced at the desk, just to make sure that he could reach it without shuffling sideways, and something caught his attention. Something that shouldn't have been there.

A small object, about the size of a matchbox, had been stuck beneath the desk. An antenna stuck out from one corner. Calum had certainly never put it there. It must have been planted, and he suddenly had a sickening feeling that he knew by whom. The break-in . . . the two burglars who had got in . . . they had done it. Maybe the entire burglary had been staged so they could hide the thing beneath his desk, or maybe one of them had just done it as a matter of course, but it had to have been them.

He knew what it was, of course. The location gave it away. It was a transmitter, hoovering up the electromagnetic radiation that came from his screens and his CPU and sending it . . . somewhere . . . for analysis.

Someone was watching everything he did on his computer, and he suspected he knew who it was – Nemor Incorporated. Were they responsible for the disappearance of Gecko, Rhino, Natalie and Tara?

And, if so, what was he going to do about it?

Rhino glanced around, assessing possibilities. There weren't that many of them.

The cave in which they were trapped was barely larger than the hotel room back in Tbilisi. The walls, floor and ceiling were bare rock, apparently hand-carved out of the mountainside by generation upon generation of Almasti. The ceiling was invisible, shrouded in shadows. In the middle of the cave was a circular depression, about two feet deep. Its sides were blackened by flames. Rhino guessed that it was a fire-pit where food was cooked, suggesting that this cave was sometimes used as a dwelling rather than a prison. There was no window, and the doorway was blocked.

'What's going to happen to us?' Natalie asked. Her voice was shaky.

'We're going to get out, that's what's going to happen.' Rhino tried to put as much reassurance into his voice as he could.

'How, exactly?' Tara asked. She gestured to the boulder blocking the doorway. 'I can't see us picking the lock.'

Rhino crossed the cave to the doorway. He placed his hands experimentally against the boulder, braced his feet against the floor and pushed as hard as he could. The boulder didn't budge. He dropped his shoulder and slammed it into the rock as if he was tackling a rugby opponent, but the thing didn't move. All he ended up doing was bruising his shoulder.

He glanced out through the gap between the boulder and the doorway. There was movement outside: Almasti going back and forth across his field of vision. He could see the shoulder of an Almast off to one side. The creature wasn't moving. It was guarding them, making sure they didn't manage to push the boulder out of the way and escape.

Straightening, he turned to the three kids. 'I know this looks bad,' he said firmly, 'but I promise you that we're going to get out of here. I've been in tighter situations than this and survived.'

'You've been in a worse situation than being imprisoned in a rock cave by a lost tribe of Neanderthals who intend killing us so that we don't tell the world about them?' Natalie challenged. 'Because that is what they're going to do. That's why the world doesn't know about these creatures – they kill anyone who finds them. That makes sense, doesn't it?'

Natalie's voice was getting shriller and shriller as she

spoke. Rhino could hear the raw edge of panic in her tone. She was on the verge of hysteria. He had to squash it, and quickly. He was painfully aware that these were just kids. He had to reassure them, but how? The situation was dire, and he couldn't immediately see any way out.

'Trust me,' he said, loading as much sincerity into his voice as possible. 'I promised Calum that we would come back from this mission with everyone alive, and that's exactly what I intend.' He made eye contact with Natalie. 'I promised your mother in particular that no harm would come to you, and I always keep my promises. OK?'

'OK,' she said in a small voice. 'But I don't know how we're going to get out of here.'

'Let me work on that,' he said.

He turned back to the doorway and pressed his face against the gap. The cave was bare – but maybe somewhere outside was the key to their survival.

Almasti were trickling down the paths that led between the caves and were all congregating in the centre of the bowl, where Rhino noticed that seven rocks had been placed in a semicircle. One of the Almasti was pushed to the focal point of the rocks by the spears of the hunting party. It was the one the hunting party had brought back – the one that had kept casting glances at Natalie as they had walked. It – no, *he* – was scrawny, malnourished, but defiant. He bared his teeth at them and snarled.

The remnants of the Almasti formed a silent and circular crowd three deep, surrounding the seven rocks, the four explorers and the one lone accused. And he *was* an accused – Rhino could see that. This was a trial.

'Actually,' he heard Tara's voice from behind him, 'I think I might have an idea.'

Rhino turned back. 'What have you seen?' he said. He left the words *'that I didn't'* unspoken, but he could tell from Tara's sudden blush that she knew what he was thinking.

'That's a fire-pit, right?' she said, pointing to the circular depression in the centre of the floor.

'Yes. Used for cooking food. Are you hungry?' He immediately regretted the barbed comment. He didn't know how they were going to get out of there, and the uncertainty was weighing his mood down. He didn't want to fail these kids.

'Well, where do the heat and the smoke go?' Tara asked.

Rhino looked around. That was a good question. There was no window, nor any smaller vents that he could see, and by the time the smoke reached the doorway it would be at head height. That meant . . .

He gazed upward. The ceiling was hidden by the darkness, but there might just be some kind of crack up there that led to the outside, a natural vent or fissure that the Almasti used as a chimney.

'I see what you mean. How did you work that one out?'

She shrugged, embarrassed. 'I build computers for fun,' she said. 'Processors give out heat. If you don't have a plan to take the heat away, then it builds up and everything fails. I assume that cooking fires in confined spaces are just the same.'

Rhino glanced sideways at Gecko. 'You're the gymnastic one – do you think if you get on my shoulders you can check out the ceiling for cracks?'

Gecko shrugged. 'I will not know until I try,' he said.

Rhino braced his legs and laced his hands together. It only took a moment for Gecko to clamber up to his shoulders. The boy's feet clamped hard on Rhino's neck. With Rhino holding on to his legs, Gecko reached up and felt around in the shadowy ceiling space.

'The ceiling is rough,' he said. 'Rougher than the walls. It feels natural. Argh!'

Rhino felt Gecko's legs shake. 'What's the matter?' he called.

'Sorry – spider web. No spider.'

'Maybe it dropped on Natalie,' Tara murmured.

Natalie brushed her shoulders and hair convulsively.

'Anything else?' Rhino asked.

'Not sure.' Gecko's voice was strained. He was finding it hard to balance on Rhino's shoulders and feel his way across the ceiling at the same time. 'I do not – Oh, wait! I can feel a breeze!'

'That's a good sign,' Rhino said encouragingly. 'Can you tell where it's going to?'

'I think it is over to the left,' Gecko said. 'Can you move across a bit?'

'I can try.' Rhino took a couple of shuffling steps.

'That is far enough. Yes, I think . . .'

The weight on Rhino's shoulders abruptly lessened. It felt as if Gecko had pulled himself up.

'There is a chimney up here,' Gecko called down. 'It is not carved. I think they took advantage of some natural fissure in the rock. The way the breeze is going through it, I think it must lead to the outside.'

Rhino's mind raced. 'How large is it?'

Gecko's next words crushed his hopes. 'I can get into it. Tara might be able to. You and Natalie – not a chance. And besides – it might narrow further up.'

'Can you explore it?' Rhino asked.

'No problem. Just catch me if I slip and fall.'

'OK.'

'What do you want me to do if I get outside?' Gecko's voice echoed down from above. He'd obviously moved a little way inside the shaft.

'You can't free us,' Rhino said, thinking as he spoke. 'There are Almasti guarding the outside of the cave. Even if you could arrange a diversion and draw them off, you still couldn't move the boulder in the doorway. I think our best bet is if you make your way back to where we were captured, get one of the headbands, make contact with Calum and get him to contact Professor Livingstone. If anyone can organize a rescue party, it's her.' He paused. 'And watch out for that other expedition – the one that kidnapped Natalie.'

'Will do.' There was a scrabbling sound from above

Rhino's head, and some fragments of rock dropped down. 'Wish me luck.'

'Good luck,' Rhino and Natalie chorused.

'I don't believe in luck,' Tara said. 'It's not rational. But good luck.'

More scrabbling from the darkness, and then Gecko was gone.

The rocky fissure seemed to close in Gecko from either side like the jaws of some carnivorous reptile. He pushed the image away from his mind. There was no time for imagination now.

His fingers scrabbled across the rock, seeking purchase. His right foot pushed down on an outcrop and he gained another few centimetres.

He told himself that it wasn't much different from climbing a brick wall, but usually he didn't have another brick wall just behind him. He was used to open spaces. Here he could feel the coldness of the rock, and feel it scrape his back as he moved upward.

The fissure smelt of smoke, and his questing fingers kept slipping on patches of soot that had been deposited over the course of hundreds, perhaps thousands, perhaps even *hundreds* of thousands of years. Gecko's head swam with the thought of how old this place was. And there was he, just a kid, daring to climb up it. He wondered how many generations had lit fires and cooked food down below, in the cave.

He also wondered if anyone else had been stupid enough to try climbing this natural chimney, and whether he might find their bones still stuck in there.

Something skittered in the darkness above him – maybe a rat, maybe a cockroach. Gecko's heart raced. Sweat broke out on his forehead. He had to wait for a few moments and catch his breath before he could continue.

What if the fissure narrowed to the width of a few centimetres somewhere up above him? What if he got stuck, wedged between the rocky walls? Would anyone down below be able to get him out? Or would he stay there until he starved to death, able to hear the voices of his friends but unable to move?

Don't think about such things, he told himself. Keep going. Save your friends.

Relentlessly, repetitively, he reached up and let his fingers find a ridge of rock or projecting stone, then pulled himself higher up the crack while using his legs to take some of the strain. He lost track of time – he might have been climbing for minutes, hours or days. A faint breeze whistled past him, cooling him and evaporating the sweat from his face and his hands. Somewhere above his head that breeze would rejoin the atmosphere, like a stream feeding into the sea – but how far above? Was he going to have to climb the entire mountain from the inside before he could get out into the open?

His fingers closed on a sharp flint that projected from the rock face thirty centimetres above his head. He braced his legs against the sides and tensed his arm muscles, pulling himself upward while his left hand reached up for the next handhold, but the flint was loose and it came out of the rock.

Gecko fell.

CHAPTER

nineteen

Sharp stone projections tore at Gecko's back and his chest, burning like acid. His hands flailed wildly, trying to get a grip on something, but it was all going by too fast! Grit fell into his eyes, blinding him. Desperately he pushed his legs outwards, as wide as they could go in the narrow fissure. For a few seconds his feet were knocked and scraped by the rough rock, but his left foot finally caught on something, halting his fall. Quickly he braced himself with his right foot and found handholds to hang on to. He hung there for a minute or more, motionless, his breath rasping in his throat. He could feel the warm sting of blood on his back, but he was alive. He was still alive!

After his breath had settled down he started off again, trying to reclaim the distance he had lost. Handhold after handhold, foothold after foothold, testing each one carefully to make sure that it wasn't going to give way.

Eventually his fingers scrabbled against what he thought for a moment was a ledge, but it must have been a large one because his fingertips couldn't find where the rock wall of the fissure continued upward. There was something beneath his fingers that wasn't cold stone, and it took him a couple of seconds to work out that it was organic. It was grass!

His heart jumped, but he tried to calm himself down. It didn't mean that he was at the top of the fissure. Grass seeds might have drifted down along with some soil and germinated in a small patch on a rocky ledge. But surely they would need sunlight – and moisture. It had to mean that he was at least *near* the top.

He pulled with his right hand, using his left elbow and his legs to push himself up. He reached higher with his left hand, trying to locate the sides of the crack, but there was nothing there. No rock.

With nothing to hold on to, Gecko was supporting his weight just with his legs. He kicked himself upward as hard as he could. His shoulders popped up above the level of the grassy surface, and he thrust his arms out to either side to stop himself sliding down again. He levered himself up and out, falling sideways on to the grass, and it was only then that he allowed himself to realize that he was out and free.

The sky was pitch black above him. The sun had gone down a long time ago, and clouds covered the stars, but the wind that blew across his face was the freshest thing he had ever experienced. He lay there for a few seconds, every muscle in his body aching, and the scratches on his back and arms burning, and then he forced himself to climb to his feet.

That was the easy part over with. He still had things to do.

As Rhino watched, the crowd parted in several places and seven Almasti walked forward. They were older than the others, grey haired, stooped and even more wizened, and they wore long robes that had been crudely embroidered with designs. They also had leather thongs round their necks, but the stones hanging there were red rather than turquoise, and more ornately carved than any of the blue ones that Rhino had seen earlier. They walked proudly to the semicircle of seven rocks and each stepped up on to one. For a moment they stood there, facing out to the crowd, and then they turned inwards, towards the accused.

Somewhere behind the crowd, drums began to beat in a regular, hypnotic rhythm. A few seconds later an ear-scratching wail started up. It sounded like cats being strangled, but Rhino guessed that it was some kind of crude bagpipes being played.

And then the trial began.

Rhino had taken part in trials before. He had given evidence before two Crown Courts and three courts martial, and as he stood there in the cave, watching the Almasti, he recognized the form and the players. He knew exactly what was going on.

The Almast in the centre was the accused. He stood there – alone, isolated – staring around at his accusers – his tribe. The seven elderly Almasti standing on the rocks were the judges, watching impassively as the proceedings went on. And the leader of the hunting party, the older Almast with the scar running down the side of his face – he was the prosecutor.

The proceedings weren't carried on in any recognizable language. Instead the prosecutor communicated with the judges and the crowd in a series of barks, yelps and snarls. It wasn't just animal noise, however. The audience understood it. Although the judges maintained their impassivity, not reacting to the diatribe from the scarred hunter, the crowd was obviously swayed. Rhino could hear them murmuring to each other, and reacting together with sudden intakes of breath as particularly dramatic points were made.

The scarred prosecutor waved at one of the other hunters. The Almast he had waved at walked forward. He was holding something – it looked like a crudely fashioned bag. The hunter handed it across, and the scarred prosecutor threw it dramatically on the rocky ground. Grain spilt across the rock, and the crowd gasped.

Tara shuffled closer to him. 'What's going on?' she asked.

'The Almast with the scarred face is accusing the other one, the one from the village, of bringing danger on the Almasti. He's saying that when the accused went out by himself to steal food from the outsiders, he attracted their attention.'

'How do you know that?' Natalie asked. She was

standing off to one side with her arms wrapped round herself, hugging herself for reassurance.

'Body language,' he replied. 'I've travelled a lot, and I've learned the way that people stand, and move, and gesture, when they are saying particular things.'

'What's the mood of the crowd?' Tara asked.

'Sympathetic. Look at them. They're half starved. Whatever the Almasti are eating, it's not enough.' He indicated the accused. 'At least he did something about it. The trouble is that the ones in charge don't seem impressed. They've kept the Almasti away from the rest of the world very effectively, and probably for very good reasons.'

One of the judges raised a hand. Silence fell across the crowd. She asked a question – at least, Rhino assumed it was a question – but what worried Rhino was that she gestured at the cave where the four of them were being held while she spoke, and then gestured at the rocky bowl around them.

'What's she saying?' Tara asked.

'I'm not sure. She's not giving away very much with her body language, but if I had to guess I would say that she is pointing out that the fact we're here is some kind of proof that the accused Almast is guilty. People outside this place know about the Almasti now. The secret is out.'

The scarred warrior spoke in reply. He waved his spear and shouted something.

'Damn,' Rhino said.

'What?' Tara asked.

'Honestly?' he replied. 'Or reassuringly?'

'Honestly. Always.'

'I *think* he's saying that there's a simple solution to that. Just kill us.'

Gecko headed down the mountainside, navigating more by intuition than by sight. It was almost pitch black. Fortunately, years of free-running had given him a kind of sixth sense: he could tell when there were obstructions, or when the ground dropped away abruptly, and he could avoid them. For the most part. He fell a couple of times, but his reflexes were so fast that he could tuck himself into a ball and roll for a few feet.

As he descended, he tried to work out how he was going to navigate his way back to where the party had been captured. Nothing came to mind. He guessed he was just going to have to trust to luck – either that or be prepared for a very long walk around the base of the mountain.

Something made a noise nearby. Gecko stopped dead in his tracks. He held his breath, hoping that whatever it was hadn't heard his approach. He waited there, counting his heartbeats, until he estimated that a minute had gone by. Should he start moving again, or was there an Almast standing just as motionless as he was a few feet away, waiting like Gecko was for some sign of movement? The only difference being that the Almast was likely to be armed.

Another movement, and this time he heard the sound of grass being pulled out of the ground. He made a soft *click* with his tongue. From out of the darkness came an answering '*Meh-eh-eh-eh*'. A goat? A sheep? Whatever it was, Gecko didn't think he had anything to fear from it, so he kept on going.

After a while he began to notice a reddish glow off to one side. He wondered for a while if it was the sunrise, but surely he couldn't have been climbing the fissure for that long? A sudden change in the direction of the breeze brought a noise to his ears: a squalling sound, like cats fighting. He slowed down, not wanting to get in the middle of a fight between mountain lions, or whatever other carnivorous creatures lived on the mountain slopes, but after a moment he realized that the sound was more like music than the screech of a wild animal. Bagpipes, maybe?

Gecko realized that he must be getting close to the Almasti village. The red light he was seeing wasn't the sunrise – it was firelight – and the bagpipe music might mean that some kind of ceremony was going on.

He hoped it didn't have anything to do with his friends.

He speeded up, and very nearly tumbled head first into a crack in the ground that suddenly appeared in front of him. It was only a sudden updraught of cold air that told him something had changed. Cautiously, he bent over and felt forward with his hands until he found the edge. There was no knowing how far across it was. If it was narrow enough, then he could jump it. If it was too far across, then he would have to walk along the edge until it narrowed, or he could find something like a fallen tree that he could use to get across.

He scooped up some stones from the ground and threw them out into the darkness with various amounts of force. Some of the stones hit a rocky object out in the darkness, and tumbled away. Others – the ones he threw more strongly – seemed to hit solid ground. He estimated that the gap was about five metres – too far to jump in the dark.

He dropped a stone into the darkness and counted heartbeats. His heart beat barely twice before he heard the clatter of the stone hitting the ground. Just over five metres, then. His best bet was to climb down and then follow the crack either left or right.

It took him less than a minute to scramble down the side of it. The ground at the bottom was flat – so flat that he couldn't tell which way to go in order to get to the foot of the mountain slope. Randomly he chose left, and ran.

It was the wrong direction. Within a minute he began to see the glow of firelight illuminating the walls of the defile. He thought he recognized the walls as belonging to the same defile that he and his friends had been pushed along before, but he kept telling himself that it might just be coincidence, that it might be a different one entirely.

Until he turned a corner and found himself staring out across a rocky bowl lined with cave mouths. Thirty or forty Almasti were gathered in the centre. Seven of them were wearing robes, and one was standing, cowed, in front of them.

Despair flooded through him as he realized he had

come full circle. He was barely seven or eight metres away from the cave where Rhino, Tara and Natalie were imprisoned.

The scarred Almast who had led the hunting party was standing in front of the seven . . . what? Seven *judges*? He shouted something in the Almasti language. As Gecko watched, he stepped towards the accused and reached into the creature's shirt, which was tattered now from all the shoving and tugging that had gone on during the journey to the cave town. The accused Almast tried to resist, but the hunter grabbed his throat with one hand and used the other to search him. He pulled something out triumphantly and waved it above his head.

'Oh,' Gecko muttered to himself. 'That's not good.'

It was Natalie's mobile phone.

The crowd of Almasti all seemed to gasp in unison. Even the judges were taken aback.

The scarred warrior spat out a stream of barks, grunts and snarls. It was clear to Gecko that he was saying something like, *Look at this! He carries the strangers' magical devices on him! He is contaminated by their sorcery!*

'*Dá um tempo!*' Gecko said under his breath in Brazilian Portuguese.

His brain was racing. He could turn round and follow the defile in the other direction, towards the place where they had all been ambushed, but that would take time, and he had a terrible feeling that the trial going on out in the bowl was coming to a climax, and that climax might involve his friends being ceremonially slaughtered. He had to do something, but what?

Gecko closed his eyes for a moment. He relaxed, as best he could, letting the moment take over. Letting his body tell him what to do, the way it always did when he was free-running.

Before he quite knew what he was doing, he found himself walking forward. He opened his eyes in surprise, but his brain caught up with his body and he suddenly realized what to do. What he *had* to do.

His sudden appearance took the Almasti by surprise. He pushed through a circle of warriors armed with spears and axes and walked straight towards the scarred warrior who was holding the mobile phone, and towards the accused. He didn't look towards the cave where his friends were imprisoned. He had a feeling they were watching him. They were undoubtedly wondering what the hell he thought he was doing. He was beginning to wonder himself.

Both of the Almasti – accused and accuser – were staring at him. It was impossible to tell what they were thinking from their half-human, half-ape faces.

Before his better judgement could come into play, he reached out and took the mobile phone from the hand of the scarred hunter.

'Thank you,' he said. 'This belongs to us.'

The warrior's empty hand was still upraised. His gaze was fixed on Gecko, wondering what was coming next.

Gecko slowly turned round, trying to meet the eye of

every single Almast – the warriors, the crowd, the judges and the two standing directly beside him. He wanted there to be no doubt about what he was doing, no ambiguity. He wanted them to be absolutely sure.

When he felt as if he had milked the moment for long enough, he dropped the mobile to the rocky ground. He heard something break, but it wasn't enough. Stepping forward, he brought the heel of his boot down on the phone. It shattered into pieces of plastic and metal.

Gecko spread his arms out wide and turned again, so that all the Almasti could see him. 'We do not mean to pollute your tribe with our magic,' he said loudly. He knew they wouldn't understand his words, but he hoped that they understood his body language, or maybe his tone of voice. 'We are here by accident. We mean you no harm.'

Silence. Every eye in the rocky arena was on him.

Natalie watched, incredulous, from the cave as Gecko spoke. She'd been momentarily shocked by the destruction of her phone, but she thought she could see what Gecko was doing.

As she watched, the Brazilian boy gestured to the rows of cave dwellings that surrounded them, and then raised his right hand to his mouth and mimed sewing his lips shut. 'I will be silent about what I have seen!' he shouted. He turned towards the cave and gestured to the Almasti guards. Nothing happened for a few moments. He gestured again, and stared around at the circle of judges. One of them nodded, and suddenly the boulder was being dragged away from the mouth of the cave.

'What is he *doing*?' Rhino breathed. 'He was supposed to be going for help!'

'Whatever he's doing,' Tara said, 'it's having an effect. Go with it.'

The guards pulled Rhino, Tara and Natalie out of the cave and pushed them towards where Gecko was standing. As they got close, they could see that he was covered in cuts and scrapes, and his clothes were ripped.

'Hi,' Natalie said, smiling uncertainly. 'Something you want to tell us?'

'Sorry,' he murmured. 'Got turned round somewhere back there.' He looked at the judges and the scarred hunter, and then gazed at his friends. He raised a hand to his mouth and tapped his lips. 'Your turn,' he said.

After a moment, Rhino nodded. He stepped forward, gestured around – a little theatrically, Natalie thought – and also mimed sewing his lips shut. 'I will be silent about what I have seen!' he said loudly.

Tara did the same. Her voice shook, but maybe that was good. Maybe the Almasti needed to see a little bit of emotion.

When it came to her turn, Natalie called upon all the resources she had developed in the school debating society.

She waved both her arms, encompassing the entire crowd and the town as well. 'I will be silent about what I have seen!' she called, her voice echoing across the bowl.

The echoes died away into silence. Nobody spoke, nobody moved.

It wasn't enough. Natalie thought that the message had got through, but it wasn't enough. Maybe the Almasti just didn't believe them.

Now it was Tara who stepped forward. She waited until everyone was looking at her, and then she bent down and scooped up a handful of grain that had spilt from the bag stolen by the accused. She held the handful up for everyone to see. Natalie didn't have a clue what she was doing.

Tara walked slowly across to the accused Almast. She reached up with her other hand and touched the turquoise stone that hung round his neck on the leather thong. She pulled it gently. The Almast stared at her. She pulled it again, still gently, and gazed into his eyes.

The Almast nodded, as if suddenly understanding what she was getting at. It reached up, pulled the thong off and held the turquoise stone out to her.

Slowly, Tara took the stone with one hand. With the other she held out the handful of grain.

The Almast tilted its head to one side questioningly, and then reached out its own hand, open and flat.

Tara tilted her hand and poured the grain into its palm in a golden stream.

Natalie could hear the crowd talking in excited tones. The seven judges were looking at each other, confused, uncertain what to do.

'What the *hell* is going on?' Natalie hissed.

'I think,' Rhino said quietly, 'that we've just told the Almasti two things – firstly that we can be trusted to keep quiet, and secondly that they can trade their carved stones for grain from the village. They don't even have to meet the villagers face to face to do it – I'm sure we can arrange some system where they can leave the stones in a safe place, and the villagers can do the same with the grain.'

'Will it save the Almasti?' she asked.

He shrugged. 'In the long term, probably not. I think they're doomed to extinction. That's evolution for you. But in the short term at least their babies can be fed.'

'Will it save us?'

He smiled. 'You know, I think it just might.'

Gecko glanced at the accused Almast. He was standing staring at Tara with his head tilted to one side.

Rhino looked around at the judges. They were conferring among themselves. Finally, one of them waved at the guards and said something. The guards stayed where they were, but they lowered their weapons. Suddenly, a lot of tension seemed to drain from the scene.

'I get the impression he's going to be all right. He may even find himself a local hero.'

'The question now,' Gecko said, walking over to them, 'is how we're going to get those DNA samples that Calum wants. Somehow, I don't think I can convey *that* message to the Almasti.'

'We don't need to.' Tara had joined them as well. She held up the turquoise stone that the accused Almast had given her. Caught between the stone and the leather thong were five coarse black hairs. 'We have the samples we need right here,' she said, 'and all it cost us was some grain.'

'And a whole load of pain and grief,' Natalie added in a heartfelt voice, 'not to mention the heart-stopping tension, but don't worry about that.'

CHAPTER

twenty

Calum realized that the team was still alive when their headbands came back to life simultaneously. He had been on the verge of calling the British embassy in Tbilisi to report them missing. His hand had actually been resting on the phone when his screens suddenly lit up. Each screen showed their faces – Rhino, Natalie, Tara and Gecko – as they all stood in a circle, looking at each other. Gecko's face was scratched, but apart from that they all looked OK, thank God. They seemed to have recovered their rucksacks, and at least two of them were holding mobile phones. In fact, Natalie was making a call as Calum watched – probably, he thought with a pang of guilt, to her mother. That was still a conversation he was going to have to have, and which he wasn't looking forward to at all.

'What happened?' he cried. 'I've been worried *sick*.'

'Lots of things happened,' Gecko replied. 'Some of which we may even tell you about.' He was smiling, as if at a private joke. In fact, they were all smiling.

Tara was looking around nervously. 'Hey, I've just had a

thought. What about the Nemor Incorporated expedition? The last thing we want right now is for them to turn up – especially after where we've been. Calum, do you know where they are?'

Where we've been? Her words sent a thrill through him. It sounded as if they had a story to tell, and he was desperate to hear it, but first . . .

He weighed the bugging device that he'd found beneath the desk in his hand. He had disconnected the battery as soon as he had found it, rendering it mute, but he could reconnect it in a few moments if he had to. And he thought he had just found a reason to do so.

'Actually,' he said, 'I think I can send them on a wild goose chase. They've had my computer bugged – that's how they were able to track you all, and how they got Natalie. They pulled your mobile-phone locations right from my system. Now I know what they've been doing, however, I can set some software running that will gradually distort your positions. When I switch the bug back on, it will faithfully transmit the wrong locations, and Nemor's team will head off into the wilderness. I could keep this going until you're all back here and they're heading into Azerbaijan.' He paused. 'Did you . . . ?' he started to ask, and then stopped. He wasn't sure whether or not he wanted to know.

'We'll tell you after we've got back to civilization.' Rhino smiled. 'But first we have some negotiations to conduct. For now, we need to get back to Ruspiri, if only to stop the locals sending out a lynch mob.' He glanced around at the other three. 'Right – everyone back in the van. Calum – I'll brief you later.'

'OK,' said Calum cautiously. He leaned back in his chair and watched as the circle broke up and they headed back to the van. ARLENE, he noticed, was still with them, trotting faithfully along with their equipment on its back.

As he relaxed, his gaze moved upward, to where one of his screens was showing a photograph that had just come in to the Lost Worlds website. It showed what at first glance was a scorpion, but this scorpion seemed to be swimming across a river, and judging by the size of the trees in the distance it was about two metres long.

He wondered how he was going to break the news to the team. He had a feeling that another expedition was on the cards.

AUTHOR'S notes

Previously, when writing the Young Sherlock Holmes books which have kept me busy over the last couple of years, I've finished off by talking about historical influences, research sources and which of the characters in the book were real and which I had invented.

This book is different. It's set in the present day, of course, which means that I didn't have to do any historical research. What I did have to do was *geographical* research, mainly on Georgia, its capital city Tbilisi and the area around the Caucasus Mountains. I was fortunate enough to visit Georgia at the invitation of the Georgian publishers of the Young Sherlock Holmes books, and I spent a wonderful few days in Tbilisi and out in the countryside (including an incredible day trip to a real prehistoric cave village which I used as the basis for the Almasti village in the book). For that reason I would like to thank Bakur Sulakauri Books, and specifically Elene and Tata, for looking after me so well. Never have I eaten so much good food in such a short space of time. Who would have thought that walnut sauce could go with so many different dishes? Who would have thought that you could make a refreshing fizzy drink with tarragon leaves? And while on the subject of Bakur Sulakauri Books, I would like to express my thanks to Nino Demuria for helping out with character and place names.

There are influences on this book, of course, but they are more literary and descriptive than factually historical. When I was growing up, I read a lot of books by a writer named Willard Price. He wrote fourteen novels about two teenage zoologists named Hal and Roger Hunt, who travelled the world seeking out wild animals for zoos, circuses and wildlife parks. The first of the books, *Amazon Adventure*, was published in 1949, and the last, *Arctic Adventure*, in 1980. I loved those books, and the strong memories I have of them have provided at least some of the impetus for writing about the adventures of Calum Challenger. Of course, writing about a boy whose pastime is catching animals for zoos, circuses and wildlife parks would be pretty unacceptable to most people these days, so Calum had to have a different, and more ecological, aim in mind.

Calum's interest in undiscovered animals is inherited, of course, from his great-grandfather Professor George Challenger. Like Sherlock Holmes, Professor Challenger was a character invented by the Victorian writer Arthur Conan Doyle. He appears in the novels *The Lost World* (1912), *The Poison Belt* (1913) and *The Land of Mists* (1926), plus the short stories 'When the World Screamed' (1928) and 'The Disintegration Machine' (1929). Although he obviously takes no part in this book, and in fact it doesn't really matter to the plot whether Calum is related to him or not, I am grateful (again!) to the family of Arthur Conan Doyle for allowing me to make reference to him.

Going back to Willard Price – when he wasn't writing adventure books he travelled on many expeditions to remote areas of the world for the National Geographic Society and the American Museum of Natural History. My father used to have a subscription to the society's *National Geographic Magazine*, which arrived in our letter box every month filled with glossy colour photographs of various animals, landscapes and geographic features. Every couple of months there used to be a folded map included in the package. I still have some of those maps, including one brilliant one that showed all the underwater mountain ranges buried deep beneath the surface of the world's various oceans. That really sparked my imagination. I learned an awful lot about the world from the *National Geographic Magazine*. In fact, I have my own subscription now, but it arrives wirelessly on my iPad, rather than in a thick envelope in the post. That's progress for you.

Another magazine I have a wireless subscription to is the *Fortean Times*. That magazine focuses not on the real world, but the unreal one. It lists and discusses various phenomena from poltergeists to alien abductions to bizarre deaths, but it takes a relatively sceptical approach to what it reports, and it always tries to seek out genuine evidence rather than hearsay, anecdotes and stories. What I like most about the *Fortean Times* is its regular articles on strange creatures glimpsed in remote forests or appearing from the shadows outside small, isolated villages – creatures either unknown to science or, perhaps, thought to have died off many years ago. A lot of things that I have read in the *Fortean Times* have influenced the way that Calum Challenger thinks in this, and future, novels.

Off at a tangent, I spent a long time when I was younger collecting a set of books called the Dumarest series, written by E. C. Tubb. The books form a continuing science-fiction series about a man searching for the lost planet of Earth, travelling from world to world collecting evidence that will help him find it (and picking up a lot of scars on the way). The Dumarest universe is pretty much alien-free and technology-light, and the books are more about the things one man has to do to survive in a series of hostile environments, and about the importance of integrity and honesty in a person's life. E. C. Tubb died in 2010, but not before actually writing the last book in the series (which runs to thirty-two novels). I loved E. C. Tubb's writing style. As a kind of tribute to him I recently decided to read all of the Dumarest books again, one after the other. I'm still going, but one thing I have learned (with some surprise) is that my writing style (if I have one) borrows quite a lot from E. C. Tubb's. If you're going to borrow, I suppose you should borrow from the best.

So, here we are. It's November 2012, and I've just

finished writing this book. In the next few days I'll start writing the sixth Young Sherlock Holmes book, which I think is going to be called *Stone Cold.* Or possibly *Knife Edge.* When I've finished that, I'll start work on the second Calum Challenger book. I have no idea what that's going to be called, or what kind of strange creature it will involve, but I am looking forward to finding out.

I'll see you then.

Andrew Lane

ABOUT the author

Andrew Lane is the author of the bestselling Young Sherlock Holmes books. These have been published around the world and are available in thirty-seven different languages. Not only is he a lifelong fan of Arthur Conan Doyle's great detective, he is also an expert on the books and is the only children's writer endorsed by the Sherlock Holmes Conan Doyle estate. *Lost Worlds* is inspired by another famous Conan Doyle novel, *The Lost World*. Andrew's main character, Calum Challenger, is the grandson of Conan Doyle's protagonist, Professor George Edward Challenger.

Andrew writes other things too, including adult thrillers (under a pseudonym), TV adaptations (including *Doctor Who*) and non-fiction books (about things as wide-ranging as James Bond and Wallace & Gromit). He lives in Dorset with his wife and son and a vast collection of Sherlock Holmes books, the first of which he found in a jumble sale over forty years ago.

Check out Andrew Lane's bestselling series!

'What a blast. Weird murders, creepy villains, fiendish puzzles, non-stop action – what more could you want from a book?'

Charlie Higson, author of Young Bond

Young Sherlock Holmes will need every ounce of courage, determination and strength to defeat enemies of exquisitely evil intent as he faces a crop of sinister, clever criminals. Find out how the legend came to be in the Young Sherlock Holmes series.